A Heartbeat at My Feet

AF513845

OTHER TITLES BY KRISTIN JUDD

As Kristin Beck

Courage, My Love

The Winter Orphans

A Heartbeat at My Feet

a novel

KRISTIN JUDD

Little a

This is a work of fiction. Names, characters, organizations, places, events, and incidents are either products of the author's imagination or are used fictitiously. Otherwise, any resemblance to actual persons, living or dead, is purely coincidental.

Text copyright © 2026 by Kristin Beck
All rights reserved.

No part of this book may be reproduced, or stored in a retrieval system, or transmitted in any form or by any means, electronic, mechanical, photocopying, recording, or otherwise, without express written permission of the publisher.

Published by Little A, New York

www.apub.com

Amazon, the Amazon logo, and Little A are trademarks of Amazon.com, Inc., or its affiliates.

EU product safety contact:
Amazon Media EU S. à r.l.
38, avenue John F. Kennedy, L-1855 Luxembourg
amazonpublishing-gpsr@amazon.com

ISBN-13: 9781662542978 (hardcover)
ISBN-13: 9781662539947 (paperback)
ISBN-13: 9781662539954 (digital)

Cover design by Emily Mahon
Cover image: © baby corn, © Vibrands Studio / Shutterstock; © Rudzhan Nagiev / Getty

Printed in the United States of America

First edition

To Jeremey, my everything,
and to my little dog, Annie, the heartbeat at my feet

My little dog—a heartbeat at my feet.

—*Edith Wharton*

PART ONE

CHAPTER ONE

CICERO

A terrier of indeterminate breeding

Campania, Southern Italy

Do you know what Plato said about dogs, my friend? If not, allow me to enlighten you, and if so, I do apologize for causing you a bit of boredom, for I know well how it feels to endure repetition. Dogs, you understand, put up with quite a lot of nonsense.

Perdonami, I digress.

A dog, Plato once said, *has the soul of a philosopher.*

I like this very much. Giorgio was the first to share this tidbit with me, and of course I wholeheartedly agreed with both Plato and Giorgio on the subject. The latter and I agreed on most everything, you see, and besides that, I have always fancied myself something of a thinker. Thinking is what brought Giorgio to me in the first place, when my story began.

Though born rather introverted, with—if I'm to be brutally honest—a tendency toward snobbery, I was as ungovernable a bundle of fluff as most puppies in the beginning. My siblings and I were born down in the village and, weeks later, herded into a sort of infant corral placed in the central piazza so our neighbors might see us, fall to pieces, and find themselves in need of a dog. Young as I was that day, I was deeply skeptical about the people appearing before me, one after another, all morning. No, they were not to my tastes at all. Several were children, and they hoisted me up in the hot sun, gripping me with their small, sticky hands, exclaiming, *che bel cucciolo!* and *ciao, ciao!* and *bau bau!* Horrifying, I tell you. Then they slung me about until I whined and, I'm ashamed to confess, bit a few with my sharp little teeth.

Later, back in the corral, several village women cooed at me, attempting to coax me forward with sugary words and ridiculous intonations. Even then I knew enough to be offended. I scooted away from their grasping hands, stifling the urge to bite them, too, and allowed my siblings to tumble in my stead.

Then, finally, Giorgio arrived.

I recall the moment well. If I may say so, he was in a dreadful state at the time. His eyes, I saw right from the start, were deeply mournful over his gentle smile. I found myself yearning to brighten them as he blinked down at me. His hair was like a bit of fog caught on his head, silvering in the afternoon sun.

"What do you call the little white one?" he asked my first owner, studying me, his bristle-brush brows drawing together. "There, in the back?"

I had no name, of course, as the rather disinterested breeder informed him.

"Allora," Giorgio proclaimed, enlivened. "He should be named Cicero, don't you think? He appears to be an intellectual. An old soul, perhaps." And he held his hand out to me, the knobs of his fingers unfolding, palm up.

I sensed it then. His heart beat within him, big and open, his essence traveling right down into his fingerprints. Sometimes a dog simply knows when he has found his match. Thus, I gathered my courage and crawled right into Giorgio's outstretched palm.

I learned, later, that it was I who rescued Giorgio that day. He took me home to his villa on the hill, which smelled of prosciutto and furniture polish and echoed with loneliness. For a man with such a large heart, Giorgio was quite dogless, you understand. A tragic combination. One I could rectify.

Even now, it pains me greatly to divulge what I must. I lived with Giorgio for eight wonderful years, yet he was not my final owner, and for this, I am at fault. I shall never forgive myself for not paying closer attention, for lapsing in my duties, for failing to take fate itself in my jaws, like my more athletic brethren snatch flying objects from the sky mid-flight.

I could have changed everything.

Yet I'll not burden you with the entirety of my tale now. Simply understand that my story began once again—a restart, if you will—many years after I rescued Giorgio, and in quite a different manner. And it commenced, the second time, in Pompeii.

Imagine me, *per favore*: a middle-aged, highly domesticated canine, lying on an ancient stone step in Pompeii. Alone. The archeological site, fascinating as it may be, was not a place I'd ever set foot before, and I was loath to find myself inhabiting it. Though I was quite sure I wouldn't live there long. For I was dying, you understand, of heartbreak.

The ruins smelled of shoes from far and wide, and trash cans that overflowed every weekend, and an uncouth collection of my species who'd taken up residence there well before my arrival. I situated myself apart from those wild dogs, who fought and begged tourists for scraps and shit indiscriminately, I'm aggrieved to report, throughout the grounds. I observed them from my stone stoop, unmoving aside from the flick of my eyes. I thought about my warm bed back home, and poetry, and the local butcher who exclaimed *ciao, bello!* every morning when we walked past, tossing me a bite of something delightful. I would likely never see him again.

There I was, a well-educated dog, with rather discriminating tastes, surrounded by mayhem and fleas. Lost in every way possible.

Lost. I shudder at the word even now. The best of dogs can become lost, *certamente*, but it was not a predicament I'd ever expected to find myself in. Not *me*, Cicero, who'd trotted alongside Giorgio with nary a leash on my glossy collar. Not me, who'd never lowered myself to chase whatever small, flighty animals crossed my path, nor pursued a scent, nor trusted a stranger. No, I'd always protected my dignity.

Even more crucially, I'd always had Giorgio to follow.

I remained frozen on my stone, gazing up at passersby, ignoring a mop of a dog who came to sniff at my unwagging tail, trying to avoid the indecency of scratching at my tiny, newly acquired residents. And I waited. It was a lonely place in which I'd landed. A low place, where the only future I could imagine was death. Dogs do die of grief, my friend, quite readily. Our hearts beat so fully for those we love that sometimes we cannot carry on without them.

Why then, you ask, did I not expire from grief in the ruins of Pompeii?

I can see from my current perch that while I believed I awaited death, I was not fully resigned to it. No, something else lurked in my shattered heart, flitting about like a shadow. Belief, perhaps. Faith. I've had time to think on it now, and you know I fancy myself a thinker.

Consider this: Perhaps sorrow cannot be separated from hope.

And perhaps, despite everything, I was still hoping to be found.

CHAPTER TWO

JOSIE

Gardner, Kansas

Josie Ballard dropped a skein of fettuccine into a burbling pot, thinking of all the ways her life was about to change. She pressed back a smile, but everything within her felt like laughter, bright as the steam rolling off the pot, shot through with sunlight. She would make dinner in this kitchen for three more nights. Three! Then she and Mark would wake up in a different house, on the other side of the world, for two entire months. It was so astonishing Josie couldn't quite grasp that it would actually happen, even though she'd been the one to buy the tickets, book the *appartamento*, and plan the itinerary.

In fact, she'd spent the entire final week of school combing through that itinerary, checking travel times and moving things around, so overwhelmed with excitement it was difficult to do her job. It had been her last week as a full-time librarian's assistant. Next fall, she'd go part-time, and she would spend the other half of her days forging a new path, finally. She wasn't quite sure yet what that path would be, but just the prospect of freedom, of *choices*, made her giddy.

Still, Josie's clientele—middle schoolers—had a way of keeping one grounded. They'd trundled through the library doors throughout those final days, predictable as mornings, slouching under their backpacks and dropping long-overdue books into her returns bin. Josie had chided a few of the worst offenders, pointing out bent pages and curved spines and moisture damage, but the kids mostly shrugged and offered her fist bumps as they departed, calling out variations of, *Have a bussin' summer, Mrs. B!*

And she'd grinned, telling them to do likewise, letting them all off the hook in the end. The kids knew she was no disciplinarian, and really, she was just glad they were reading at all. She'd taken the full bins back to the shelves, recalling all the library books her own son had lost, or left out in the rain, or forgotten in the netherworlds of his successive lockers. Yet Charlie, now finished with his second year at college, was still a reader. It was important to remember what really mattered, Josie had mused, humming to herself as she knelt before the shelves. And all through her organizing and alphabetizing, her mind had drifted to Italy.

Now, with the last day of school behind her and the library doors finally locked, everything was about to happen. At forty-two years old, Josie was on her way somewhere new. *New.* The word sparkled.

"Hey, Jo?" Mark called from the front door, banging it open, interrupting her thoughts. "Can I get a little help with the groceries?"

Our last groceries in Kansas, Josie couldn't help thinking as she pivoted toward the stairs, calling, "Coming!" She'd been thinking this way for two weeks now. She'd had her last haircut, her last trip to the pharmacy, her last trash day. This was ridiculous, of course; they'd be back home in August. Still, Josie had been nearly nowhere all her adult life, and she couldn't help but let a little romanticism seep in.

"I have pasta on the stove. You grabbed marinara?" she asked as she hurried down the stairs. "And snacks for the trip?"

He nodded over the grocery bag, his gaze distracted behind the flash of his glasses, and Josie felt, as she often did, that he wasn't fully seeing her, that his mind was still snagged on some crag in his day. His tie rumpled where he clasped the bag to his chest, and his tall, slender frame stooped over it. He looked exhausted, and Josie realized that the ache in her heart might be guilt. Mark had always worked hard, but this trip, this audacious trip she'd dreamed up, had saddled him with extra pressure. He'd been putting in overtime at the insurance office, running numbers and securing accounts for his absence, even though he planned to work remotely from Italy. She knew him well, and she knew he was worried.

He was such a good man.

"Do you know," she asked as she stretched up, giving him a quick kiss on the cheek before hoisting the bag into her own arms, "how much I adore you?"

His lips quirked up in a smile. "I have an inkling." He loosened his tie, rubbed at the slightly silvered stubble on his jaw, and turned toward the driveway, calling, "Two more bags," over his shoulder.

Josie scaled the stairs, the marinara jar clinking against something else in the sack, her thoughts running. Even if the trip caused some extra pressure, wouldn't it be good for them in the end? After two years with an empty nest, their days had become as bland as unbleached flour. They needed something—excitement, or fun, or novelty. The pasta was bubbling over when she dumped the groceries on the counter, and she was fanning it and wiping up the overflow when Mark reappeared with the final two bags.

"How was your last day?" he asked, joining her next to the pot. She glanced at him, watching the steam fog up his glasses, catching what she could see of his blue gaze. It was as if he'd come back online, as if he was suddenly hers again.

"Chaotic," she said, pivoting to lean against the counter opposite him, the pasta under control. "But I just kept thinking about how it was my last full day there. Mark, I can't even believe it, after all these years—"

She stopped talking because his smile faded. He lifted his glasses slightly, wiping at the lenses, and Josie's elation sank within her chest, shrinking like a pricked balloon. She'd known him long enough to sense when something wasn't right, when something was coming.

"Jo," Mark said, and she could feel it, salting the air. Outside the window, the sun dipped behind the neighbor's trees, sucking the golden light right out of the kitchen. "About that." He sighed, and she filled the silence.

"I already told them," she said quickly, trying to avoid the trap she felt descending. She knew where this exchange would go and how it would end. It had become something of a pattern over the years—Josie taking steps to leave her job, and Mark telling her, as departure drew closer, that it wasn't possible after all. "The administration is expecting me to come back only part-time—"

"Can you undo it?"

He stared at her, his brows tented over his glasses, his blue eyes earnest. And she hesitated. Yes, she could. Of course she could. The school was desperate for her to stay, actually. She was only an assistant, but the librarian, it was commonly known, wasn't fond of work, and Josie had stepped into many of her roles, balancing the entire library on her own slender, poorly paid shoulders.

She bit her lip, her mind racing. It had just seemed like time, finally, to pursue something new. Josie's mother had died early in the year, and her father had insisted on giving her some money her mom had tucked away. And with that money, it had seemed like Josie finally had a window to leap through, a chance to change her life. Maybe even to open a little flower shop somewhere, or at least work in one—a dream she'd long nurtured.

"We've been talking about me going part-time for so long . . ." she said, trailing off, her gaze searching the linoleum as if she'd find direction there. "I thought it was a firm plan, that I could finally make a change with mom's gift—"

"I know," Mark interrupted. He sighed even more heavily than before. "It's just that we need the money for other things, Jo. Charlie's making noise about medical school in a few years, and my work is slow—you know it's been slow. And now we've taken on the expense of this huge trip. I don't know why we're even doing it, honestly."

Josie felt the words like pins. Mark had planned the trip with her, months ago. Months ago, he'd been nearly as excited as she was. They figured he could work remotely, and that if they rented a single apartment for the summer, they could keep their costs low. It had seemed, after twenty years of longing for an adventure, almost reasonable.

"I spent all day crunching numbers, Jo. The quarter just didn't go like I thought it would, and we need your income."

She nodded, feeling the steam from the boiling water roll against her back, moistening her neck under her ponytail. And even though her heart bent with disappointment, she knew he was right. The trip was for her, after all. It was her dream. *Her* doing. She couldn't ask for so much all at once, surely. Maybe it was wrong to ask for so much at all. So she nodded again, unable to say the words but already knowing she'd call the principal in the morning, explain her circumstances, and he would call the district office on her behalf, and nothing would change when she got back.

But still, they were leaving. Her heart straightened out a bit. She managed a smile, and Mark leaned forward to kiss her on the forehead. She still had Italy. She would figure the rest out later.

"Mind if I take a shower?" His lips brushed her forehead. "We can talk about it more over dinner."

She nodded a final time, and he turned, vanishing down the hallway.

Josie sighed and stared through the steamy window at the setting sun. The window was single-paned, and paint bubbled around it from condensation. She would need to fix that when they got back. Also, the dingy front door could use some touching up. She wanted to cry, but she stifled the urge. "It's all right," she whispered aloud, even though the idea of another full year in the school library opened a sinkhole within her. She turned to the grocery bags. The pasta had three minutes to go. She'd unpack.

It wasn't that she hated her job, she thought as she opened the fridge, tucking a carton of milk in beside half a cooked chicken. She loved both the kids and the books, certainly, but they were only a small part of her days. The rest involved the photocopier—always breaking—and never-ending sorting, and the damnable computer carts with their constantly missing power cords, and the ever-evolving technology that seemed to overtake the library a bit more each year, pervasive as black mold.

She went back to the grocery bag, piled a handful of yogurts into her cupped forearm, and returned to the fridge. She'd done everything wrong, of course. She frowned, stacking the little containers. She'd gotten pregnant too young, at only twenty-two, then gotten married, and had duct-taped her life together ever since. Not that she'd change it; Mark was the love of her life, and Charlie? He was her sun, her reason. She'd build her universe around them a thousand times over if she had to. She'd shelve books and organize computer carts for eternity if it allowed Charlie to shine.

She returned to the grocery bag, nearly empty now, and saw a receipt waiting at its bottom. Mindlessly, she fished it out, hip against the counter once more, and glanced at the total. It was a habit, built from so many years of shopping sales and stretching groceries. Josie knew what things should cost, nearly to the penny, and she scanned every receipt.

And so, she was scanning this one, her mind humming on a different frequency altogether, consumed with thoughts of school next year, and her life, and all the many paths she'd never take, when she got to the final sum and frowned.

Why was it so high?

She straightened a bit, flattening the curl from the paper to study it closer. She searched the column of items, her heart beating a bit faster, though she didn't know why. And then, there it was.

In the middle of the grocery list, tucked in between the yogurts and trail mix for the airport, was something out of the ordinary.

Roses, two dozen, $39.99

Josie glanced from the receipt to the grocery bags, her heart leaping against her sternum. No roses. As if they might be hiding, she found herself detaching from the counter and pawing through the remaining two bags, her sense of dread expanding like a flood within her, rising, just getting started. *Roses.* Why would Mark have bought *two dozen* roses?

Behind her, the stovetop timer began to beep. Steam billowed, the pasta water leaped from its pot, and Josie felt as if she were waking up.

Her pulse pushed all conscious thought from her skull, and she left the kitchen with its shrieking timer, hurried down the stairs so fast she nearly tripped, and grabbed Mark's keys from a hook by the front door. She moved as if by remote control, as if someone else were directing her steps, telling her what to do while confusion robbed her of the ability to think. She found herself jogging down the front walk, clicking the fob to Mark's Prius in the driveway, sickness creeping into her belly. What on earth could that receipt mean?

She opened the passenger door, ducked her head in, and scanned the pristine interior.

Nothing.

Then she rounded on the hatchback, pressed the key fob again, and watched the hatch lift before her.

There, tucked against the back seats as if they'd been kidnapped, twenty-four roses stared up. Josie blinked, glancing at the house where Mark was currently showering, scrubbing his woolly torso with soap and probably whistling a tune, oblivious. Josie's hands shook. Could the roses be for her? Could they have something to do with the bomb Mark had just dropped about her remaining full-time next year, with the disappointment he knew would follow? Could they be to celebrate her last day of the school year? Or could they be a gift heralding their upcoming trip?

No, she thought reflexively. Who bought two dozen roses for someone who was leaving town in three days?

A note was tucked into the bundle. Josie plucked it up, glancing at the roses that seemed, somehow, accusatory, as if it were *she* who'd trapped them in this warm, felted darkness. Breathing deeply, she flicked the tiny envelope open and retrieved the handwritten card within.

Hey Babe, it began, and the pit of Josie's stomach opened as if to some yawning, internal abyss. Never, never once in their twenty years together, had Mark called her babe. *I know the next two months are going to be hard. I'll miss you every single day. You just need to trust me, Jen. I promise that everything we've planned will happen when I get back, and in the meantime, here are two dozen roses, a dozen for each month I'll be gone, to remind you of what's next. Love and a hundred kisses, M.*

Josie staggered back as if the car had burned her, the note pinched in her fingers. Her thoughts spun so fast she was dizzy. She looked at the house she'd shared with her husband for two decades, the house where they'd raised their son together, her mouth open in shock. Overhead, a summer moon rose in the pale, bluing sky.

And Josie knew she'd been right all week. She'd been right, damn it. Her life was about to change.

But it was going to change in the manner of a car wreck, or an earthquake, or a hurricane. She squeezed her eyes shut, everything she thought she knew whirling around her, and tried to breathe.

Josie Ballard was forty-two years old, standing in the vicinity of a traitorous Prius and an even more traitorous bundle of roses, under a moon that shone like a nickel above her familiar, tired, split-level home.

And there, in her own driveway, which she'd lined with tulips and daffodils, where she'd taught her son to park a car and ride a bike, where they'd drawn pictures with sidewalk chalk and once, long ago, where she'd passed over the threshold as a new bride—there she was, in the place she knew best, utterly and completely lost.

CHAPTER THREE

Josie

Gardner, Kansas

Josie wasn't sure how she mustered the courage to do it.

She wasn't, after all, known for courage.

She felt as if she'd been hit with a cannonball, there in the driveway, as if her chest were so blown open that wind whistled right through it. Still, she made herself walk back to the Prius. She picked up the roses, holding them by the stems gingerly, as if they'd crawled into the hatchback and died. With the note pinched in her other hand, she walked up to the front door.

Mark was in their bedroom, a towel wrapped around his waist, running a hand over his wet hair and whistling as she approached. His glasses were off, his T-shirt-tan dark from his many hours spent biking country roads. As Josie paused in the doorway, watching him, a thought hit her like a fresh bullet. Had he really been biking all those weekends? When he pedaled away like a middle-aged man rekindling his boyhood, where did he actually go?

Mark turned just as she felt her knees weakening, and, taking three desperate steps backward, she stumbled onto the love seat opposite the bed. He looked happy as he turned, in the moment before he took her in. But then his gaze fell on the roses, and the note. And, like Josie's, his mouth dropped open.

"Who," she croaked, her voice abandoning her. She cleared her throat. "Who is Jen?"

Mark stood so still it was as if someone had pulled his plug from the socket. Josie could sense his mind darting around, seeking a way out. She let the roses drop to the carpet between her feet, a few petals exploding outward as they landed.

"Nobody," he sputtered, and Josie met his stare. In a flash, she saw the two of them as they'd once been, so many years ago, before she'd found out she was pregnant, before she'd dropped out of college to live in their first little apartment with baby Charlie, before they'd married and bought the house in one fell swoop, their toddler in tow, expanding their lives into a proper adulthood. She remembered the way it had felt to be so young, to be held in his arms, cradled as if he were an oyster and she the pearl. She remembered the way they'd shared their fears and hopes with one another, drinking wine and eating Thai food in her dorm-room bed. The way they'd laughed until they'd cried, and dreamed, and loved. The promises they'd made.

How had they traveled from there to here?

Again, she cleared her throat, holding her husband's stare. "Tell me the truth, Mark."

He looked from her to the floor. A full minute ticked by before he spoke.

"I was going to tell you after the trip." He sighed, then shrugged. "Do you remember Peter's mom?"

Peter's mom? The mother of one of Charlie's childhood friends? She gaped.

"Well, we reconnected at a corporate event a few months ago. It turns out she's a local businesswoman, too—a Realtor. We didn't mean to, Jo—I swear to God. But we've fallen in love." He sat down on the corner of the bed, the towel fanning out between his hairy legs. Josie was still trying to comprehend his words, the use of *we* and *love* utterly undigestible. There was nowhere for her in that sentence. She was *nowhere*. And yet she'd been here all along.

"I meant to drop those off before coming home, but I ran out of time. I'm sorry, Jo."

She shook her head, freshly stunned. Was he apologizing for his carelessness with the roses or his affair? For a second, she wanted to plead with him, to take an eraser to everything that had just happened. *You're supposed to love me,* she wanted to sob. She, who'd had his baby, and washed his boxers and bike shorts, and made his dinners, and reminded him to pick up his prescriptions, and attended his work parties and smiled at his friends and colleagues who only rarely remembered her name. She wanted to echo his words, spoken in the kitchen just moments ago.

Can you undo it?

Cold rinsed through her, like rain. Had he pressed her to remain full-time at the school library so he could leave her more easily? Additional questions followed: Had he actually been working overtime all these months, or had he been somewhere else? Was he actually worried about money? Or was he just trying to extricate himself from her, like an octopus from a net, tentacle by tentacle?

Amid the accumulating questions, Josie picked just one to ask.

"What were you going to tell me after the trip?"

Mark raised his head from his hands, his cheeks reddened, his eyes bright, and she knew before he said it.

"I want a divorce."

Without thinking, Josie stumbled to her feet. She felt like she might be sick, or like she might detonate into a thousand tiny pieces. She passed Mark where he was perched on the mattress, catching sight of herself in the bedroom mirror: Her hair, no longer blond these days but a sort of light brown tinged silver at the temples, had fallen out of its messy ponytail. Her face was as pale as a plate, aside from a slash of pink flaming across her freckled cheeks. She wore a plain white T-shirt and jeans in the same wash she'd bought for years. Suddenly, Josie wanted to hit that mirror with a hammer, to shatter this reflected moment. Instead, she went to the closet while Mark watched. She lugged her suitcase out and tipped it onto its wheels. She'd been so excited about the trip that she'd packed early, checking and rechecking her lists. Her passport was in her purse.

She was ready to go.

"Jo?" Mark ventured, standing up, his towel loosening. "What are you doing?"

She said nothing, lugging the suitcase across the carpet, forcing it to roll, intent on the hallway. When she reached the stairs, Mark drifted in her wake, his voice growing more urgent.

"Josie. Don't be crazy! Can you just sit down for a minute so we can talk?"

No, she could not. She wrestled the suitcase down the stairs while Mark stood at the top with his hands on his hips, still in his towel, shaking his head as if he was witnessing lunacy. And maybe he was.

Josie didn't know, and she didn't care.

"Just give me one goddamn minute, Josie!" he repeated as the suitcase bumped onto the landing, but she didn't slow. All she knew was that she needed to get out of this house, and away from her husband, as fast as possible. Somewhere behind him, the oven timer still beeped.

At the door, she turned, finally meeting his baffled gaze. She felt the tears gathering within her, but she froze them into ice. She would not cry—not yet.

"Don't follow me," was all she said, and then she opened the front door.

~

Three days later, Josie sat on the bench seat of her dad's old farm truck, clutching her purse to her knees, watching planes rise up in the cloudless sky and arc into the distance. They were nearing the airport, finally, and her nerves lifted higher with each departing plane. Her dad, hunched over the wheel beside her, maintained his usual stream-of-consciousness chatter, though it was peppered with uncharacteristic bafflement.

"I just can't believe that after all these years—twenty *years*, Jojo—old Mark wasn't the man I figured he was," he said for at least the fifteenth time, shaking his head, his knobby knuckles tightening on the wheel. He frowned under his mustache, glowering at the road unspooling beneath the tires. "Far as I'm concerned, that husband of yours can take a long walk on a short dock." He shook his head, his brows coming together like dual toothbrushes. "You know Aunt Mildred never did like him? She had a way with people—men, especially. Could see through 'em like a clean window—"

"Dad," Josie ventured, "I don't want to keep rehashing—"

"Now, see here," he interrupted, heedless of the normal back-and-forth rules of conversation, lost in his own currents of thought. "You know I always liked him, Josie girl, always thought he was a good kid. Even when he knocked you up before putting a ring on your finger, which took your mom a spell to get over, let me assure you, I liked him . . ."

He talked on, and she stared out at the road skipping by, willing herself to remain patient as he recounted various episodes of her broken life. This was just her dad's way of working through it, of comprehending that his daughter had been shucked like tassels from a corncob. It wasn't in his nature to comprehend it. Josie's parents had forever been on her side, had been ludicrously proud of her even when she'd failed to achieve much at all. Her father, now her lone parent, simply couldn't make sense of the fact that her marriage—one of her only true achievements—had failed, too.

So he was compelled to discuss it. Over and over.

"To leave you, Josie?" he continued. "You? Hot *damn*. The man's antenna might be up, but he's surely not gettin' all the channels."

When she'd landed on her father's doorstep three days earlier, suitcase in hand, she got through a mere sentence of explanation before her dad turned, rather stiffly, headed back into the house, and started searching for his ever-misplaced phone. At first, she'd just been glad he wasn't searching for his rifle. When he'd located the phone, she had to physically take it from him to prevent him from calling Mark and voicing whatever outrage was cohering behind his deepening frown.

Now he was preparing to launch into a familiar stream of invectives, a stream she'd heard more than once, when she interrupted. "I know," she said over the engine's rumble, surprised when he fell momentarily silent. "I know what he is, Dad."

But did she? Had she ever really known the man she'd married?

The question had hounded her for the last three days as her dad trailed her around the farmhouse and ranch, nursing a mug of Folgers coffee, repeating statements of fury and dismay. If anyone had seen it, Josie knew, onlookers would imagine her dad was in the throes of early dementia. Yet she knew that wasn't the case. He'd always been this way. He spoke in well-worn idioms at least half the time; he had an arrow in his quiver for just about every quirk of human behavior, a saying for any occasion. And now all those arrows were aimed at Mark.

"I just think," he muttered, as if to the air, "he's proven himself to be the wrong end of an ugly horse. That's all I'm saying."

An image of Mark flashed in Josie's mind, and pain pounded alongside her pulse. She saw her wayward husband's half grin, his swift humor rising behind it. She saw his hands, gentle and brown from the sun. His eyes, overlarge behind his glasses, the exact same blue as their son's.

Charlie. For the hundredth time, she thought about Charlie and how he knew nothing of what had transpired in the last three days. Her darling boy, who'd likely been immersed in his biochem lab at the exact moment his parents' lives blew apart. None the wiser.

And the worst thought of all: At some point, they would have to tell him.

"Well, Josie girl," her dad said, slowing as they ascended the long curve of highway heading to the departure gates, "you go over there and have a wonderful time, kid. Have an experience. Leave that bastard in the dust, where he belongs."

She nodded, meeting her dad's eye as he risked a glance away from the road. His face was as lined as the ancient leather boots he'd pulled on every day for several decades. He was coming into his busy season, old widower that he was. There was hay to cut and cattle to feed. He still managed the ranch she'd grown up on, though now it was half the operation it once was, and he had younger, paid help to bring in the hay and care for the animals. Still, soon he'd be busier than a one-armed paper hanger, as he'd assured her several times while they drank Folgers together on the porch. She knew he didn't want her to worry about him, and he knew that she did. They both knew he was lonely out on the ranch. All he had to treasure, anymore, were days gone by.

And Josie, who would soon fly far, far away.

The airport terminal loomed, and a sign declaring DEPARTURES appeared over the slowing line of cars. Josie's stomach clenched. A surge of anxiety rolled through her like a breaker: She was really doing this. Could she do this? She hadn't been anywhere, aside from a couple of corporate trips for Mark's work, all her adult life. She was middle-aged, and she had no idea how to manage in a foreign country where she didn't speak the language. She had no idea how to navigate public transport, or foreign grocery stores, or airports, or really anything at all.

Alone.

Her anxiety ratcheted up. All the times she'd imagined herself in Italy, she never imagined that.

For a second, Josie thought she'd throw up right there on the floormat of her dad's old truck. She bent over her purse, closing her eyes and breathing deeply as they pulled to a slow stop alongside the curb. Would she be able to navigate the airport? She was embarrassed to admit, even to herself, that she'd spent the morning watching videos on YouTube to learn what to expect. It was shameful for a grown woman to be so inept in the world, wasn't it? Yet she'd been so busy raising Charlie, so busy navigating the terrifying challenges of his childhood, that everything else had fallen away. And later, she'd spent her days supporting Mark, and stretching dollars, and minding middle schoolers, and watching her mother die.

She'd had no time—no time at all—to learn everything she imagined a normal grown woman should know.

"Josephine."

Her father's voice was quiet, yet it splintered through her revolving panic. His hand, calloused and arthritic, landed on her knee.

"Jojo. Listen."

She opened her eyes, glancing at him sidelong.

"You'll be just fine, kid." His voice was as low as a tenor's, gravelly as an old man's. Which he was, of course—sometimes she didn't see it. A lump rose in her throat. "Just fine," he repeated. "You get out there and live. Take this chance. God knows you've earned it."

She nodded, and he wiped a tear from the creases under his eyes with his free hand. Her own eyes filled.

"And if I kill him," her dad said, a glint in his gaze, "I'll letcha know."

Josie laughed through her tears, her father patted her knee with an air of finality, and, as if synchronized, they unbuckled and hoisted themselves out of their opposite doors. Moments later they convened at the truck's dusty tailgate. Her dad heaved her gigantic suitcase down, waving away her offers of help, and wheeled it, now decorated with a few stray stems of hay, into her waiting hands.

His face creased, a thousand lines re-forming, and his eyes twinkled brightly.

"Go get 'em, Jojo."

An intercom echoed somewhere in the background, and travelers streamed toward the terminal, moving purposefully through the doors, and yet time seemed to pause. Without planning it, Josie fell into her dad's stiff embrace. He patted her back with his knobby hands and kissed her cheek, his mustache rough on her skin.

"You can do anything anyone else can," he whispered. "And more."

She nodded, wiping her cheeks, and found the handle of her suitcase. He saluted her as if she were going to war, and they both chuckled. And then she found herself stepping away, pulling breath into her tightening lungs, and she wheeled the suitcase toward a pair of glass doors.

They opened, beckoning her onward.

Josie turned once more to glance back at her dad, alone beside the truck, his hands propped in his pockets. He nodded. And she thought of her mother, who'd been endlessly brave, refusing to complain even once through months of radiation and chemotherapy. When she'd lost her battle, she'd left Josie a notebook filled with gardening advice, just in case Josie ever opened the flower shop she'd dreamed of since she was little—a dream long since abandoned. Also in the notebook, there was a cashier's check representing every penny her mother had squirreled away over the years.

It was, of course, how Josie found herself bound for Italy now.

And so, unnerved and alone as she was, she had to go.

She glanced at the kiosks appearing before her, guarding the baggage drops like the little self-checkouts at the grocery store, inscrutable. The noise of the airport melded into a low, continuous hum around her.

"I can figure this out," she whispered to herself, approaching a kiosk, knots in her stomach. There was this, and then the airport itself, and then her connecting flight at a different airport, and the airport on the other side, and the taxis and trains and buses, and the new towns and strangers and an apartment she'd have to locate, all alone.

All of it, on her own.

For many years, Mark had figured such things out. She hadn't planned it that way, hadn't meant to let him take over—there was just always so much to do every day, between work and home, groceries and lunchboxes, laundry and music lessons, baseball and playdates, grade checks and college applications, and the accursed, never-ending laundry. So they'd divided and conquered.

And now Josie didn't know how to do approximately half of life.

She breathed, forcing down her rising anxiety. It might not leave anytime soon, she knew. So, as she tapped on the kiosk's screen, gripping her suitcase with her free hand, she thought of a message she'd seen on coffee mugs and, if she recalled, a poster in the middle school guidance counselor's office.

If the fear won't go, it read, *you'll just have to do it afraid.*

CHAPTER FOUR

Cicero

Pompeii, Italy

Loyalty is a concept not all humans understand.

Giorgio, however, did, and I've long suspected that it's what brought him back to my side.

This hypothesis makes sense to me because, of course, loyalty is nothing short of a dog's driving life force, an overwhelming blend of love and duty and purpose that shapes canine existence. It's powerful stuff, I tell you. And *certamente*, I am quite sure that my undying loyalty to Giorgio was reciprocated, emphasis on the *undying* bit.

Are you confused, my friend? I can sense your multiplying questions. What happened to Giorgio in the first place, you might ask? After eight long years of inseparable friendship, why were we parted? How could *I*, treasured companion that I was, inhabitant of a grand house on a hill, have become one of Pompeii's cast-off mutts?

Allow me to explain.

I lost Giorgio on an evening in early June.

We sat outside on our *terrazza* at twilight, as we always did, watching rivers of orange and blue merge like a confluence in the sky. The vanishing sun set fire to distant hills, burnishing them gold, yet I knew darkness would soon overcome even such vivid light. I'd seen it every evening of my life, *infatti*, for we sat out there in any kind of weather, bidding goodbye to the day. There was a pergola covered in grapevines that kept us dry when it rained, and the open *terrazza* for evenings like that one in June—warm and lovely, as if day was happy to welcome its old friend, night.

"I've been thinking of a poem this evening, Cicero," Giorgio said, leaning back in his wooden chair, making it creak. "Listen to this line, *ragazzo mio*, by Rumi. 'The moon stays bright when it doesn't avoid the night.'" His eyes, a bit glassy that evening, reflected the sky. "Do you agree with Rumi here, Cicero?"

I glanced up from my sheepskin bed, always positioned next to whichever chair he inhabited, and cocked my head. I stared at him ardently, my way of assuring him that *sì, sì*, indeed, I agreed with the poets of old on many things. And I agreed with Giorgio on *every*thing. Does any of this surprise you? Are you a bit baffled, a bit disbelieving to learn of a literate dog? I could not parse through the pages myself, of course, yet by my eighth year I'd consumed many a collection of poetry, many a book.

All my life, Giorgio had read to me. Sometimes he read an entire novel aloud, glancing over its cover to catch my gaze at poignant moments, and other times he tossed tidbits from poems or stories, much like he fed me nibbles from his meals. Giorgio, you see, regarded me not as a mere pet, but as a friend who could listen. I had no spoken language with which to respond, *certo*, but I managed to share my own thoughts with a cock of the head, a meaningful stare, or a well-placed bark. He knew I had them—thoughts. Unlike many humans are wont to do with those of us who travel on four legs, he never underestimated me.

One of Giorgio's big hands cradled a fine glass of red wine that night, like every night. The other came down to land on my head and rub me gently about the ears. I have always rather liked my ears. They pop off my skull, ever alert, but at the tips, they fold down as if nodding politely. They suit me well, as do my tidy little paws and bright brown eyes. I have been told a time or two that I resemble a noble British breed—the Jack Russell—which cannot be entirely my lineage, as my mother looked nothing like a terrier. Yet such is life, full of surprises.

Giorgio and I always paid considerable attention to our appearance. We used to check ourselves in the mornings before departing the villa, turning this way and that before the mirror to make sure his shoes were shined and my collar properly buffed, appreciating the dapper image we cut together, a gentlemanly pair. Then we'd stroll down to the village, settle at a streetside table, and enjoy a cappuccino and a bowl of *latte*, respectively. Each day was the same for us. Our habits were as reliable as the sunset, as constant as the coming stars.

Yet, that evening, everything changed.

I do not appreciate change, as you might imagine.

As I lay there on my sheepskin bed, my eyes closing in reverie as Giorgio petted my velvety ears, I missed what I should have noticed. I was lulled by the peace of the moment. This, I tell you, is my life's greatest regret.

I should have known.

Dogs, you may have heard, can sense things that are beyond the scope of human perception. We can feel not only the heartbeats in those around us, but also their goodness or lack of it. Some of us can smell cells that have gone awry within a body, or the acrid stench of encroaching illness. I am more of a poet than a scientist, at heart, yet even so, I'm aware of the invisible biological drama in the world around me, the intricacies of the unknown. Most animals are; humans are unique in their ability to muzzle their intuition.

Still, I ignored mine that night. I must have, because I failed to sense the seizing in Giorgio's heart, the struggle. I failed to discern his slowing, spasmodic pulse. I failed to alert him before it was too late, to bark for help, to run for a neighbor.

In sum, I failed my dearest friend entirely.

One moment my eyes were closed, the last, lowering shafts of sunlight warming my nose, and the next Giorgio's glass was shattering before my paws, a thousand sparkling shards spraying out amid spilled wine that spread like blood.

And Giorgio, my Giorgio, jerked thrice in his creaking chair and then became utterly motionless.

For nearly two days, I didn't leave him. I remained on the *terrazza*, moving gingerly around the broken glass to lick at his slack hands, nose his elbow, and even climb up on his bony lap, which was never our custom, and bathe his face in frantic kisses. Then I curled up there, on his cold thighs, fully aware of what had befallen us, yet unable to accept it. He had died. *Died.* No, it couldn't be, I argued with myself. For if he died, how could I live on?

I would have stayed there forever if the owner of the village café hadn't appeared, concerned at the interruption to our daily ritual. He shuffled through the grand house and out onto the *terrazza*, his dark eyes widening.

"Madonna mia!" he exclaimed, bursting into a clumsy run. *"Oddio. Oddio!"*

Later, many more people appeared, trickling in one or two at a time. And even later still, they took Giorgio from me, and I was no longer half of a pair.

~

How on earth, you're surely wondering, did he return to me?

Once again, my dear limited human, there is much you don't understand. Settle back and listen well, if you will.

It happened on the evening of my tenth day in exile, while I lay on the ancient stone stoop that had become my bed in the wilderness of Pompeii and waited. As I've mentioned, I didn't realize then that I was awaiting not death, but Giorgio. That deep in the shards of my broken heart, some part of me believed he would return.

Now, do understand, this was not a conscious thought. I would not have thought this consciously, for if nothing else, I am a sensible dog. Most people do not return once they have died.

Most.

"Cicero," a voice called faintly, interrupting my restless dreams. My head shot up, and I breathed in the sultry evening air. Something tickled my whiskers like an eddying wind.

"Cicero, come! Come, *ragazzo mio*!"

My small heart pounded in my chest, and I sprang up from my stone bed, staring in the direction of the voice. It was Giorgio—I'd recognize him anywhere. But how could it be? Someone whistled.

The sound was a bit unusual. Both the voice calling my name and the whistle seemed more like an echo than anything close, anything real. It sounded like Giorgio was trapped in a cavern far away. Did some part of me understand, even then? Did some part of me recognize what was to come?

I bounded off my stoop, sniffing the air, my gaze darting about the ruined city spread before me. An ancient road spooled from my feet, the paving stones bigger than me and worn smooth by passing centuries. Buildings—if you could call them that—lined it, their brick walls rising, partially intact, along the road. A few wild dogs lay in the shade of the crumbling walls on the lee side of the sunset, where the stone was cool. One, a scruffy old fellow, glanced at me with lidded eyes, then lifted his head to watch something emerge from the shadows down the lane.

Someone.

I cocked my head, ears up, sniffing the air fervently. It was Giorgio! I took in his familiar ambling gait, hitching a bit due to his bad knee, his hand raising to give me a wave, his shock of silver hair catching the slanting sun. But then, even as I burst into a wiggling, ecstatic run, I noticed the changes. It wasn't only Giorgio's hair that was silver now. His entire figure was silver and shimmery, like a drop of water passing through light. I could see him, yet he wasn't fully there.

And he had no odor.

This was most alarming of all—the absence of aftershave, shoe polish, and coffee breath—yet it did not stop me. I ran to him, my entire soul a streak of electric joy, and as I leaped up to land in his outstretched arms, the world seemed to slow. I sailed toward Giorgio, as I had every time he came home from a rare, dogless outing, sending me into a slingshot's arc upon his return. My entire heart propelled me into his arms, which I could not wait to feel closing around me.

Yet they didn't.

Like a shuttlecock missing a racket, I arced through the sunlight and shadows and tumbled onto the ancient paving stones.

I hit with a thud, rolling twice, and lay there for a stunned second. Then Giorgio was at my side, crouching over me, casting no shadow.

"Cicero," he gasped. "Cicero, my boy. Are you hurt?" Again, his voice sounded strange, as though he were far away and not right there next to me. The old mutt resting in the shade cocked his head, studying Giorgio, and then sighed as if he'd seen it all.

I shook myself out of my shock and stood, wiggling again with a joy I couldn't suppress despite my mounting confusion, my expanding dread. He reached out as if to pet me, yet I did not feel his hand.

"Merda," he murmured, and his familiar face, lined as a map that's been in a pocket, crumpled. He looked as if he was caught somewhere between smiling and weeping, his translucent eyes heartbroken. Yet I sensed no heartbeat within him, none at all. My comprehension was catching up, quickly, and my spirits sank with his. Still, I bowed as if to play, wagging fiercely, trying to reassure him. I barked, just once, as if to echo his sentiment: *Shit.* Truly.

"I haven't figured this out yet, Cicero, my boy. You must forgive me, little friend."

Again, I tried to climb into his arms, to lick his face, a reflex I couldn't suppress. But when I jumped up on my hind legs to do so, I touched what felt like a cold draft of wind before falling back onto all fours. *Sì,* this is how it would be. I understood, well enough. I was a dog, after all—the mysteries of the unseen world were not unfamiliar to me, as you recall. But such mystery swallowing *Giorgio*, my lifelong companion, was destabilizing. I confess it took me longer than it should have, out there on that ancient road, to grasp what had happened. To accept it.

I knew ghosts existed, *certo*. I'd never sought them out and had never seen one quite so clearly, yet they hovered around villages and farms here and there, lost and wandering. There was even one in Pompeii. Only one, mind you—the original inhabitants of the ruined city had likely departed long, long ago. The lone ghost hung about the Casa degli Amanti, but he kept to himself. They all did, in my experience. Ghosts largely ignored the living, and we ignored them.

Now, for me, that would change.

"Don't trouble yourself, Cicero!" Giorgio exclaimed, taking pains to brighten his voice, to reassure me. "You must not worry. I am here, even if I'm not quite myself." He held out a hand, turning his swollen, silver knuckles over in the fading light, briefly examining them. Marveling. *"Sono io,"* he muttered, then batted that hand as if to say, *What did it matter?* He was different, but he was back.

"I've been searching for you, *ragazzo mio*. When I found myself waking up—because that's the only way I can describe it, Cicero, I awoke a few days ago, as if from a coma. I was on our *terrazza*, in the chair, all alone. It has been terribly confusing, I tell you. Anyhow, after I made a bit of peace with the—" He hesitated, again holding up his hand and turning it over, a gesture I imagined he'd performed countless times in recent days. Then he sighed and carried on. "After I came to terms with my situation, I set off to find you. I went to my son's house first, if you can believe it. Why are you not there, Cicero? I spelled it out in my will, dear boy. He had my car, such as it is, but not you! I could not have been clearer. I'm an old man, you see, I knew I might—that this might—" He could not seem to say the words, but I thought them: *You might die*.

Because yes, he had absolutely died. And now he would haunt me.

And, as my own bewilderment faded to acceptance, I was beyond delighted. He was back! Things would be different, *certo*. He could no longer pet me, and he could not carry me, either, but that was fine. It had never been our way, after all. We were gentlemen, dignified and reserved.

I glanced once more at the shaggy mutt who'd witnessed our reunion, but he'd already gone back to sleep. No dog is overly surprised by the presence of a spirit, just as we're unsurprised by wind, or birds, or shifts in the weather. Ghosts are not to be feared, my friend. They are simply people who could not leave this world because their hearts were not quite finished with it. That's how I understand them, anyhow. And they're *always* human. I suppose animals know they're meant to travel on, and so they do, posthaste. Mind you, the vast majority of people depart as well, a fact made clear by the relatively small number of souls left hanging about. Where do they all go, you ask? Who knows? Even Giorgio, dead as he was, missed the signal for whatever turn he was meant to take. He couldn't explain it, even when he tried.

My theory? I believe he couldn't yet leave because he was worried about me. This makes absolute sense.

There was, also, the small matter of his son. I had nothing but disdain for the man, but Giorgio would be no more capable of abandoning him than he was me. Because Giorgio, like any good dog, and the best of humans, was nothing if not loyal.

CHAPTER FIVE

Josie

Napoli to Sorrento, Italy

Josie stared out the train window, spellbound, her hands gripping the handle of her suitcase where it sat propped between her knees. She tried to breathe. This was the final step of her journey to the *appartamento* she'd booked so many months before. She couldn't believe she'd nearly made it.

Also, she couldn't wait. The train, which had surely been built well before she was born, lurched between impossible speeds and precipitous stops, over and over, adding more and more commuters from various graffitied platforms. It was crowded beyond reason, the air trapped within the carriage as stifling as hot breath. Sweat tickled Josie's lower back, wetting her T-shirt, and she kept having to wipe away stray hairs that stuck to her glistening face. People packed the aisles, and in the seats surrounding Josie everyone's knees angled around her ridiculous suitcase. She yearned to apologize for this whenever a local traveler looked askance at her luggage, eyes just shy of rolling, but she couldn't remember what to say. So she kept her gaze on the window.

Outside, scenery slid by as the train rocked south. Residential buildings spread in every direction, pastel-colored blocks stacked against each other and the abruptly rising hillsides. Laundry flapped between balconies, and the streets below hummed with cars, mopeds, and people. Occasionally, the ocean flashed in passing gaps, silver in the afternoon sun.

Josie hadn't imagined the city and its environs would be so *big*, so sprawling. An image of her own suburb, with its tidy storefronts and surrounding neighborhoods, all laid out on a grid, hung in her mind. Beyond those leafy streets, fields spread like rumpled quilts in every direction. If you were to walk among them, you'd hear nearly nothing.

This place, she thought, couldn't be more different.

She'd merely glimpsed the actual city of Napoli when she'd taken a taxi from the airport to the Stazione Centrale, yet in that glimpse she'd witnessed an overwhelming cacophony. Streets teemed with people walking, talking, texting, and shouting. Car horns pealed, warning pedestrians to clear the way, which, to Josie's horror, culminated in several near misses. Her own cab driver had taken a rather loose approach to whatever traffic rules existed; when confronted with congestion, he'd simply stepped on the gas, rocking the tiny taxi up onto a cobbled sidewalk, trusting those on foot would leap to safety.

Once in the train station, it had taken Josie several tries to locate the Circumvesuviana Treno, the name of which she'd written down in the notebook she'd created to house her itinerary, and notes, and dreams for all she'd do in the next two months. Eventually, she'd found the stairs down to its platform, under the main station, and figured out how to purchase a ticket having likely, by then, missed more than one departure. Still, she'd made it. She was where she needed to be, on the dingy Circumvesuviana, winding toward Sorrento, her heart in her throat.

Was she really doing this all by herself? Had she ever done anything so independent in her life?

No. That was the simple answer. Perhaps she'd spread her wings a bit when she'd first landed at college, ages ago, but there had been people she'd known there, and the familiar Midwestern landscape surrounding her, and parents she could call whenever the need arose. And, only a few months after arriving at school, there had also been Mark.

Mark, who'd steered her life alongside his ever since. She'd been like the sidecar on a motorcycle.

She glanced at the seat beside her, inhabited by an old woman in a black skirt and heavy shoes, a purse like an anvil on her lap. The woman nodded, though the scowl never left her face, and Josie smiled nervously. If life had gone according to plan, Mark would have been in that seat. What was he doing now?

Her heart ached for a beat.

He'd called, of course. His number was on her missed calls log, in fact, over and over, along with one from her best friend, Ellen. She'd call Ellen eventually—when she was ready to discuss her shock, her grief, her humiliation. But she would *not* call Mark. Pain sharpened within her, like a paper cut on her heart. Was he with his new—what? Lover? Fiancée? Both words made Josie want to gag, just a bit.

And questions hounded her alongside the pain. For the first time in her life, Josie could no longer picture her future. When she returned from this trip, would she live in her own house? Would she work at the middle school until she retired someday? *Could* she retire someday? She didn't know. Her budget had always included two incomes—hers meager and Mark's better, built from years of work she'd enabled him to focus on while she managed everything else. She tightened her grip on the suitcase. When she'd imagined growing old, it was always with her husband on the motorcycle beside her.

And now here she was, middle-aged and seated next to a stranger.

"Dove va?" the old woman said suddenly, interrupting Josie's spinning thoughts. Josie met her stern glare, trying to parse meaning from her question. Perhaps the old woman had seen something akin to panic on her face, and this, a distraction, was an act of pity.

Josie shrugged, grasping for the phrases she'd plucked from months of practice, but they seemed to have left her. The woman, apparently intent on receiving an answer to her query, persisted.

"*Forse* Positano?" she said. "La Costiera Amalfitana?"

She spoke so fast Josie could hardly separate the words. The old woman's scowl deepened, but her voice was kind when she tried again. "Sorrento?"

"Sì!" Josie leaped on the word, repeating it for affirmation. "*Sì, sì.* Sorrento."

"Ah," the woman said, her jowls wiggling as she nodded. "Sorrento *è una città bellissima. Non è più molto lontano.*" She reached over and patted Josie's knee, a gesture that inexplicably raised a lump in her throat.

Josie blinked, nodding as if she'd understood, and the old woman managed a smile.

Moments later, the woman began to shift on her heavy shoes, straightening her skirt and hoisting her gigantic purse as the train slowed to a stop. Then she heaved herself up, paused before Josie, and bestowed one more encouraging pat, this time on the shoulder.

"Buona fortuna, signora."

With that, the old woman was gone.

A few stops later, Josie saw a sign bob past the window. STAZIONE DI SORRENTO. Her heart beat harder.

She'd made it.

~

Josie walked from the train station into the heart of Sorrento, her suitcase bouncing along in her wake, her spirits brightening with every step. The small city, perched above the glittering Mediterranean Sea, was everything she'd imagined it might be.

She wound through narrow, cobbled streets lined with citrus trees and bistro tables, where people sat drinking wine and coffee shaded by clusters of jaunty umbrellas. She emerged into a central piazza, passing under the flags of a dozen nations flapping in the breeze, their poles framing a glimpse of blue sea. Palm trees swayed against stately, pastel-hued buildings, shops lining their ground floors selling watches, handbags, shoes, and pastries. Then more cobblestoned lanes opened before Josie, thick with pedestrians, mopeds buzzing down wider avenues. Josie looked everywhere as she walked, sometimes turning all the way around to gaze up and down, mesmerized.

Soon enough, she found herself moving into quieter streets, approaching the neighborhood where she and Mark had booked an apartment, ages ago. She read street names as she passed block after block, checking her progress against the map on her phone. And then, close to where she was meant to turn, something snagged her interest: a gelato shop.

Josie realized, all at once, that she was not only hot, but famished. Decision made, she detoured toward the shop.

Half a dozen people crowded inside the *gelateria*, and Josie's nerves tightened a bit with the resulting tumult. She tried to recall how to order gelato in Italian, something she'd specifically practiced. *Un gelato, per favore.* She stepped up in line, searching the case, aware of the server behind the counter staring at her as she hurried to pick flavors. Another bumbling tourist, she imagined him thinking, with her oversize suitcase and clumsy Italian. Still, she tried.

"Un gelato, per favore," she said, adding, *"Pistacchio* and *cioccolato."*

Moments later, she stood among the waiting throng, having managed to pay. A bowl with green and brown scoops appeared on the counter, and Josie retrieved it, nodded her thanks, and hurried back into the sunlight.

She'd done it, she thought, as she took a bite of chocolate, fully aware that this small sense of triumph was silly. How hard was it to order an ice cream? Still, she'd traveled all the way to Sorrento by herself, and now she'd purchased something in a different language. It was a beginning.

She started down the cobbles, buoyed, and a voice rang out behind her.

"Cosa fai?"

She turned, blinking in the sunlight, trying to separate the words. A man, oddly, seemed to be in hot pursuit of her. His leather shoes clicked the cobbles as he narrowed the gap between them, frowning behind a pair of dark-rimmed reading glasses. "What," he said, taking in her suitcase and switching languages, "do you mean by this? You stole my gelato." His heavy brows lifted with the question.

She glanced down at her cup, her cheeks heating up. "I didn't steal . . ."

He shook his head, gesturing widely with one arm, his other arm restrained against his chest in a blue sling. *"Menta e cioccolato,"* he said. "This is what you're eating, no?" He looked incredulous, shaking his head as if to say he'd had enough of her nonsense.

Josie glanced at the untouched green scoop in her cup, her heart sinking. It was very, very green. "I'm sorry—" she began. "I thought it was pistachio—"

He interrupted with a wave of his free hand. *"Non è importante."* He puffed air through his lips, his dark eyes roving the street, clearly still exasperated. "But you must pay attention, *sì*?"

Josie nodded, fumbling for her purse. He was, she realized, irritatingly handsome. He had a strong, stubbled jaw, wore a button-down shirt behind his blue sling, and creased slacks. His hair lifted in the breeze. He looked like a man who should be on a yacht, not haggling over ice cream.

"Listen," she said, "I'll pay you for it—"

He waved her off before she could retrieve her wallet. "Certainly not. But you must try a little harder, *sì*? Pay attention. Many of us live here all the time, *capisce*?"

Josie's mouth fell open. She wanted to tell him that this was quite an overreaction, that really anyone, tourist or not, could have made such a mistake, that perhaps he was being a bit of an asshole. But he turned abruptly, apparently finished with her, and strode away.

Josie was left with flaming cheeks and melting gelato, her simple triumph deflated.

"Good grief," she murmured to herself as she finally located the address of the apartment she'd rented, trying to shelve the entire interaction. She paused before the correct door, glancing up and down the quiet lane, so narrow that sunlight didn't slant all the way to the cobbles. Instead of shops and cafés, the street was lined with residential doors, flowerpots flanking a few of them, and the walls were heavy, in places, with bougainvillea. It was as welcoming as it was serene, a place Josie could imagine people living.

A place *she* could live.

She punched the code she'd been given into a keypad on the door, pushing thoughts of the man from the *gelateria* away, suppressing the persistent sense of her own ineptitude, waiting for the lock to click. It did, and Josie exhaled with relief. Then she made her way into a small courtyard of swept paving stones, dotted with potted lemon trees and rosemary and ringed with floors of apartments. Across the pavers, a flight of stairs beckoned, and Josie lugged her suitcase toward them. She struggled up, one laborious step at a time, passing doors and clearing two flights before she found hers.

When she stepped inside, her sense of relief finally spilled over like water in a glass. The apartment was cool compared to the hot day outside, and dim, and sparsely furnished. She let the door close behind her with a heavy click, taking in the living room with its simple wooden table, a single couch, and a lamp. The space had high, stuccoed ceilings, speckled marble floors, and a small kitchen off to one side mirrored by a bedroom on the other. She could just see the bed, made up with crisp white sheets; in a wave of comprehension, she realized how tired she was. Soon, she'd take a shower and a nap, and then she'd figure out what was next.

Anxiety kindled at that thought. What *was* next? Josie thought of Napoli, with its teeming streets. She thought of Rome, which seemed so far off, so complicated. What if she just made the rest of this adventure easy and safe? She could stay in this quaint town, near this apartment, for two months. Couldn't she? What if she did away with the lengthy itinerary she'd planned, full of day trips and overnights and transportation and a million things to navigate all on her own?

Across the living room, a wide window glimmered beyond closed wooden shutters, and Josie went to it, her steps echoing. She unlatched the window, pushed open the shutters obscuring the glass, and gasped. Before her, an array of jumbled rooftops rolled toward a strip of bright-blue sea. Josie stared at the Mediterranean, stunned by a view much more impressive than the rental website had led her to believe. She pivoted, taking in the apartment anew, now bright with daylight.

Her phone began to ring in her right hand. And Josie, unmoored by her ping-ponging emotions, answered it reflexively, without thought, as if it would only be Ellen, as if nothing had changed in her life and calls were not to be avoided.

"Jo? Oh my God, Josie—I've been trying to reach you for days."

It was Mark, of course.

"Where are you?" he demanded, and her heart began to pound as if this wasn't her husband, but a stranger. And maybe, in some ways, that was true.

She mustered her voice. "I thought my dad would've told you—"

"He won't answer my calls, either," Mark said, cutting her off. "I thought about just driving out to the ranch, but I don't even know if that's where you are. Are you staying with him?"

She shook her head, her stare fixed on the Mediterranean, and tried to marshal her voice. "I'm not. I'm in Italy, actually."

For a long moment, there was no sound on the other end of the line. Josie's emotions battled like bumper cars within her. Hadn't he guessed she'd gone to Italy without him? When she took her suitcase and left him, did he imagine she'd also abandon the trip she'd anticipated for so long?

"I never thought you'd go alone," he said finally. "Christ, Jo, it's lucky you're not lost in Europe right now. You're not, right?"

She frowned, the bumper cars crashing. "I'm standing in the apartment we rented."

"Christ," he repeated. "I should just come over there. You can't do this trip alone—"

"Of course I can—"

"Jo, listen." He hesitated for a second, then sighed. "I don't feel comfortable with you traveling alone, and I know you might think I'm not allowed to say so, with everything that's happened, but it's the truth. Don't take this the wrong way, but you go around with your head in the clouds most of the time. And you get so flustered—you'll be a target for anyone who wants to take advantage of a tourist."

"I'm doing fine—"

"I should just come. I'll buy a new ticket tonight and be there by the weekend, and we can hash things out. You left so fast we didn't even have time to talk."

Abruptly, the bumper cars halted in her chest.

"You mean," she said, her voice toneless, "about you divorcing me?"

"N-no," he stammered, "I mean, we have a lot to discuss, sure, and I don't want to do it over the phone. And anyway, everyone expects me to be in Italy, Jo. Charlie thinks I'm there with you now. What's going to happen when he calls and finds out you went alone?"

She hesitated. Her heart seared at the notion. "I guess we'll have to tell him."

And that would be it, she thought. The true end. She thought of Charlie and the anguish this would cause him. The way his carefully built world would collapse.

Mark was quiet for a long time. Had he not foreseen that divorce would be painful? Or had he not been serious about divorcing her, typical of so many men with a woman on the side? Perhaps, in finding the flowers, Josie had forced his hand and now he was scrambling, trying to keep his secret from his friends and coworkers, trying to mitigate the damage.

"Whatever happens," he said finally, "you're still the mother of my son, and my friend, and I care about you. That will never change."

Wouldn't it? What was he talking about?

"Everything will change," she countered. She felt as if she were freezing, slowly, cell by cell. "Everything already has."

"No," he said quickly, clearly knocked off-balance. Josie was never cold. She was never abrupt. "It doesn't have to, Jo. I'm not even sure what I want yet . . ." He trailed off, hearing himself, and she connected the dots.

Of course. The affair wasn't new for Mark. It was only new to Josie, only a matter of urgency to her. The facts of Mark's life had merely tilted a bit when she'd discovered them, while for her, the entire universe had upended.

"Do not come here." She stared out at the sea, watching waves scud across its surface, feeling lost and off-balance, feeling sure of nothing except the fact that Mark could not come here, to her apartment. She couldn't stand to see him. "If you do, I'll have the landlord change the locks."

And with that, she hung up.

Her entire chest felt carbonated, like she was a pop bottle set to explode. She thought of the itinerary she'd drawn up, and in a daze, she went to her purse and pulled out the notebook she'd pored over for months.

She would do it, she decided at once. All of it.

She'd only change where she'd planned to start.

On the Circumvesuviana train, she'd seen the stop for Pompeii. She'd been planning to visit the archaeological site in two weeks, but now she'd bump it up. She knew how to get there, after all; she simply had to retrace today's steps and disembark about halfway back to Napoli. It was manageable.

Yes, Josie thought, bolstered. She needed to find her confidence and prove, to herself and everyone else, that she could make her way in the world.

And she would start with Pompeii.

CHAPTER SIX

Cicero

Pompeii, Italy

My will to live returned with Giorgio.

The night of our reunion we slept inside, bedding down in the Casa del Poeta Tragico upon Giorgio's suggestion. He loves a good tragic poet, I tell you. There was no bedding to be had, of course, so I turned in wistful circles on the ancient stone floor, scratching at the mosaic under my paws, thinking of my sheepskin bed back home.

"Safer for you in here," Giorgio muttered, settling beside me. "With all those big mongrels out there, Cicero."

Indeed.

Could we not return to our own house? I curled into a tight ball, nestled against a wall, and blinked up at Giorgio, willing him to intuit my question. Now that he was back, what prevented us from inhabiting the villa on the hill, as we always had? It came to me almost as soon as the question formed: Giorgio could live there surreptitiously, *certo*, regardless of any forthcoming residents. I, unfortunately, lacked his new stealth.

I huffed at the thought, for it was my house as much as it was Giorgio's, and though I was but a terrier, I should have inherited it. Who would live there now? His damnable son?

"Ah, Hugo," Giorgio muttered, as if he'd read at least a bit of my thoughts. He sat next to me with his legs crossed, something he'd never been able to do in life with his bad knee. He didn't seem the least bit tired, either, and I found myself wondering whether ghosts sleep. Outside, the moon climbed the sky, and he scowled into its silver light, glowing a bit as if he himself were a flake of moonlight, cast off.

"I'm finally putting the pieces together. Hugo left my house—after I'd *died*, mind you—crashed my car, broke his arm, and lost my dog. That's how it happened, *sì*?" He glanced at me, as if for confirmation. "I saw the car, in Sorrento, and the arm, but didn't put it all together until now. *Gesù Cristo.*" Again, his gaze met mine, and the frustration softened under his frothy brow. "Forgive me, for you've had quite an ordeal, my boy, if my assumptions are correct."

They were, more or less. For half a second, I thought about the crash. It had occurred on the autostrada, not far from where I now lay in exile. In a flash, the catastrophe returned to me—the sun too bright, Hugo beside me shouting curses, an oncoming car, screaming metal, and the world rolling over and over, turning upside down. Me, running, my paws raw on hot concrete, my heart vibrating like a violin's string. Just the memory doused me in a fear so cold I could not breathe, so I shook my head to knock it away.

Best not to think of such things.

"He's back in Sorrento," Giorgio continued, his frown so deep wrinkles boxed his mouth. "Twiddling his thumbs, I expect. Not getting on with life even now, at forty-five years of age, with both parents dead and everything to do." He sighed, the sound like gravel in water. "I worry, Cicero. I worry about my boy."

My head shot up. Which boy did he mean? Irritation pricked my very soul, for of course I knew he spoke of Hugo, that miscreant, who was *not* his good boy and not the one he should be fretting over. No.

When Hugo abandoned his father, I'd stepped into the vacancy, filling the hole in Giorgio's battered heart. And I, *veramente*, would never abandon anybody.

Giorgio quieted after that, and I watched him as if searching for clues. What would become of us? What was he planning? Though sitting, he seemed to hang, ephemeral as the moonlight pouring through the Casa del Poeta Tragico's incomplete roof, neither here nor there. As I drifted off, the worry on my dear friend's face grew ever brighter, and I stewed alongside him in my dreams.

~

The next morning was one where nothing seemed to go as it should. The world was a puzzle full of misshapen pieces, and Giorgio and I wandered through it, seeking food.

"You're looking a bit bony there, *ragazzo mio*," he'd said as I stood up in the first shafts of dusty sunlight, shaking myself off. If it were possible, anguish became even more clear in his translucent face. "What have you been eating, eh?" He glanced around the cool, quiet house, cocking an ear as if listening to the stone. "Tourists' scraps?" he guessed. "Garbage?"

I huffed, mortally offended. There was a reason I looked thin—unlike so many of my species, I would never lower myself to eat garbage. Well, not *old* garbage, anyway, and I certainly wouldn't push over a trash can as I'd seen a rather large, curly-haired mutt do two days earlier. Yet I must confess that I'd found a bit of salami stuck in a crack behind that can, after the mutt departed, and that I ate. Oh, how we fall.

During my exile, I'd also partaken in a bite of *panino* shared by a German schoolgirl, and most crucially, the little piles of dog food left by Good Samaritans nightly. Every evening a different car pulled up before Pompeii's entrance, from which someone emerged lugging a bag of cheap dog food. These saintly volunteers seemed to have little in common aside from a love for lost souls. Without them, I likely would have expired the first week.

Still, eating piles of kibble strewn across the cobbles, with no bowl in sight, was not my idea of dining. Even worse, I'd had to shoulder my way in to procure any of it, braving the masses of my flea-ridden brethren, and I never came away with a full stomach. So yes, Giorgio was right: I was famished.

"Shall we go to the *ristorante*?" he asked, and I sprang up at the suggestion, almost giddy. Reality, you see, still came in rather inconsistent waves.

When we arrived at the café, which I'd sniffed around many an afternoon, we realized something in tandem: Giorgio couldn't secure food any more than I could. Gone were the days of ordering a cappuccino and a bowl of *latte*. Gone were the days of whiling away a morning at a bistro table, a pair of gentlemen, welcome anywhere.

"I thought he might toss you something," Giorgio whispered as we stood outside the restaurant, staring inside moments after having been, quite literally, kicked out. When we'd arrived, he'd strode in straightaway, and I'd followed, only to be rudely shooed from the counter. *Vai via!* the server had spat, wielding a kick that, thankfully, only grazed my rump.

Now Giorgio stood shimmering on the patio, crestfallen. "I imagined we would go in," he persisted, "and he would see that you're hungry. What kind of man doesn't feed a hungry dog?" He stared for a long moment at the man in question, bored behind his counter, awaiting the tourists who would soon flood the ruins.

Giorgio's despondence was heartbreaking, yet his shock did not surprise me. After a lifetime of being noticed, wooed, and waited on, it takes more than a week to expect something different. But I was getting it. These days, I was merely a stray dog, and he a ghost. We were welcome nowhere.

It took two more hours for Giorgio to come to a decision.

"I cannot take care of you." He said this, finally, like a confession, after we'd been patrolling trash cans all morning, seeking something like the salami I'd once found. "I can do nothing for you, Cicero."

The sorrow in his voice was as heavy as the heat pouring over us. I halted, staring up at his silvery shape, somewhat difficult to see in the searing light of day.

I yearned to tell him: He was still everything to me, even in this odd state of affairs.

"Ecco," he sighed, "sit, *ragazzo*. Sit here, alongside me, and we shall have a chat."

I perched on the street while Giorgio lowered himself, his knees popping out around him like downed tent poles. I did not like the resignation in his voice, the worry. I could feel something coming.

"Ascoltami," he said. "Listen. I know you will not take this well, Cicero, but I think you must find a new owner."

I froze. I barely blinked, my eyes stinging in the sun.

"Hai capito?" he asked. Giorgio had always been eccentric in this way. His belief in my ability to comprehend him used to provoke eye rolls and gentle teasing from his friends in the village; humans always underestimate the rest of us. Now he gestured to the wider world, as if seeking evidence. "What can I do? Can I feed you? House you? No. And look at all these people wandering around here. *Alive.* What if one of them wants a nice little dog like you?"

I glanced at the people streaming around the ancient streets and buildings. They stared at their phones and guidebooks, squinted at informational plaques, and wandered into the ruins like aliens tentatively exploring a new planet.

No. I could not adopt one of them.

"They cannot all be from far away," Giorgio said quietly, his gaze skipping between the drifting tourists. I sensed his thoughts: He didn't want anyone to take me abroad. No, he wanted a local. Perhaps he intended to tag along?

"I also cannot stay here all the time," Giorgio said, giving me a hard stare. "I have to take care of some other things, you understand. And I don't know if I shall be here permanently, Cicero. What if, one day, I simply vanish? Poof?"

I sneezed, allergic to the very idea.

He looked from me back to the tourists, falling silent for a long, long time. I didn't like it, I tell you. I didn't like all the things he was thinking, all the thoughts I could sense as if they were rancid, rank as the tin garbage cans heating up in the southern sun.

"You will not do it if I'm here, *sì*?" he said eventually. "*Capisco*, Cicero. *Capisco.*"

With that, Giorgio let the subject drop, and we continued wandering around the stifling ruins, aimless. The sun rose and dipped back toward earth. We dodged big dogs, sought shade, and finally, at the end of the day, emerged when a volunteer appeared with my nightly kibble delivery.

For the entire day, I felt as if I were walking on a tightrope, but I did not know why.

Now I do. *Certo.*

Because I went to sleep alongside Giorgio in the Casa del Poeta Tragico once again that night. I watched him in the slowly arcing moonlight, until my eyes could stay open no longer.

And when I awoke, Giorgio was gone.

CHAPTER SEVEN

Josie

Pompeii, Italy

Right from the start, Josie's day veered toward the unexpected.

She arrived at Pompeii successfully, getting off at the correct stop and finding the entrance just as the ticket booths were opening. She waited in a snaking, sunlit line, surprisingly long for so early in the morning, and her mind galloped off in unwanted directions. It had been doing so since she woke. Really, her thoughts had begun to run wild the moment she hung up on Mark, and though she'd tried to steer them, Josie found she couldn't. Her mind went where it wanted, and apparently, and quite unexpectedly, what it wanted was Mark.

Also, apparently, it wanted to leap right from denial to mourning. Which was very inconvenient, seeing how today Josie was supposed to be setting out boldly into this new country, proving that she could move forward without her husband.

Her husband. Tears leaked from her eyes as she stood in the line labeled *biglietti*, and she blotted their corners and slid her sunglasses down. Why was this happening now? Had she held back her feelings for so many days that her walls had finally begun to spring leaks? She'd also cried on the train ride, failing to stifle her tears the full forty minutes, the sign for the Pompeii Scavi station blurring upon approach. Josie was furious with her lack of control. Now she tucked her guidebook into her tote bag, freeing her hand to again wipe at her cheeks, hoping people in line weren't wondering about this weepy American in their midst. All around her, tourists shuffled forward in groups of two or more, chatting in various languages, sharing cereal bars and bending over maps and phone screens, their foreheads touching as they peered at something together.

And no matter how hard Josie tried to force him away as she stood there, surrounded by strangers, Mark crept into her mind.

She saw his face, so familiar, his smile quirking up and crow's-feet crinkling around his eyes. She saw flashes of him from years past. There he was, stringing lights on the Christmas tree, stepping back over and over to make sure they were perfect. And there he was with Charlie on his chest, asleep in a baby carrier. She remembered how Mark used to duck to kiss their son's little hatted head. If she closed her eyes, she could feel his hand in hers, his grip strong. She thought of the way he ate muesli every morning, pouring milk into the bowl first. For twenty years, she'd teased him about his out-of-order cereal habits, and he'd responded by encircling her waist with his muscled arm and pulling her to him.

Twenty years. And then, without invitation, a newer memory flashed: the hatchback opening and the roses staring up, shockingly red in the twilight, transforming her into a fool.

How had she misunderstood her life so thoroughly?

She stepped forward in the ticket line, nearly there. *"Un biglietto, per favore,"* she whispered under her breath, drawing up the phrase she'd practiced. One ticket, please. Just one.

Loss hit her over and over, like waves on a beach.

Moments later, the woman in the booth slid her a ticket, failing to smile amid her murmured, *"grazie,"* and then Josie was set loose in the park.

The first surprise came within minutes: Pompeii was absolutely enormous. Josie had studied her guidebook and watched travel videos, but she knew, walking into the ruins, that research hadn't done it justice. Ancient roads scrolled before her, intersecting each other in grids, lined with building after building. She wandered farther in, thoughts of her life falling away in the face of the strange world opening before her.

The ruins were not only vast, but far less ruined than she'd realized. Josie stepped through a doorway, wandering into a building that had once been a house, pausing before a fresco still vivid on the wall. She took it in: The painting was of a woman, her head ringed in olive leaves, her eyes, Josie thought, rather startled. Who was she? Josie stared at the woman's lovely, worried face, questions falling around her like the ash that had once blanketed the city. Had this woman really lived? What had her life been like?

Eventually, Josie made her way out of that first house, threading through clusters of tourists, drifting about as if in a dream. The day was heating up, already. She would need to develop a plan, she thought, to see everything. In a moment, she would retrieve her guidebook, the map, and the audio recorder she'd rented at the ticket booth. She wanted to see it all, to learn all she could. But for just a bit longer, she'd simply take it in.

She was *here*, in Pompeii, a place she'd dreamed of seeing for so long.

Josie spotted an overhang on the next street, sheltering a display she'd read about—casts, a handful of several collections dotting the ruins. As she neared, her breath shallowed. The casts were actually shapes of human beings, people who'd lived in the doomed city and had been encapsulated, on the fateful day, in hot ash. The cavities their bodies once inhabited had been discovered by archeologists, filled with plaster, and thus they'd become casts of humans frozen in their dying moments, forever bracing against disaster.

Haunting, Josie thought. That's what it was.

She bent slightly before a glass case, studying the figure within it. The person lay prone, covering their eyes. She thought of fate, vibrating through human lives like a plucked string.

"Howdy."

A voice splintered her thoughts, and she jolted a little, straightening. A man approached the glass case, giving her a nod, and she felt it the way all women feel such things. She knew, somehow, that he was coming over to see her, not the cast.

"Quite a thing, isn't it?" he asked, standing a bit too close as he bent to peer in.

"It really is," she said, noncommittal. The man's belly hung over his shorts as he stooped, frowning at the frozen human, his face florid in the rising heat.

"Place is a trip," he said. "A real goddamn trip."

She shrank away, just a bit, trying not to appear overly rude, though she wanted to cease the conversation before it began. Had he sought her out because he could tell she was American? She glanced down at her outfit: capri pants, walking shoes, a white T-shirt. Her hair was in a loose braid on her neck, bits of it falling out and sticking to her face. Did she look as Midwestern as he did? He turned to regard her, his eyes flicking up and down, and suddenly Josie felt her loneliness like a garment. It was like a dress, sticking to her in the heat, impossible to strip off.

"Where you from?" the man asked after a moment.

She forced a smile. "Kansas. You?"

"Texas." He grinned. "Panhandle area. Go Chiefs, am I right?" He chuckled, and she shrugged. "I'm here for work, actually," he continued. "Staying in Naples for a couple of months. Where you staying?"

Josie glanced over her shoulder as a fresh bout of intuition hit her: She had the distinct feeling that she was being watched. Was it because of this stranger's attention?

"Sorrento," she said, taking another step back, smiling apologetically despite herself. "Just down the line a bit."

"Sorrento!" he boomed. "I want to get down there to sample some of that *limoncello*. You tried that yet? Sorrento's famous for it." He barked a laugh. "There's nothing I like better than sampling the local booze."

Josie's smile persisted, her good manners like a reflex, and still she couldn't shake the feeling: Someone was *watching* her. She glanced around, taking in the hordes of tourists outside, the guides walking around with their little flags held aloft, the odd single person drifting about. She saw nobody's eyes on her, in particular.

"You traveling alone?" he asked.

"Yes," she said, realizing too late that she should lie. She moved farther from him, taking in a frescoed wall, preparing to leave the man before he found a way to adhere to her, which somehow she knew he would, given half the chance, like glue. And as she moved away, she allowed the thought she'd held back all day to creep in. It had been there, lurking in her mind from the moment she'd left her husband. It was a question, whispering over and over beneath all the tumult, awaiting its moment.

If Mark wanted to take Josie back, to undo all he had done, would she say yes?

Yes, her heart beat out in an instant. There was longing behind the word, and fear. *Yes.* To no longer be adrift, unattached, unsure of herself in a world where she'd never had to be alone? It would be a relief.

Josie sighed, nodding toward the American and stepping back into the hot sun of the ancient street. Yes, however disappointed she would be in herself, however defeated, Josie knew she would take Mark back.

If, of course, he even wanted her.

CHAPTER EIGHT

Cicero

Pompeii, Italy

Sorrento.

It was all I could think of as the day heated up, and tourists streamed into Pompeii, and I was, once again, alone.

Giorgio must have gone to Sorrento to oversee his son. *Sì,* that had to be it. Hugo was the only remaining family member who, despite being an ungrateful shithead, merited haunting. Pardon my language.

This realization left me with only one option. I, too, would embark for Sorrento.

Understand this, my friend: My entire life had revolved around Giorgio. I'd risen every morning at the foot of his bed, then spent all my waking hours keeping him firmly in sight. I sat nearby while he ate, observing as his fork lifted and fell, my attention rapt. I trotted alongside his footfalls, matching his pace. I listened while he spoke, tilting my head to take it in. I watched him. He was the sun, and I an orbiting planet.

Lest you think me overly vigilant, or, at worst, obsessive, you must remember: I'm not only a dog, but a *terrier*. Of indeterminate breeding, *sì*, but I have a terrier's disposition nonetheless, and we are nothing if not devoted. Rather single-minded, some might say.

And so, you see, I simply had to find transport to Giorgio's new location.

The only problem, really, was that I had no idea how to do so. The question vexed me all morning as I toured the ruins in search of breakfast, hugging close to walls and peeking around corners as if awaiting an ambush. As a little dog in a big world, caution is a constant necessity. I could not afford to be waylaid.

Find Sorrento, I thought as I sought breakfast and, finally, slumped against a half-crumbled wall in defeat. *Then find Giorgio.*

The heat of the day increased exponentially, and I leaned into the bricks at my back, panting and hungry. Fresh questions arose. Once in Sorrento, how would I locate Giorgio? His new state rendered him odorless, a critical obstacle. Scent was how I found everything: thrown sticks, the little treats Giorgio used to hide around the villa when I was but a pup and craved diversion, my way around the village and surrounding countryside, and now, food. Without scent, I had nothing to search for aside from Hugo, the *cretino*. I wasn't sure I could find him, however, even if I wished to. What did he smell like? I tried to remember but could conjure only high-octane fuel and the kind of sweat born of panic. No, I reasoned, that wouldn't do; he surely didn't smell like that in normal circumstances. The most useful bit of information I'd retained regarding Hugo, really, was a hazy memory of a door he'd once shut, rather hard. Was it his door? And was it blue? I snuffed at the thought, colors not being my strong suit.

A new question hit me like an errant ball. Would Giorgio be able to find me again if I left Pompeii? Or would I be well and truly lost then? The sun climbed the sky as I ruminated, watching tourists stop to peer in at a display of calcified people shielding themselves from imminent doom. Dreadful, I tell you, the things that enrapture humans. I blinked, wondering how Giorgio had found me in Pompeii to begin with. I'd been something like the proverbial needle in a haystack, so how did he turn up on my ancient block? Did ghosts sense something the rest of us miss? Or had Pompeii simply sprung to mind when he'd pondered lost dogs? We all seem to wash up in the ruins, after all, like flotsam in a stream.

Perhaps it didn't matter, I decided finally, shifting my paws on the hot stone. I watched as a trio departed from a glass case sheltering a body, and a lone woman took their place. She paused before the frozen figure, bending to study it, her gray eyes wide with something like wonder.

Sì, I thought absently. I'd made up my mind. I'd take charge of my situation.

A man joined the woman before the plaster human, and I tilted my head, mildly interested. He wore a collared T-shirt and white shoes, and I shuddered to imagine what Giorgio would say about such choices. The man said something to the woman in a language I didn't understand, and I watched as she glanced at him, the wonder fading from her gaze. No, I realized, they were not the pair I'd assumed them to be, not like me and Giorgio. The woman smiled tentatively, shrinking away from his booming voice but replying, nonetheless. She was a small human, with a warm expression, a freckled nose, and hair that shone golden, in places, when the sun hit it. She reminded me of a dog that, when approached, rolls over to show its belly—not an unwelcome trait in the canine world.

But then she spoke again, and I tilted my head so hard the world tipped sideways. "Sorrento" spilled from her lips, clear as a dinner bell. It was surrounded by other words, but then the man echoed it, confirming what she'd said. *Sorrento.* She nodded with the word, tucking loose hair behind her ears, taking another small step backward in her tennis shoes.

I stood, shaking off the heat as if it were a blanket. My mission clarified before me.

This tourist, with her self-deprecating smile and surprisingly intelligent gaze, was my ticket. *Sì!*

She would get me where I needed to go.

CHAPTER NINE

Josie

Pompeii, Italy

Josie walked out into the heat of an ancient street, trying to shake the sensation of being watched, when a small white dog appeared before her. He approached purposefully, halting in her shadow as if arriving for an appointment.

"Hello there," Josie said, smiling as the dog stared up at her, cocking his head. "Where did you come from, little fellow?"

His head cocked further, so he was looking at her fully sideways, and she had the distinct impression that he was trying to parse her words. She laughed a bit, shrugged, and as the American man emerged from the alcove behind her, she turned abruptly up the street. She hurried through several clusters of tourists, glancing back to see if the overbearing Texan trailed in her wake, relieved that he didn't. The little dog did, however. He trotted along as if he belonged to her, his short tail held like a comma over his back, his ears bobbing with the movement. *Strange,* Josie thought. She'd seen several dogs lounging among the ruins, but none had shown interest in the tourists. She turned down a side street to cement her departure from the Texan, glancing back as she did. The dog turned, too.

It was a quieter street, and Josie paused after a few steps, pivoting to inspect her petite pursuer. He came around to her front and sat neatly, like one might expect of a show dog or a service animal.

"What do you need, little sir?" Josie asked, crouching to regard him eye to eye. He did not fall all over her, like a typical dog might, panting and wiggling in the halo of her attention. No, he regarded her as earnestly as she did him, blinking his bright marble eyes. She stifled the urge to reach out and pat his perky head. Were you supposed to touch the wild dogs of Pompeii? She'd read about them, the abandoned dogs who ended up living amid the ruins. Sometimes they'd been dropped off by people who no longer wanted them, as if the archeological site were a giant humane society. Others had been born wild, growing up in these ancient streets, sleeping in alcoves, and begging for food. They were, Josie mused, a bit like deer living in residential areas: used to humans, able to coexist, and eager to benefit from carefully tended roses and hostas—or tourists' lunches in this case—but not quite domesticated.

Nonetheless, as this little dog stared up with an intensity that made Josie feel as if she was missing something, she thought he seemed like the most domesticated creature she'd ever encountered. He had speckled brown ears that flopped over at the halfway point, and aside from a few caramel-colored patches across his body, he was largely white. And clean, strangely, as if he regularly partook of the Roman baths.

"Would you like to tour the ruins with me?" Josie asked, feeling instantly foolish. Yet he stood, his stare still fixed upon her, as she rose from her crouch.

So Josie shook out her map, drew a line with her finger to the forum, and set off.

The dog paced alongside her like a show pony, his posture jaunty, and again Josie wanted to laugh. He was, she decided, a nice surprise; she would enjoy his companionship for as long as it lasted. And, as she wove into the forum, pulling out her audio guide for the first time, she felt a little less alone in the world, a little less heartbroken.

The day heated up, and Josie moved through it like a person in a particularly wonderful dream. She walked into ancient houses, marveling at the mosaics covering floors and walls, the designs impressively preserved and fascinating in their detail. She listened to her audio guide as she passed structures that had once housed storefronts, or food vendors, or residences. She toured the Roman baths, marveling as her audio guide described plumbing that had warmed the floors with radiant heat before spilling into spas. She walked through a brothel, taking in descriptive paintings on the walls that, her audio guide informed her, were meant to serve as menus. Josie made a face and, without meaning to, she thought of Mark and Jen and had to pinch her eyes shut for a second.

"Jen," she whispered as she left the brothel, uninterested in lingering there. She glanced at the dog, who met her gaze as if commiserating fully. What was Jen like? Josie had prevented herself from contemplating this other woman as much as possible over recent days, but now the questions came, intrusive and unwelcome. She vaguely remembered a tall blond woman with severe bangs, from the days their sons had played together, but it was an age ago. Was she adventurous? Assertive? Was she things Josie herself was not?

The notion stung like a wasp.

It had become, quite inexplicably, late afternoon. The streets were unbearably hot, the crowds thick, and Josie stood among them for a long moment, unmoored, Jen strolling through her mind like a vagrant. The little dog stood so close to Josie's ankle they were nearly touching, and she suspected he was waiting for her cue to carry on. She glanced down, and he looked up.

"How would you feel about some lunch, pup?" she asked, realizing she'd forgotten to eat.

He blinked, cocking his head.

"All right, then. Let's find something, shall we?" She turned and crouched, looking him in the eye. "You've come with me this far, so you may as well join me for a bite." Without thinking, she extended a hand, and the dog moved into it like a ball into a glove. He closed his eyes while she pet his small head, and the constriction around her heart eased once more.

"Let's go have a look at that restaurant." She stood back up, and he positioned himself next to her ankle.

Josie followed the map to Chora Cafè, located behind the Temple of Jupiter, bemused. Where had this little dog come from, with his impeccable manners and vast self-assurance? She glanced down at him, walking alongside her as if on an invisible leash, and smiled. Had someone owned him, trained him, and then abandoned him here? It was unthinkable, really.

When Josie neared the doors to Chora Cafè, which was something like a cafeteria, misgivings overtook her. Again, she glanced down at her new companion, fretting. She didn't want to leave him outside alone. Which, she realized immediately, was ridiculous. He *lived* here, for God's sake. But still, what if she went inside and he thought she was gone, that she'd abandoned him, and he gave up on her, too? What if he left, finding a new tourist to follow? The thought made Josie feel surprisingly bereft.

She hesitated, then bent and scooped the dog up into her arms. He stiffened for the briefest second and then relaxed into her embrace. It was like carrying a baby, Josie thought, heading inside and thinking of Charlie, so long ago. The warm, soft weight of him in her arms, his jolly eyes following her. Pain beat into her heart.

Good lord, Charlie. She would have to call him soon. He likely thought it was weird she hadn't called yet, that his phone hadn't rung with her number once in over five days. She tried hard not to be overbearing, but she still called every so often.

When Charlie had left for college, she'd encouraged him to go, hugging his broad shoulders and pressing comforters and day planners and toiletry kits upon him, happy for him to have a chance to spread his wings. And yet, as she'd hugged her little boy, who'd become a man, she couldn't help but think of him as he'd been—her child, with his birdlike shoulders and combustible grin. Her boy, who'd once had to sit routinely for blood draws, his fist clenched as the phlebotomist sought a vein, his eyes on Josie as she told him jokes or flipped through a copy of Calvin and Hobbes, her heart breaking. Her child, who had once occupied a hospital bed, who had been breakable and scared and was now so strong. So big, and wonderful, and off in the world like a sailboat at sea.

As he should be.

It was everything she'd wanted for him. It was the future she'd imagined as she'd held up those comic books, forcing a laugh, as she'd ordered pizza to his hospital room, and invented nicknames for doctors, and wept when he finally fell asleep amid the beeps and whirs of machines.

And now she couldn't tell him what Mark had done. She could not tear a patch from the sail that propelled his boat, finally, a sail he'd earned. No, she would not do anything that might cause his boat to list. She clutched the little dog closer, feeling his tiny heart beating against her.

She simply couldn't.

At the counter, the server swept his gaze over Josie and down to the dog in her arms. Josie braced, imagining that he would take one look at the terrier and point her toward the door, but he didn't. Apparently unfazed by her furry companion, he simply waited for her to order. Josie glanced quickly through the case of food before her. There, a sandwich. That would do, and she knew how to order it.

"Un panino, per favore." She hesitated, then added, "Prosciutto."

Wordlessly, the server retrieved a sandwich from the case, and Josie paid quickly, struggling to extricate her wallet with the dog in her arms. Minutes later, she was back outside on the hot street.

She took her sandwich and her newfound friend and backtracked, making her way to the amphitheater where she figured she could sit and eat.

"Would you like some cheese?" she asked once there, seated in a spot with a bit of a breeze, the dog beside her. Together, they ate the panino and stared out at an amphitheater where gladiators once fought, the rings of stone seats capped by a horizon of shadowy mountains. Josie tried to imagine the ancient fighters, their swords clashing against the backdrop of hills and greenery, interrupting birdsong and whispering wind. Humans, clearly, hadn't evolved much. The dog sat against her hip, following her gaze as if they were in conversation about the past and all it meant. He accepted bits of her sandwich politely, never once snatching them from her fingertips, though hunger was clear in his rapt expression.

Was he an unusual dog? Josie had never owned a dog as an adult. There had been farm dogs spotting her childhood, back at the ranch, of course. But Mark was fiercely allergic to all animals, so they'd only ever had a pet fish, which Charlie had named, amusingly, Thunder. Even that was short lived; in Thunder's third month at their house, he jumped from his tank after a cleaning and vanished down the drain.

An unwelcome voice fractured her thoughts.

"Hey there! Hey, Kansas!"

Josie jolted, understanding, before she'd even located him down below, that the American man had found her. There he was, making his way up into the amphitheater seats, his big belly impeding his climb. His face was ruddy in the hot day, though the sun had recently begun its downward slide.

"Thought I'd lost you!" he called, nearing, and Josie's stomach soured. The last thing she wanted was to spend her final hours in the ruins with this man.

The dog, still resting against her hip, began to growl. She felt his body tense beside her, though he didn't move. Only the sound signaled his distaste, low and rumbling as a thunderclap in his throat. Josie glanced at the dog, catching his gaze. "I hear you," she whispered. "I feel the same."

"I was thinking," the Texan boomed, flopping down on the bench seat as if she'd offered it to him. "We should get some dinner before heading our separate ways. What do you think?"

The dog leaned harder into Josie. She smiled. "Oh, I think I'll just head home."

"Come on," the man said, as though they knew each other, and she was letting him down. "Just a drink, then. You're not going to leave me hanging, are ya, Kansas?"

She stifled the urge to roll her eyes. He didn't even know her name, for God's sake. How could she owe him anything? "I'm sorry," she said, readying to stand. "I just can't."

The man stood, too. His nose was red, and Josie wondered whether he'd resisted sunscreen, or spent his afternoon in Chora Cafè drinking. He had the puffy, mottled look of a person accustomed to overindulgence. She sidled past him in the narrow seats, trying not to touch him, and indeed she could smell the alcohol. He must have found his *limoncello*. She was nearly past when he reached down, shockingly, and cupped her right butt cheek, giving it a firm squeeze.

Josie reared back, stunned, and he chuckled and held up his hands in a "how can you blame me?" sort of way.

"When in Rome," he began to say, but before he could finish, the little dog, following in Josie's shadow, leaped at the man's yet outstretched hand. He flew up like a collie after a Frisbee, latched on to the hand that had palmed Josie's bottom, and bit down hard.

The man unleashed a torrent of curses as he jerked his arm back and forth, flinging the dog around like a tug toy before hurling him to the ground. The dog rolled once in the dirt and hit the stone of the amphitheater seat, releasing a stunned yelp.

"Goddamn!" the man howled. "You goddamn mutt!" And he heaved himself forward, preparing to kick the tiny, shivering dog, when Josie stepped in front of him, moving without thought, and punched him squarely in the face.

"What the fuck!" the man shouted, and Josie bent, her knuckles throbbing from the impact, and scooped up her little dog. Utterly stunned at everyone's actions, including her own, Josie took one last look at the Texan, who was now cupping a nose that spilled blood down his polo shirt, and then she ran.

The dog panted in her arms as she hurried down the amphitheater steps and wove through a tour group, her tote bag bumping against her side. She spilled out onto a quieter lane, yet couldn't slow. Her heart pounded hard in her chest, and she continually glanced back to see if the drunk American was in pursuit.

She was nearly to Pompeii's entrance when she slowed, panting alongside the dog, her head swimming. Good lord—had she really hauled off and punched that awful man? The dog nosed her chin, giving it a perfunctory lick, and she met his gaze and laughed once. "I *hit* him!" she whispered to her small friend, marveling. But what would the man do if he found her? Worse, what would he do to this sweet, noble fellow in her arms? The dog blinked up, earnest, and Josie felt sure he was wondering the same thing.

"Well, that's it, then," she said, decision made.

She moved into the shade of a building, glancing around to see if anyone was watching, and crouched down to open her tote bag. She removed her guidebook, making space, and met the dog's intent gaze. "In you go," she whispered, lifting and settling him. He required no convincing. He folded himself neatly into the bag, nestling amid her wallet and keys, his head poking out the top. Josie hoisted the tote onto her shoulder, concealing his face as much as possible with her arm, and aimed for the entrance.

She held her breath as she exited Pompeii, bracing for calls of protest that never came. She wasn't sure if you could just *take* one of the wild dogs, yet she had. And now she would take him with her on the train, hoping once again that nobody would notice him, that nobody would complain.

She glanced down and met his watchful stare.

"I don't know what we're going to do," she whispered, and he listened gravely. "But I couldn't leave you there, pup."

Worry shadowed her minor triumph. She'd made off with an illicit dog, but now what? What if someone discovered him in her apartment?

And if his presence went unchallenged in Sorrento, what would she do at the end of the summer, when it was time to return to Kansas?

Even as these questions rose, she replayed what had happened in her mind, over and over again: the tiny dog, leaping to attack an imposing man on her behalf. The man's giant white shoe aiming for him.

And, as she made her way to the train platform, her decision hardened.

She simply would not leave him behind. That was all she knew right now, looking down the tracks, her tote bag snug under her arm.

She would figure out the rest later.

CHAPTER TEN

JOSIE

Sorrento, Italy

Life, Josie learned rather swiftly, was better with a dog.

For the first time in Italy, she didn't feel lonely on the train. Instead, she hugged her pup close in his tote bag and stared out the window alongside him, murmuring observations, here and there, about the passing world. He tilted his head when she spoke, listening as if every word was important, following her gaze.

When they arrived in Sorrento it was nearly evening, the sun was going down, and the dog remained patiently alert in the tote as Josie left the station and threaded her way into the cobbled streets. Her mind moved at a clip as she walked: She would need to purchase dog food, straightaway, and a collar and a leash. Perhaps, she mused, flea shampoo was also in order. Where could she find such things?

As she entered Piazza Tasso, with its twelve flags listing in the soft evening breeze, she spotted a woman walking what appeared to be a Bernese mountain dog, who, despite being clipped, panted heavily in the lowering sun. Josie hurried across the piazza, pausing as a pair of mopeds crisscrossed in front of her. She caught up with the woman and dog near a grove sheltering the statue that gave the piazza its name.

Torquato Tasso, a rather dapper, Shakespearean-looking figure, gazed about with his marble eyes, and the woman passed under him, her dog plodding along behind her like a plow horse.

"Excuse me," Josie called, then switched her language. *"Scusa, signora!"*

The woman turned, took Josie in, and then her gaze fell upon the little head poking out of the tote bag.

"Ah!" she exclaimed, *"che carino!"* She grinned, flashing a lovely smile, faint lines crinkling at her temples. She was perhaps Josie's age, and she walked her dog in a pair of heels, slim trousers, and a silk tank top crowned with a sweater tied around her shoulders. She looked like she'd fallen straight from the pages of a magazine.

"Grazie," Josie said, then, her Italian depleted, switched reluctantly to English. As the woman caressed the dog's protruding head, he closed his eyes, enjoying her attention, so unlike his reaction to the Texan. He, too, must have sensed the woman's warmth right away.

"Do you speak English?" Josie asked.

"A bit-*a*," the woman said, her gaze flicking up, her smile easy. She lifted a hand and touched her forefinger to thumb, as if to say she had only a pinch of English. "How can I help?"

"I need to buy some things for my dog, but I don't know where to find them," Josie said, relaxing as the woman cocked an ear, somewhat like the terrier in her tote did, and thought. "A leash," Josie added, pointing to the strip of leather tethering the panting Bernese. He looked up at her with gentle, doleful eyes, his tongue dripping on the flagstones. "And a collar, and"—she cupped her hands to mime a bowl—"dog food."

"Ah!" the woman exclaimed, brightening. She pivoted, gesturing to the streets departing the piazza like spokes. "You go down Corso Italia, *sì? Sempre diritto. Sì?"*

Josie nodded, listening hard.

"And you find, on your left-*a*, *un negozio*. It is a *supermercato, sì?* But they have a few things for the dogs." She nodded, as though to encourage Josie's comprehension.

"Corso Italia," Josie echoed, and the woman nodded again with enthusiasm. *"Grazie."* Josie wished she knew how to say more, hoped her smile conveyed her gratitude. *"Molte grazie!"*

They parted, the woman turning to call, *"Ciao ciao!"* and Josie marveled at how much easier everything seemed now that she had her little companion.

Twenty minutes later, she emerged from the supermarket with shampoo, a hot-pink collar, a matching leash—all they'd had—and a bag of dog food. Her tote, nearly bursting, also contained some human food—cheese and bread and tomatoes that shone like oversize jewels. The dog trotted along once more at Josie's ankle, his head darting about as he took in his new surroundings.

She located her apartment, raised her eyes in silent thanks when the courtyard was empty, and hurried upstairs to fix dinner for herself and her pup. Soon, she mused as they stepped inside the cool living room, she would need to name him.

And, for the first time in a week, everything felt all right.

~

As the days unfurled after her trip to Pompeii, Josie's confidence seemed to expand, inexplicably, outward. She decided to rewrite her itinerary that first morning at home with the dog, moving things around a bit so she could figure out how to incorporate him into her future travels. She would see, she decided, if any hotels allowed dogs in Rome, where she hoped to travel in August. Perhaps the room she'd already booked wouldn't turn away such a small, polite pup? If not, she mused, it might be possible to smuggle him in. Of course, so far he'd seemed welcome everywhere they went, but she wasn't sure if such tolerance toward pets extended to all of Italy.

She glanced over her plans, thinking. Day trips seemed entirely possible; he could again ride in her tote on trains, which had caused no one to look askance. She glanced at him, lying in a sunny spot, curled up tight. For a week, she decided, she'd simply stay in Sorrento so they could get to know one another. She would see the entire town, get used to shopping and dining anywhere that would allow a dog to lie at her feet, and explore the beach and cathedrals and lemon groves she'd read about.

And that's what she did.

The dog came along with her everywhere, either walking on his leash or bobbing along in her tote bag, behaving as if he'd never been a stray for a day in his life. He never barked, never tugged, never did his business anywhere but the most convenient locations. Instead, he looked around gamely as they saw the sights. He was both mannerly and enthused, as though he, too, was a tourist. And everyone they met was kind and talkative, eager to fawn over her adorable companion, happy to welcome him and Josie to their town. When people met her now, they no longer saw a tourist, but a woman.

It was, she marveled, all quite delightful.

The only stressful moment in those first days occurred one morning when Josie emerged from a *pasticceria*. She carried a small paper bag containing a *cannolo* for her and a biscuit for the dog, which she planned to eat down at the beach, gazing out at bobbing, colorful rowboats, wheeling seagulls, and swimmers in the sparkling sea. Tomorrow, she'd been thinking, she would don her swimsuit and take her dog for a dip. Hopefully he liked the water. She was imagining this, and turning down a road that would deliver her to the shore, when her phone rang.

Charlie flashed on her screen.

Josie froze. She was surprised, really, that it had taken him this long to call. And somehow, for the past few days, she'd thought very little of home and the catastrophe that was now her life there. She'd avoided calls, even from her best friend, Ellen, a language arts teacher at the middle school. Josie knew Ellen would be horrified on her behalf when they finally talked, but she dreaded discussing all that had transpired since school ended. She dreaded the rumors that would fly back home once she did. She could imagine Ellen talking it over with her husband, aghast. She pictured the ladies in their book club, furious on Josie's behalf, cupping their wineglasses and dialing her number, ready to offer support. She wanted none of it.

No, Josie wanted to pretend, for as long as possible, that nothing was amiss, that all would be well.

Now she looked down at her screen, struggling with whether to answer it, the dog regarding her gravely, as if he understood her turmoil. What did Charlie know? Had he spoken with his dad? And, suddenly, it all came flooding back: Mark and Jen, the lies, the roses.

Josie felt sick, and the call went to voicemail.

She listened to her son's message as she continued down the street, passing under a pair of swaying palms, a tangle of emotions tightening in her chest. She felt the dog's eyes on her, analytic in their intensity.

"Hey, Mom," Charlie began, clearing his throat. "I don't want to bug you—I know you're off on your adventure and everything. Just thought I'd say hi, and that I hope you and Dad are having a great time. He's not answering, either, but I'm actually not sure what time it is there. Maybe you're asleep."

Her nerves loosened.

"Anyway, I just realized I hadn't chatted with you for a while, and I miss hearing your voice. Things have been good, but intense—these summer classes are no joke. But I aced my last lab, so doing good."

Josie glanced at the dog, giving him a reassuring nod.

"Call me when you can," Charlie finished. "Love ya, Mom!"

She locked the phone and gazed out at the morning glimmering before her: the palms whispering overhead, the vivid bougainvillea tumbling over a wall, the cobblestoned road that would take her to the sea. She exhaled.

"He doesn't know," she murmured, as if to the dog.

For now, it was enough.

~

The next day, everything changed.

Josie set out again in the morning, her tote bulging with a towel, sun hat, and book. She wore a sundress over a bathing suit, and the dog paced along in his pink collar. Her heart swelled with the warmth of the morning. She imagined what the day would bring: a swim, a long morning reading under an umbrella, and a late lunch at a seaside bistro table, perhaps, with her dog at her feet.

He really needed a name, she mused as she wove down a quiet lane she'd yet to explore. It was lined with orange trees, residences, and the occasional shop or bar. A neighborhood, she surmised, frequented mostly by locals. She glanced about as she and the dog descended, heading to a different beach than the ones she'd visited, a bit farther away from the center of town. Josie didn't mind. She enjoyed a good walk.

The dog, for his part, seemed particularly excited. He pranced along, his steps light, his nose flicking back and forth as if the air were scented. Josie smiled, watching his ears bob, and then suddenly, for the first time ever, he tugged on the leash.

She was taken aback and followed as he pulled her toward the side of the street and into the shade of an orange tree. Did he need to do his business? Josie glanced at the tree he seemed to be aiming for, flinching and giving him a gentle tug. Because it, and the next half dozen trees descending the road, were hemmed in rings of carefully cultivated flowers. A heavyset woman hoisted a watering can a few trees down, pausing to glare at the dog, and Josie picked him up. She nodded at the gardener as they passed, well aware of the work that had gone into those flowers.

"We'll find you a different tree," she whispered, but as she continued on down the street the dog strained over her shoulder, gazing backward.

Josie was just about to round a bend in the lane when a voice erupted behind her.

"Aspetta!" a man's tenor shouted. *"Aspetta, per favore!"*

She turned, and there, a few blocks up the street, a man had emerged from a blue door. The woman with the watering can paused, watching with interest. The man jogged down the cobblestones, the door left ajar in his wake, holding an arm up as if hailing a taxi. The other arm, Josie noticed with expanding dismay, was fastened to his chest in a sling—as it had been the first time she'd encountered him.

"Aspetta!" he called again, and then something about her appearance caused him to switch languages. "Wait, please!" he hollered, overloud.

Did the asshole from the *gelateria* remember her?

Josie stood in the speckled shade, holding her dog close, bracing as if for a wave on a beach. What could this man possibly want? He rounded on her, panting slightly in the heat, his eyes startled behind his dark-rimmed reading glasses.

"You," he said. He looked absolutely incredulous, rubbing at his stubbled jaw with his free hand while shaking his head, his brown eyes wide. *"Madonna mia,"* he sputtered, then appeared to search for additional words. A sea breeze bumped up against them both, tousling his boyish hair.

Josie took a step back, hugging the dog a bit closer. She didn't like this stranger's intensity, the way he looked at her as if she were a rather confounding puzzle he needed to piece together.

"What is it?" she finally asked, completely off-balance.

He inhaled and shook his head, finding his words, starting again. "You are holding my dog."

PART TWO

CHAPTER ELEVEN

Cicero

Sorrento, Italy

Under normal circumstances, I have impeccable manners. I rather pride myself on restraint and self-control—on, in a word, *domesticity*.

That said, when faced with imbeciles, one must act. And should such an imbecile tread over a person's good, dependable heart, like Josie's, the gentlemanly thing to do is, well, attack. Thus, I was not sorry when I bit that *bastardo* in Pompeii, with his loud voice and wandering hands. And all too soon, I found myself in preparation to bite another. Needs must.

It was, I hesitate to admit, somewhat invigorating.

Are you surprised, my friend, to hear me refer to Josie in such a manner, considering I'd only just met her on the day of the first bite? Do you fear my loyalty was too easily bought, secured merely by a shared *panino* and a jaunt in a tote bag?

I do adore that tote bag.

Nonetheless, you mustn't doubt me. For my fairly instant devotion to Josie sprang from something deeper, something truer than mere convenience. Before encountering her, I could not have imagined that any fresh human might sidle their way into my shattered heart. No, I tell you, never would I have believed that someone could creep into the vacancy left by Giorgio, claiming space. Yet Josie did.

Were they alike, you might ask?

Allora. In a word, *sì*, though as with most things in life, it's a bit more complicated than that. Upon first impression, you certainly would not think so. Giorgio was old and white haired, tall and so slim his joints seemed overlarge. Josie was very small, in comparison, her thick hair spilling over her shoulders, her colors a range of brown and gold right down to the freckles spattering her nose—though, I must admit, that impression might be due to my canine vision. Giorgio was gregarious, a friend to everyone he met. She was shy. He was fashionable and she was, well, American.

Yet they both had wide, generous smiles, quick in coming. Even more important, they had unfailingly kind hearts. And there was something else, too, which is a bit more challenging to explain. I shall try: Giorgio and Josie both looked at the people and creatures they encountered and really *saw* them, if you know what I mean. Do you? Have you ever met a person who, while regarding another, makes them feel absolutely seen? Such people are rare, indeed.

Like Giorgio, Josie was one of them.

Our first week together was bliss. She either carried me around in my tote bag or allowed me to jog alongside her wearing my new, shiny leash and collar. You might expect me to have been offended by the leash, because I certainly did not require one. Yet when I saw how other dogs donned them with pride, strutting alongside their humans, I was swayed. I'd never experienced life as a city dog, you see. Very soon, I took joy in flaunting my loose leash amid the busy streets, something most of my brethren cannot maintain. As a dog of some intellect, I never pulled it taut. There's nothing wrong with showing off a bit, my friend. Simple pleasures, and all that.

Nevertheless, there came a day when I did pull on the leash. *Sì*, we were walking along a street that seemed, somehow, familiar. A memory strolled through my mind as we passed under a sun that was already hot, the cobbles under my paws warming. Josie, I must tell you, was fastidiously thoughtful about my delicate toe pads. Whenever the cobblestones burned, I would flick my paws up and toss her a plaintive look, and she'd scoop me up posthaste. Aside from saving my toes, I enjoyed the view from her arms.

Scusami—I've veered off topic. That morning, a breeze tickled my ears, and the birds trilled enthusiastically overhead, and all seemed well with the world. But then, the street on which I found myself walking prickled my senses, quite strangely. It was like static crackling the air, tickling my whiskers. What could be causing this odd sensation, I wondered? My nose shot around, imploring the breeze to deliver familiar scents. I began to hope, my friend. *Sì*, I pined for a whiff of shoe polish, a hint of coffee breath, though I knew poor Giorgio no longer smelled like much of anything. Even so, I found myself searching for what I thought of when I pictured him: aftershave, leather, the tang of red wine.

I had not stopped searching for him, you understand, not for a minute. I loved Josie already, *certo*, but it was a new love, and my devotion to Giorgio had gone nowhere. In fact, I could, I was astounded to realize, love two people at once. Thus, as Josie and I toured Sorrento that first week, stepping into cool churches and exploring gardens and frequenting cafés, I never stopped seeking him. I likewise searched for his son, my disdain for him notwithstanding, for I suspected they would be found together. So you see, Josie's touring of Sorrento benefited my secret mission, indeed.

On the morning of the, shall we call it, *ill-fated* encounter, I was searching for Giorgio as vigilantly as ever. And on that street, something whispered to me. It wasn't until we passed the blue door, nestled between a pair of rustling orange trees, that I became certain.

Thank goodness dogs can see the color blue.

Hugo's door, from all those years ago, slammed in my mind.

I pulled on the leash.

Josie stumbled along behind me, caught off-balance, speaking her nonsense. A few of her words had begun to stick in my nimble brain, by then: *dinner*, *walk*, and *who-is-my-good-boy* among them. All the rest was gibberish, I'm aggrieved to report.

Anyhow, I tugged, she came, and then she picked me up and I watched the door pass. I stared at it, fading in our wake, and searched for any sign of Giorgio. I nearly whined, scanning the empty air. Nothing shimmered, nothing called.

Then, the door opened, its blue flashing. And a man appeared, one-armed and ridiculous.

Hugo.

At first, I was excited to see him despite my hatred of the man. I searched for Giorgio in his wake, certain he would waft through the blue door any second. For where else would he be? Who else would Giorgio haunt, if not me and Hugo? Though the fact that he would linger in Hugo's life, and not mine, was an insult so dire I chose not to dwell on it.

Giorgio, however, was not there. I saw no ripple of silver, heard no familiar laugh. I strained my ears, sniffed the air, frantic to catch an echoing, *Cicero, ragazzo mio!* ringing down the street. Was it there, somehow? Had I simply missed his voice, his essence, his presence? My heart beat hard against Josie's shoulder. She turned to regard Hugo, to speak in her odd language to him, and I ignored them both. Only vaguely did I recall that Hugo had lived in another place, once. That he'd added a language to our native tongue, a fact that delighted Giorgio, who, like me, conversed only in Italian. His admiration for Hugo spurred piteous jealousy in my noble heart.

But no, I could not listen there in the street, under the orange trees. Because that noble heart of mine, I tell you, was devastated anew.

Giorgio was nowhere.

I had come all the way to Sorrento, found Hugo behind his blue door, and Giorgio was not there. Was he in Pompeii, calling my name at that very moment? Had I lost him again? Had I made the second most irreparable mistake of my life in leaving the ruins?

I studied the street for a long time, looking up and down. If I were human, I would have wept. No, there was no Giorgio.

Only, I am sorry to say, Hugo. His detestable son.

CHAPTER TWELVE

Josie

Sorrento, Italy

Josie took a step back as the man standing before her frowned, his heavy brows drawing together over his reading glasses as if he'd stumbled upon a particularly perplexing algebraic equation.

"That dog," he reiterated, "belongs to me. Where did you get it?" Clearly bewildered, he raked his uninjured hand through a head of hair that yearned to curl in the humidity.

"He can't possibly belong to you," Josie sputtered, matching his bewilderment, trying to ignore the way her dog began to sniff the air, as though someone were frying bacon. "What a ridiculous suggestion!"

She thought of the other time she'd crossed paths with this well-dressed local; despite his aura—a blend of something like a polo player, a wine connoisseur, and a mountaineer—he'd been a little unhinged, then. And now, she decided, he had gone so far off-kilter he was like a door listing in the wind. She took another step back, a bead of sweat tickling her spine under her sundress, and blinked up at him in the dappled light. Overhead, leaves murmured in the breeze.

As if their thoughts were somehow synchronized, her accuser's expression brightened, revelation dropping into his gaze. *"Gesù Cristo,"* he exclaimed, "I know you, *vero*?" A stunned laugh escaped his lips. "You're the woman who snitched my gelato. *Menta e cioccolato, sì?*"

Snitched? Where did he learn his, admittedly impressive, English?

"Oh, for God's sake," she managed and, abruptly, the dog ceased sniffing the air, apparently sensing that his time had come to join this exchange. He began to growl.

"It was a simple mistake," Josie added over the expanding sound, long and low, vibrating through the little chest in her palm. "We both ordered brown and green flavors."

The man shrugged. "First the gelato. And now you have my dog." He shook his head, his brows again lifting over his readers. "*Madonna mia.* The universe laughs, I fear."

"This is not your dog," Josie insisted, unamused. "Listen to him! He's obviously terrified of you."

"Not at all." The man chuckled, as if to suggest that when the universe can't be beat, perhaps it should be joined. "No, no, he's not afraid. He simply hates me. Isn't that right, Cicero?"

Abruptly, the growling ceased. The dog cocked his head, ears perked, his stare nailed to the stranger attempting to claim him. "See that?" the man said. "Cicero!" The terrier's head cocked even more, so far to the left he appeared broken.

Cicero? A bit of dread rose in Josie. Her dog seemed to know this name. Very well, in fact. And, she had to admit, it fit him. Worse yet, if Cicero was in fact his name, perhaps this man wasn't an unhinged stranger. Perhaps he did, indeed, have a claim on her little friend. The dread expanded.

"Allow me to introduce you," the man persisted, dimples framing his smile, suddenly cheerful as if, Josie thought, he'd won a sparring match. "This dog who you allege to own is called Cicero Caruso, and I am Hugo Caruso. *Piacere.*"

He reached out for a handshake, but at the same instant Cicero's growl sharpened into a bark, and Hugo snatched his hand back as if he'd encountered a viper. He chuckled, shrugging.

"But why does he hate you?" she managed, swallowing, trying to force down the darkness within her. She could feel the dog's—*Cicero's*—heart beating against her cupped palm. "I don't understand." Suddenly, she wanted to cry, because she *didn't* understand, and she couldn't imagine giving up her dog, and, deep down, she was starting to believe that there was something to this man's—*Hugo's*—assertion. But who on earth wasn't adored by their own dog?

"He's only been mine for a couple of weeks," Hugo confessed. "He was my father's, and I inherited him, and then I promptly lost him." His tone grew gentler, less adversarial, as though he'd noted the shine in her eyes. "Where did you find our little fugitive?"

"Pompeii." Josie took a shaky breath, her thoughts racing. "He was among the strays."

"Pompeii! *Madonna mia.*" Hugo rubbed at his stubbled jaw, frowning as he took this in. "*Sì, sì.* Why did I not think to look there? *Madonna!* Is this not remarkable? The universe, I tell you, is having a laugh. Why did you bring him from Pompeii to Sorrento?"

Josie shrugged, struggling to voice the answer: She'd fallen in love with him, obviously. She held Cicero a bit closer, thinking of how he'd slept on the pillow next to hers all week, curled up tight. Of how his bright eyes watched her, always, as though he was trying to guess her next move. Of the many times he made her giggle each day.

"I was not far from Pompeii when I lost him," Hugo marveled amid her silence, shaking his head. "I returned to the area many times. I hung posters. There is a reward—*aspetta*, I can give it to you. Would that help?"

His gaze met hers, and she realized that he had glimpsed her breaking heart in that moment, which only made it worse. Before he could backpedal, humiliated tears stung her eyes, and Cicero unlatched his wary stare from Hugo and sniffed Josie's chin, worried. And with that, the tears she'd been pressing back, for so many reasons, spilled over entirely. With them, everything else Josie had walled off tumbled through her like an avalanche: the reason she was alone in Italy, the reason the pillow beside her was available, the reason she failed to answer her phone and pooled her focus on adventures and sunshine and Cicero. The way she'd been pretending, really, that everything was all right, that *she* was all right, that she belonged here, with this dog who was never meant to be hers. She thought of her bedroom, back in Kansas, and how those damnable roses had hit the carpet while Mark sat on the bed they'd shared for twenty years. A bed that, now, another woman likely inhabited in her absence.

Josie did not belong in Italy. But really, she didn't belong anywhere anymore.

"Dio mio," Hugo whispered to himself as she pressed a hand over her eyes, crying silently in the sunshine, feeling Cicero's pulse beating faster in her other palm. Tenderly, the dog rested his little head on her shoulder. Josie sensed Hugo, hesitating before her, likely more perplexed than ever by the emotional breakdown unfolding before him. And that, considering the circumstances of their acquaintance, was really saying something.

"Listen," he ventured finally, speaking cautiously, as one might in a hostage negotiation. "I don't even know your name. Would you tell it to me?"

"Josie," she sputtered, still shielding her eyes. She was *crying* in front of a stranger. One whose ice cream she'd snitched, and then, as if raising the stakes, one whose dog she'd claimed as her own. *Hell's bells,* her father would say. She inhaled, trying to reassemble her composure. "Josie Ballard."

"Josie." Hugo let it sit for a moment, allowing her to breathe and sniff her way back to civility. When she met his eye, briefly, he added, "Were you going to the beach when I stopped you?"

She nodded, wiping tears from her cheeks.

"*Allora.* What if I join you and Cicero for a bit? We can get a cappuccino, take in the sea, and discuss our situation. Perhaps we can sort something out."

Josie's foolish heart leaped at the notion. Sort something out—did that mean she could, potentially, keep the dog a little longer? "You can explain what happened," she supplied, finally managing to hold his gaze, and Hugo nodded.

"I can indeed. Wait here." He held up a palm like a traffic warden, as if he felt she was in need of explicit instruction. "For just a moment, *sì*? I'll go and close up my shop, change my clothes, and by the time I return you will feel better. And then we shall set off and make a proper introduction."

She nodded, and he reached out for a conciliatory clap on the shoulder. Yet his hand had barely lit upon her when Cicero erupted in a freshly outraged growl.

"Watch out," she found herself saying as Hugo whisked his hand away a second time. "He's been known to bite."

"*Vero,*" Hugo agreed. "The little demon."

And, as he turned to saunter up the hill, shaking his head as he went, both he and Josie stifled a chuckle.

~

"Fate has thrown us together, Cicero and I," Hugo said as they ambled down the lane, nearing the beach. They turned a corner, the Mediterranean flashing between a pair of cypress trees. "He truly despises me, so I'm not sure how we'll ever get along. But my father passed away very suddenly, a few weeks ago, and he asked that his dog go to me." He lifted his hand to emphasize a shrug. "Duty commands me to take him."

This, of course, changed things. His father had *died*, only recently?

Josie glanced at Hugo, surprised not only by the revelation, but by the lack of emotion in his tone, the detachment. Yet she saw, in his expression, a twist of pain. When he'd mentioned inheriting the dog, earlier, she'd imagined an infirm father, one who needed support. She'd not imagined that Cicero had been part of a literal inheritance.

"I'm so sorry for your loss," she said quietly, giving Cicero a pet. "You must be devastated."

Hugo nodded perfunctorily, and for a moment they walked in silence.

Josie couldn't fathom what it would be like to lose her father unexpectedly, nor the resulting grief. She'd watched her mother die, certainly, and it had been like surviving a series of little earthquakes for years, her heart breaking again and again until, finally, her mother was gone. Even so, she'd had time to say goodbye. There had been years to prepare, to forge a kind of peace with the hole her mother would leave in her wake. Everything that needed to be said had been.

"How did he pass away?" Josie found herself asking, not intending to pry, yet curious nonetheless. The dog continued to rest his head upon her shoulder as they walked, and Hugo glanced at her fully, his brown eyes catching hers.

"A heart attack. The man drank too much wine, ate too much meat." He sighed and shook his head, signifying long exasperation. "It was not a shock."

She nodded, and they turned another corner. She wondered about his mother, but asking another question felt like one too many. Josie did not, after all, know this man. The sea opened before them, just down the path, and Hugo tipped his chin in the direction of a beachfront bar.

"Care for a cappuccino? Espresso?"

She smiled, letting the conversation go for a moment. "Cappuccino, *per favore*."

"Prego." And, before she could offer him a couple of euros, he peeled off to head for the counter.

Josie chose a bistro table. It was perched on a patio that overlooked a beach full of umbrellas sheltering the first sunbathers and swimmers of the day. The sea glittered like a thousand stars burned on its surface, and gulls dipped and eddied overhead. The sand was cupped by the curve of rocky, hilly land, its humps and terraces jumbled with bright buildings and swaying palms. Josie breathed in the salted air. Cicero curled into a tight ball on her lap, and some of the tension left her, like fog evaporating in the sun.

When Hugo returned, he had to do so twice to transport the pair of frothy cappuccinos in his one good hand. Josie took him in the second time he approached the table, and for a moment it was as though she were seeing him anew: his black swim trunks topped with a button-down white shirt, the top open enough that she sensed a smooth chest beneath his blue sling, the sleeve rolled up on his functional arm. He smiled, his gaze newly affable behind his glasses, his hair catching the wind.

And she couldn't help but think: If only Mark could see her now. Not the truth of the moment, however. Just a curated snapshot of Josie sipping coffee by the sea with a beautiful man, her sundress catching the breeze, a purse-size dog on her lap. A dream.

Of course, nothing here was as it appeared.

Hugo sat down, pushed her cappuccino across the table, and sighed.

"*Allora*, I will tell you the whole story," he began, and she leaned forward a bit, as if focusing on a lesson at school. "My father died, and he left me everything, including his dog and his car. I went to retrieve the car and old Cicero, here, a few days after. And then, on the autostrada, not far from Pompeii, a stupid tourist was looking at his phone while driving, trying to interpret a map, and he hit me rather hard." He puffed air through his lips in apparent disgust. "The car spun twice on the road, crashed into the rail, and I broke my arm." He lifted his sling slightly, as if to demonstrate. Josie, freshly stunned, opened her mouth to say something, yet found herself lost for words.

"Cicero was unhurt," Hugo carried on, pausing to take a sip of his cappuccino, "but his leash was stuck in the bent door. I'd bought it for him, and the moment he was in my care that leash was on, because I was sure the little renegade would run away from me. We have never"—he leveled a rueful gaze on the sleeping dog—"ever been friends. Anyway, the stuck leash was too tight to maneuver, so I had to take his collar off to free it, and the moment I did, he leaped through the open door, in a panic, and ran."

"Good lord," Josie said without thought, imagining the dog streaking down the autostrada.

"Truly. Though I had more expressive words for it. I went after him for a bit, but very quickly the pain in my arm became too much. So I returned to the car to deal with the tourist who'd hit me, and then an ambulance came to take me to the hospital, and by the time I could search for Cicero, he'd vanished."

Now it was Josie's turn to puff air through her lips. There was no way she could avoid returning his dog. Not with a tale like that. She pet Cicero's small back, clean white with caramel patches, and imagined saying goodbye, a lump returning to her throat. She tried to take a sip of cappuccino, to deflect her rising emotions, but it hurt to swallow.

"Now, you must tell me," Hugo said, watching her carefully under gathered brows, changing tack. "How long are you going to be in Sorrento?"

She managed a smile but couldn't mask her sorrow. "Two months. Well, a little less, now."

"Ah." He nodded, frowning in thought, murmuring, *"due mesi"* as if to himself. Then, he paused to take a sip of his coffee, eyeing her, and again changed tack. "I must apologize regarding the gelato incident."

She nearly laughed at this, her emotions tipping over again. He studied her, his lips quirking in suppressed amusement. "Of course, you should have checked to make sure you were taking the correct cup—"

"Oh," she sputtered, "for God's sake."

"*Sì*, I'm sure God had an opinion. Gelato is serious in Italy. You must pray for forgiveness, at the very least."

She laughed despite her dipping spirits. "Why don't you let me buy you a new one, and we can bury the hatchet?"

"Bury the what?"

"It's a saying about axes—oh, never mind." She batted a hand. "I actually have no idea what it means."

"About *axes*," he repeated, shaking his head in mock exasperation. "You make no sense. Anyhow, I was fed up with tourists the day of the gelato, considering one had recently crashed into me on the autostrada. Perhaps . . . I overreacted."

"Perhaps." This time, Josie chuckled out loud, and the smile Hugo was trying to suppress broke loose. Dimples nipped his cheeks. For a moment, they simply regarded one another, no longer enemies, yet still at an impasse. And Josie understood. It was time to offer him the dog. That was the right thing to do, the only answer now. The cappuccinos were nearly gone.

"You can have Cicero back, of course," she said finally, feeling every word. The wind whipped at her hair, and she tried to tuck it behind her ears, to think of other things, to avoid any new tears. "He's clearly yours. And maybe it's like you said, but instead of laughing, the universe found a way to return him to you."

He nodded, his brows gathering again over his perceptive gaze. She filled the momentary quiet.

"I'm very sorry that you lost your father, Hugo. I hope caring for his dog will bring you some peace."

He released a rueful laugh. "Peace?" He shook his head. "No, Cicero absolutely will not bring me that. And to be honest, you mustn't feel too sorry for me." He shrugged, and something like regret passed through his troubled eyes. "We were not close, in truth. I hadn't seen my father in many years."

Josie blinked. *Years.* She thought of her own father, with his silver mustache and booming laugh, his arthritic hands and stiff body, the way he heaved hay bales around, nonetheless. His old boots, the smell of Folgers, his gentle bemusement when regarding the wider world. She couldn't imagine not seeing her father for years. Not mourning him.

"I said goodbye long ago," Hugo added, as if this was explanation enough, frowning as he glanced out to sea. "All I feel, to be honest, is duty. It's why I searched for Cicero." The dog, tugged from his snooze by his name, lifted his head to blink at his adversary. Hugo sighed. "It's why he matters to me."

And Cicero, gathering himself, resumed his low growl. For the first time, Josie leaned close to his soft, freckled ears and shushed him. Cicero blinked, his gaze darting between Josie and his nemesis across the table.

"*Dio mio.* What am I going to do with him, though?" Hugo shook his head, at a clear loss. "Perhaps I should just give him to you, my father's wishes be damned. But when you fly back to America, what then?"

I could take him, Josie couldn't help but think, yet she knocked the notion away. Even if she could manage the logistics of such an outcome, it wouldn't be the right thing to do. That had become abundantly clear.

The man sitting across from her was in pain; he'd lost his father, it seemed, in more ways than one. And perhaps the small, opinionated dog sitting on her lap could provide some healing.

"I can't bring him home with me," Josie lied. She could not take the possibility of catharsis away from anyone.

"Hmm," Hugo said after a moment, studying her. "You're here through August."

Josie nodded, trying to follow his train of thought.

"What if," he said slowly, "you keep Cicero through the summer. And in return, you help me get to know him?"

Hope kindled in Josie's heart. "I could help you make friends," she ventured.

Hugo laughed. "That's ambitious. I would be happy if he simply tolerated me. If I could get close to him without requiring first aid afterward." He nodded, gaining momentum. "So, for the summer you can have him, and I won't have to worry about him biting me every time we pass each other in the hall, or his ceaseless attempts to escape. *Madonna*, I cannot imagine having to feed the little beast. Or walk him."

Josie giggled, and the frown fell away from Hugo's face, bit by bit, his expression loosening.

"And the shop!" he exclaimed, joining her laughter. "He would scare away every customer."

"If you happened to be there antagonizing him with your existence, yes he would. I've never seen a dog with such a grudge."

"He would murder me in my sleep, if he could."

"Without hesitation." She chuckled. "But listen. I think this could work. I can help you do right by your dad." She smiled, but a bit of guilt nudged her. She wasn't being completely honest. This was, of course, not entirely altruistic on her part. "And," she added, "I feel I should tell you, I sort of need the dog in the meantime. This arrangement helps me, too."

He studied her for a second, biting his lip in thought. "I gathered as much."

He didn't ask anything further, for which she was grateful. Perhaps, she mused, taking a final sip of cappuccino, she could do some good, here. She could sway Cicero—she was sure of it. They would start with exposure, and positive reinforcement, and by the end of the summer she'd leave a happy dog, one who might bring Hugo some joy. Josie thought of the ways she'd gotten through her own mother's death, the way help sometimes fell from unexpected places. And, of course, there had been much unsought help when Charlie was little, when she'd needed it most. She used to think that's what grace was, really: little bits of bread dropped by the universe, showing the way.

Now she could be one of those precious bits for someone else. And so could Cicero.

"Va bene," Hugo said, running his usable hand through his hair. "It's decided. We shall meet off and on while you're here, *sì*? I can show you around, if you like. Cicero will join us, and perhaps if he thinks we're friends, he will take to me."

"I'm sure he will."

"We'll have some fun," he said. "I'll be your tour guide."

"Va bene," Josie ventured, grinning, and a gull wheeled overhead, dipping close to their table. Hugo reached over to collect her empty cup, but when his hand neared, Cicero's lip curled menacingly, showing his tiny canine fangs.

"Good lord," Josie said at the same time Hugo sputtered, *"Dio mio."*

It would be fun, Josie thought—for some of them, anyway.

CHAPTER THIRTEEN

Josie

Sorrento, Italy

A few days after their *cappuccini* by the sea, Josie was on a call with her father when she received a text.

"I've been wondering, Jojo," her father was saying, speaking louder than was strictly necessary, "whether you've gotten yourself up to Rome yet?"

"Not yet," she said as her phone dinged in her ear, signaling the arrival of a text. "I plan to go in August. I'll send you pictures when I do, Dad."

"Good, good," he said, and she could hear the creak of his porch rocker in the background. She pictured him, taking in the night air while they talked; he sounded, she realized, unusually tired. They'd already covered the ranch, the weather back home, the weather in Sorrento, and now he seemed to be winding down like an old watch.

"How late is it there, Dad?" she asked, concerned. "I didn't do the math before I called."

"Oh, I'd say coming up on eleven, but you know me. Bit of a night owl these days. I'm just worn out because I spent the day setting a fence right—it was wobbly as hell, Josie girl. I should probably hit the hay.

And I suppose I should get off this porch before the bugs eat me alive. Some of them are big enough to burn diesel this year."

She smiled. "All right. But I'm going to send some pictures of the town I'm living in now, okay? Look for them tomorrow. Can you remember how to view them in a text message?"

"Oh sure, sure," her dad said, not sounding sure at all. Josie shrugged to herself, reminded him to put on some sunscreen and a good hat for the fence building tomorrow, knowing he'd skip the sunscreen. And as she ended the call, the text popped up.

Meet me for passeggiata tonight? Perhaps I can try holding the leash.

She chuckled, typing back, How brave! Count us in.

~

It was twilight when Josie stepped from the apartment's courtyard into the street, with Cicero on his leash, a few minutes early. Yet Hugo was already coming down the cobbles, two cups of gelato in hand, one held awkwardly in his slinged palm.

He grinned. "*Pistacchio e cioccolato* for you," he said, "but would you take both for a moment?"

"I thought it was my turn to buy gelato," she protested, taking the cups, and he shrugged, dimples deepening.

"This way, you remain in my debt, Giuseppina."

"Giuseppina?"

"Italian for Josephine. Is that not your full name?"

Giuseppina. She smiled. "It is. You're right."

"*Brava*—this is what I like to hear. Now, to make friends." He reached into his pocket and knelt before Cicero who, apparently, hadn't quite registered Hugo's appearance. "And a treat for you, too, sir." He held out a little dog cookie, smiling playfully.

If a dog could glare, Cicero managed it. He took two steps back, running into Josie's shins, and a growl like a freight train rolled through his little chest.

Hugo shook his head, pocketing the bone, and stood. *"Madonna,"* he murmured. "Do you know, Cicero, I bought a whole bag of treats this afternoon? Just for you?"

Josie tried to clear the laughter from her voice. "I'm sorry," she began, but Hugo held up a hand.

"No, no, this is between us. Unless, of course, you've been telling him how awful I am."

"Absolutely. Just awful." She returned his gelato, taking a bite of *cioccolato* as they started up the street.

"Allora," Hugo said, adopting the air of a guide. "Every evening, we embark on a *passeggiata* here in Italy. Have you joined in, while you've been here?"

"Once or twice. Do you go every evening?"

"Sì." He shrugged. "Unless I'm otherwise busy. It was one of the things I missed most, when I didn't live here."

She looked at him fully, her curiosity piqued. "Where did you live?"

"England. Just outside London, for many years."

She took him in for a moment, strolling beside her in his white shirt and slacks, his hair lifting in tufts, his reading glasses absent. This revelation fit like a puzzle piece, creating a larger picture of the man, explaining his impeccable English. He took a bite of gelato, glancing around the lit street, his eyes dancing as if appraising the view.

"But I always missed home. Tell me, what brought you to Sorrento?"

Josie shrugged, belying the truth. So many things had brought her here: a lifelong yearning to travel, a desire to see famous sights and works of art in person, a burning need for adventure, an even greater need to escape her philandering husband.

"I always wanted to live abroad, at least once." She smiled. "Italy was my top destination."

"And do you like it, so far?"

"Oh, I'm completely in love with this place," Josie answered without thought. "If I could, I'd never leave." As she said the words, she realized how true they were. Though this, of course, was a fantasy.

Hugo nodded. "*Capisco.* There's nowhere else I'd like to be, either."

They turned a corner, merging into the foot traffic of Corso Italia. People strolled in both directions, some hand in hand, others walking strollers and dogs, all of them passing under buildings awash in yellow lamplight. It was still the gloaming hour; overhead, the strip of visible sky was a watercolor of blues, steadily darkening. And yet the evening was warm, its breeze ruffling skirts and ponytails and the awnings of shops, still open.

"Must you leave Italy, then?" Hugo asked as they threaded into the crowd.

She glanced at him, taking in the faint smile on his lips, just a curl in the corners. She felt as if he'd seen past her words, glimpsing the yearning she'd always hid so well within.

"I mean," he amended, "if you love it so much, why go so soon? We only live once, *sì*?"

A laugh escaped her, and Cicero glanced up to check in. He was trotting along sedately, tolerating Hugo's presence, though every now and again he looked at the man and bristled.

"If only life were so simple," Josie said. "I have too many responsibilities to stay longer, though. I have a son in college, and a job. A house." As she spoke, she wondered whether she *would* still have a house. Would she and Mark sell it? A tiny knot of dread formed, deep within her, at the notion. What would she be able to afford, if she had to find a new place? Her job, too, flitted through her mind, tightening the knot. At just the thought of the library, she felt as if she could smell its signature blend of carpet and books and inconsistent teenage hygiene. She could see it, too: cold on a winter day, the fluorescent lights buzzing overhead while snow fell outside, encrusting cars in the parking lot.

If only life were simple.

Josie scraped up the last of her gelato, and Hugo held out his hand, offering to toss her empty cup. When he wove back to her, his brown eyes hinged on hers for a moment. "Tell me about home." Again, he seemed to study her. He, too, was assembling a puzzle. "Where are you from?"

"The Midwest. Are you familiar with it? Right in the middle of the country—we live in a suburb of Kansas City. It's really its own small town, though."

"And what do you love about it?"

She smirked, knocked off-balance. "Funny question."

"Is it?" His brows lifted in puzzlement.

Josie chewed her lip, thinking. Just now, *love* wasn't a word that rang true regarding home. "Well," she said after a moment, "we have incredible lightning storms in the summer."

"Lightning."

"Yes—the skies are enormous back home," she continued as they wove through a group of gray-haired tourists, pausing until the street reopened before them. "In the summer, we have glorious sunsets, and so many stars, and when storms roll in over the plains, the lightning comes with them. We used to watch the entire sky come alive with lightning bolts. It was both terrifying and strangely beautiful."

"Like the gods, fighting," he said, catching her eye.

"I suppose."

Hugo shrugged, his lips tipping into a half smile. "I've always rather loved mythology."

"Me, too." She did, truly. When Charlie was small, she'd read all the Greek myths to him before he could read himself. She looked at Hugo sidelong. "And what do you love about where you live?"

"Everything." He puffed air through his lips, a habit, she was learning, this time signaling the enormity of such a question. "But I will show you, instead of telling you. That's the deal we brokered, in exchange for your help with this little monster, *sì*?"

"*Sì.*"

Ahead, a store lit up the street with its yellow awning, open front, and assortment of yellow-hued items spilling out toward passersby. Josie glanced at Cicero, an idea forming. He'd been perfect for the entire walk, so perhaps it was time to experiment. "Listen," she said, "can you hold the dog for a minute while I duck into this shop?"

She handed the pink leash to Hugo, who took an involuntary step backward at the sight of it, his eyes widening.

"Oh, he's not going to hurt you!" she scolded, laughing.

"Easy for you to say." Hugo took the leash, looking warily at Cicero who, for his part, didn't appear to notice the exchange. Instead, he was staring down Corso Italia, head tilted, focused on something Josie couldn't see.

"I've been wanting to buy a bottle of *limoncello*," she added. "Use my absence to make friends."

Before he could protest, Josie turned and went inside, waving as the cashier called, *"buonasera!"* from across the shop. She perused the shelves, found a slim bottle with lemons on the label, and was back out on the street within minutes.

When she emerged, it was to find Hugo standing against a wall, barking commands in Italian while Cicero leaped forward and backward like a dog possessed, snapping at his shoes and pant legs.

"Holy shit!" Josie sputtered. "Cicero! Stop!" She hurried across the street, snatching the dog up mid-bite, and like a teakettle lifted from the burner, his snarl died out. "My goodness!" She glanced, astonished, from Hugo to Cicero, who reached up to lick her chin in apology. "Are you all right, Hugo?"

"Che diavolo!" he whispered, catching his breath and shaking his head. A group of teenagers snickered as they walked by, looking over their shoulders to study the purse-size dog.

"I'm all right." He bent, fingering a torn hem. "He's like a wolverine."

Josie had no idea what to say. "He's usually such a sweet little dog," she managed.

"Sweet." Hugo straightened, laughing. "That's the wrong word, Giuseppina. *Mio Dio.* I suppose he thought I was kidnapping him." He shook his head. "It's going to take a lot of walks, my friend, to fix this. I hope you're committed to this little project."

"I am."

Like him, she spoke with a hint of jest, but she meant it. She loved Cicero. How could she hand him over to Hugo in six short weeks unless something changed profoundly?

"How did you get him to like you?" Hugo asked, gesturing for her to fall into step alongside him once again, his pant leg flapping.

Josie hesitated. "Honestly," she said, "I didn't have to try. He doesn't usually hate people the way he—" She stopped herself, blushing.

"The way he hates me."

She nodded, and Hugo shook his head, ruminating. "It's almost like he knows something. Like he was listening, all along . . . but how could that be?"

"I think," Josie ventured, "animals understand a lot more than we give them credit for."

"*Sì.*" Hugo sighed. "I suppose they must. Now, let's get you and the little demon home."

~

Three days after the *passeggiata*, Josie woke up to a text inviting her to Positano.

Car is fixed, it read, and I have an errand to run. Care to join me for lunch in Positano? Bring the beast.

She found herself smiling as she texted back, inquiring about the time and place he'd prefer to meet, wondering how Cicero would handle a car ride in such close proximity to his great enemy. Still, a guided trip to Positano sounded lovely, and it aligned with her larger plans to boot.

Her larger plans involved, of course, her itinerary. She glanced from the bed where she still lay, cast in a shaft of morning light, out to the kitchen table. On it, her notebook waited. The one she'd spent countless hours poring over, planning and scheming and dreaming, writing down all her intentions for this special, once-in-a-lifetime summer. The one she'd been afraid to open since arriving in Italy, because it meant doing so much alone. The week she'd decided to spend in Sorrento, putting her itinerary on hold, was more than over. The notebook beckoned.

She was, however, a little less afraid now. She glanced from the notebook to Cicero, asleep on the pillow beside her, curled in his customary ball. Positano was on the itinerary, as was the sightseeing involved in getting there, so today she would do both. Check, check. Eventually, she'd work her way up to Naples, Rome, and Florence.

Ten minutes later, Josie settled into a chair by the window overlooking the sea, still silver in the morning light, a mug of coffee steaming in her hand and the notebook close enough to thumb through. She'd taken to waiting for Cicero to rouse himself. She woke with the dawn, but he preferred the sun to hang fully in the sky before rising, which was an hour away, yet. She'd just gotten comfortable, and was about to take her first sip, when her phone rang.

The names of people it could be ran through her mind: Mark, Charlie, her father, Ellen, or one of a handful of other friends in Kansas. None of whom knew about Josie's crumbling marriage. Her phone had become an object of dread, something to be fastidiously avoided.

Nonetheless, she had talked to Charlie twice, briefly, in the last week. She'd lied to him like a con artist, and felt dreadful about it, but she would have felt even worse had she told him the truth. *Dad and I went to the beach this morning,* she'd said on the day she'd had coffee with Hugo by the sea. *The water was wonderful.* This last bit, at least, had been true: She'd taken a swim in the wake of Hugo's departure, and it was bliss.

Luckily, young people have limited imaginations when it comes to their parents, and Charlie had rounded out the conversations with descriptions of his summer classes, which he'd opted to take this year instead of coming home. Ever ambitious, he was bent on building an impressive transcript, and on fitting in labs and prerequisites that filled up quickly during the regular year. But he also mentioned other things: repairs he'd had a friend make to his car, a girl he'd noticed, a camping trip he was planning. And, typically, these chats sparked both worry and relief in Josie. Relief that Charlie was finding time for some fun, and worry about heartbreak and binge drinking and cliff diving and bears.

But your friend knows what he's doing, right? Josie had interrupted, anxiety flickering. *The car's completely safe?*

Charlie assured her it was, and she'd nearly told him to drive it to Mark, to have his dad check it out, but caught herself just in time.

And that brought her to the name on her screen, now. *Mark.*

Josie sighed. She had to talk to him, whether or not she wanted to. They needed to figure out how to handle the situation with Charlie in a more forward-thinking, more appropriate, more *adult* manner. At what age, she wondered, would she feel like an actual adult—a woman who, as her father might say, had her shit together? Was she alone in feeling like she was forever growing up?

Another question flashed as Josie frowned at her ringing phone, hesitating. The same question had banged into her mind lately, like a fist on a door, every time she thought of Mark, confounding her more than any other. After everything their child had been through—indeed, after everything *she and Mark* had been through—how could he have betrayed her? How could you witness someone's soul ripping in two, how could you watch them march through the no-man's-land of a fear so deep and cold it seemed to belong to another world, how could you stand on the dark banks of the River Styx with your wife, wrestling your child from the currents, and then go on to *betray* her?

They had been through hell together, and he'd tossed her away.

"Josie!" Mark exclaimed when she answered, as if he'd won something in a slot machine. "You picked up."

"I did. Look, I don't want to talk—"

"How are you? Christ, I've been worried."

She frowned harder, staring at the sea, watching it brighten as the sun rose somewhere in the east. She lifted her feet onto the coffee table and took a sip from her steaming mug, making him wait.

"I'm fine."

Now it was his turn to hesitate. "What have you been up to there? Are you seeing all the things you planned out in your little book?"

"I am." Josie glanced at Cicero through the open bedroom door, and as if they were tethered, he opened one eye, tracking her, his head yet unmoving on the pillow. "In fact, today I'm going to Positano with a new friend." She didn't know why she said it, but it felt unexpectedly good. If only Mark, who may well be about to go to bed with another woman on the other side of the world, could see the friend she meant. "His name," she found herself saying, "is Hugo. He's a local."

For a long moment, the other end of the line was silent. She could only hear her husband breathing, faintly, far off in his own time zone. Josie felt like she'd placed a screwdriver into a screw, and slowly, deliberately, had begun to turn.

"Jo," Mark finally stammered. "How did you meet this guy?"

"That's none of your business." Josie glanced again at Cicero, still staring at her from across the apartment like a little Yoda, sending her strength.

"How are you getting there? To the town you mentioned?"

"His car."

"Jo." Mark's tone shifted from surprise to one of authority. It was how he usually spoke to her, as if she were a teenager in need of guidance. "Is that wise? Look, I know you might think I'm saying this out of jealousy, but I'm actually worried about your judgment here. You can't know him well, after what? A couple of weeks? And now you're planning to get into a strange man's car, in a foreign country, and drive off to God knows where?"

"To Positano," she interrupted.

"Nobody would miss you if you vanished." His voice was deadpan. "Not for a long time."

"Well," she said, frustrated by his tactics, but also knocked off-balance. Was there any truth to what he was saying? It was strange, certainly, how much Cicero hated Hugo. A bead of worry hardened within her, deep down, but she ignored it and said, "I'll have my attack dog with me, so nothing to fear."

"What? Your attack—"

"Look, Mark, I have to go. I'll text you later about Charlie—I've been lying to him, telling him you're here, and I know you have, too, and that can't go on forever. We need a plan. But right now, I need to go."

And without giving him a chance to respond further, Josie hung up on her husband.

~

Later, as Josie and Cicero walked through Sorrento, passing through shadows and shafts of light dividing the narrow lanes, she worried. She wore a citrus-yellow sundress, had her hair in a loose bun in anticipation of sea winds and lunch out, and was heading toward the planned meeting point, Hugo's shop. And, despite her flippant response to Mark's concerns, his words had hit their target with a resounding thwack. As he knew they would, certainly.

Josie *wasn't* sure this was wise, in fact.

She really didn't know Hugo at all. If asked, what could she say about him? Could she expound on his career, his childhood, his marital status, his history? No. She didn't even know what type of shop he ran, for God's sake. All she knew about Hugo Caruso was that he'd once lived in England, he'd once had a father, and now he had a dog who hated him with a vengeance.

Cicero had hated only one other person since they'd met—the Texan. This, surely, was a bad sign. Wasn't there lore about animals and their ability to judge character? Was Cicero trying to tell her that Hugo was a con artist, a member of the mafia, a violent psychopath luring her into a trap?

She thought of Mark. Lord knew her intuition had been off in the past.

Her chest tightened with anxiety as she turned onto the street lined with orange trees. Hugo's blue door was just a few blocks down. Not far. Cicero glanced up at her, and she met his earnest gaze.

"Should we turn around, pup?" she whispered, watching him blink in response.

But Cicero didn't turn around. He swung his eyes from Josie to the road and trotted steadfastly in the direction of the blue door.

Riding a tide of uncertainty, Josie followed.

CHAPTER FOURTEEN

CICERO

Sorrento, Italy

"Ragazzo mio!"

Giorgio's voice rang out as the blue door jingled, closing behind me and Josie, his words hitting me like wind.

My friend, I must confess that, for a moment, I completely lost my senses. Josie released my leash when I tugged, rather hard, and I ran, as if my tail had connected with an electrical outlet, abandoning all thought in a searing burst of joy. Giorgio was back! I'd found him! I zipped around the store once, twice, three times while Josie laughed, bewildered, and Giorgio called out. Finally, his voice broke through my frenzy, pulling me up to a shaky halt.

"Cicero! *Calmati! Calmati!*" he hollered, laughing. "Sit, boy!"

I skidded into a spot of sun, blinking and panting, my heart bounding in my chest. I wanted to leap into his arms, to cover him in kisses, but his words coursed through me like a sedative.

"Sit!" he repeated, and I did. "You must act normal, *ragazzo*. Hush, my friend."

As I recovered my senses, the shape of my dear companion clarified before me, his silvery outline distorting the window behind him.

Giorgio is back.

The words fell into me like raindrops into parched earth, bringing relief. Yet I realized, as I caught my breath, joy and relief were not all I felt. No, strangely, there was something else, wriggling like a worm in dry earth, surfacing. But what?

For two weeks, I had despaired over Giorgio's absence, privately mourning every day I failed to locate him and then picking myself up the following day to try again. And here he was, hovering before me, acting as if nothing had happened at all. The strange feeling I was experiencing, for the first time ever regarding my dearest friend, hardened into five words that roared abruptly through my mind. Not to be rude, but in that moment, I longed to ask only one question: What the actual fuck, Giorgio?

In the absence of words, I remained stuck in place for several more breaths, as if rigor mortis had taken hold of me, as if I was the dead one. *I've been so worried,* I yearned to shout. I'd thought we might never reconvene. I'd thought, this time, he might *actually* be dead. Well, you know what I mean.

Yet here he was, grinning as if nothing at all had happened, dropping to kneel before me.

Giorgio's joy faded a little. "Cicero," he coaxed, "you're not angry with me, are you?"

You're damn right I was angry. Still, I tilted my head, listening. And despite my hurt, I could feel the thaw starting already as I stared into his beloved, silvery map of a face. His bristle brows shot up, and he slapped his bent knee, making no sound at all.

"But look, Cicero! You found a pretty lady in my absence, did you not? How can you be upset when you walked in on her leash, eh?" Josie glanced at me quizzically here and there, but she'd wandered off, perusing the shop. Giorgio chuckled, and I strove to subdue my tail, which started an uncalled-for wag. I was not ready to give in fully, not yet. I needed him to be really, *really* sorry first, sorry enough that he would never leave me again.

For his part, Giorgio already seemed to have moved on from feeling contrite. He was looking at me no longer.

No, my friend, it confounded me to realize that Giorgio, my ghostly companion, stared not at me with a strange new fervor in his eyes, but at *Josie*.

CHAPTER FIFTEEN

Josie

Sorrento, Italy

The door jingled when it opened, and Josie stepped inside, looked around, and gasped.

For a long moment, she stood as if she were a character in one of the graphic novels her middle schoolers used to read, frozen in her frame, her expression stunned. It took Hugo's voice to reanimate her.

"Josie?" he called down from a flight of stairs. She heard his steps moving faintly overhead, wondering whether he lived up there. "Is that you? I'll be down in a moment!"

"Okay," she managed, distracted by her surroundings, turning a full circle to take them in.

Hugo's shop, of all things, was a *bookstore*.

Cicero, for his part, appeared to feel the same way Josie did. Upon entering the shop he burst into an excited run, tugging the leash from Josie's fingers, spinning and wagging and running in frenzied laps as if he recognized the place. And just as Josie was coming back online, he settled in a patch of sun, panting, seemingly taking it all in.

The space was light and cheerful, the shelves rising to meet high rafters overhead, all of it a heady mix of an old, old building and a fresh new vision. Josie stepped over to a shelf, running her hand across it. It looked handmade. As did the counter, decorated with a leafy dieffenbachia and a pair of tiny cacti. The walls were white, the door blue on the inside as well, the entire shop like something Josie would have dreamed up herself.

Much of her worry fell away in that moment. Book people could be many things, but they could *not* be ax murderers. She knew this wasn't a strictly scientific observation, knew Mark would roll his eyes in exasperation if he had a window into her head, but she didn't care. Josie had known countless book people in her life as an assistant librarian; she trusted this metric.

Cicero remained in his sun patch, his ears perked, and Josie imagined he heard Hugo walking around upstairs. She was happy enough to wait. She wandered the shelves, running her hand over spines featuring titles she could not read. Then she came to a shelf dedicated to gardening and plants, and she knelt, her yellow sundress falling in a bell around her.

She pulled a book from the shelf and stood, flipping pages. It was in Italian, of course, but as she took in the pictures, she surmised that it was about Mediterranean plants, or perhaps xeriscaping. She studied the pages, intrigued, mentally naming the cultivars she recognized.

Hugo appeared, trundling down the stairs with a leather bag slung over the shoulder of his good arm, his glasses catching the light.

"You didn't say you owned a bookstore!" Josie exclaimed as he reached her, unable to stifle her enthusiasm.

"Didn't I?" He joined her at the gardening shelf, an amused smile spreading all the way to his gaze. "What did you imagine I did for work?"

Josie shrugged. "Well, if I were to listen to Cicero, general villainy, I suppose." She, too, felt a smile playing over her lips.

He leaned against the shelf, settling in for a minute. "Cicero, apparently, thinks I'm far more exciting than I truly am." He gestured. "You like it?"

She could see his pride as she answered. It was there in the purse of his lips, the light in his eyes. She spoke the truth. "I could not imagine a more perfect place." She shelved her book. "I've worked in a library for much of my adult life, actually, so any place with books feels like home to me."

"Ah, *anch'io*," Hugo said, "*anch'io.*"

"Have you had this store for long?" Josie asked, her attention wandering back to her surroundings.

"Since I returned from England, about ten years ago." Hugo shrugged behind his slinged arm. "But I wanted it for far longer. And you—did you always wish to be a librarian?"

"No," Josie admitted, though she'd loved books and libraries all her life. "Actually, what I wanted to be, more than anything, was a botanist. I studied botany at college, a long time ago."

"A botanist," Hugo said, brows lifting, apparently delighted. "I should have guessed! I can often guess the secret selves of visitors by where they settle in my store."

"The secret selves?"

His lips quirked into a half smile, and he seemed a little shy as he caught her eye. "The real person, *sì*? The person hidden underneath everything life has piled on them."

Josie nodded, considering this. Hugo's secret self, she thought, was clarifying before her, a man with a soft heart beating beneath that blue arm sling.

Cicero suddenly broke from his trance, releasing a single, frustrated bark, apparently directed at the wall. And with it, both Hugo and Josie broke from their thoughts as well. She frowned at the little dog, still sitting in the sun, oddly absorbed by the wall rising before him.

"Is he all right?" Hugo whispered, amusement clear in his voice.

"I'm sure he's fine," she said, not sure at all, wondering whether she should worry before deciding against it. Cicero looked as he should: small and alert. What, after all, could be amiss?

She shrugged. "He probably just saw a ghost."

CHAPTER SIXTEEN

Cicero

Sorrento, Italy

Giorgio glanced from me to Josie, watching intently as Hugo, who'd appeared seconds before, spoke with her. The *bastardo* said my name amid his senseless banter, as did Josie, but I could comprehend nothing else. They both gestured around the shop and grinned like a pair of fools. *Fools.* The unbidden word pricked me with guilt, and I tried to reverse course, to shift my observation of them into a new light. Because Josie, of course, could never be a fool. No, I decided, I was simply seeing the *bastardo's* influence on her.

"They like each other," Giorgio whispered, interrupting my stewing. My head tilted hard at the notion. What did he mean, they liked each other? I, for one, didn't appreciate the implication. But Giorgio, never a man to withhold thoughts, expounded on them.

"Well done, Cicero! Do you know, my boy, that this is exactly what Hugo needs? You've brought him a nice girl to warm his bed, eh? Bravo."

I was shocked, I tell you. Furthermore, I vehemently disagreed regarding the referenced needs. Josie had me to warm her bed, thank you very much, and I didn't give a flying fuck about what Hugo might need.

My goodness, it all made me testy. My language, I assure you, is normally quite refined.

Ignoring my dismay, Giorgio carried on, his gaze on Josie and his son. "It has to be a sign, surely? Her sudden arrival on the end of your leash *must* be a sign of some sort, telling me which way to go. What I'm to do."

I was about to bark again, lodging my protest, when he added, "I've been quite lost, you know." And he looked so abruptly sad, so completely bewildered, that my fury diminished. This was Giorgio, after all. I'm better at maintaining grudges than most dogs—terriers excel in this area—but I could not stay angry with my best friend for more than a minute.

He ran a hand over me that I couldn't feel, and my tail got the better of me, wagging under a pet that felt like a frigid wind.

"We have a job to do, *ragazzo mio*," he murmured. "And I will need your assistance. That must be why I'm still here, eh, boy? To help my son patch his broken heart. To help him live before I die completely."

Perhaps not, but *Dio mio*, who cared? Giorgio was with me once again, and he loved me, and that was enough. He needed me, too, apparently, though for what I could not fathom.

Things were very odd, indeed.

Hugo and Josie approached, looking at me strangely as I wiggled under a pair of silvery hands they couldn't see and I couldn't feel, my tail wagging like a frantic metronome nonetheless.

"Cicero?" Josie ventured, worry clear on her face, and Giorgio's booming laugh obscured whatever else she said, loud even in its new hollowness.

"Ragazzo," he managed, chuckling, "behave normally, *per favore*. She's looking at you like you've grown another head! We need her to trust your sensibility."

Josie plucked up my leash, and Giorgio rose to stand on his ephemeral legs, preparing to follow the living from the shop. Time to go, apparently.

"Shall I tell you what we're about to do, my boy?" Giorgio asked as we emerged in the bright morning sunlight, blinking. I glanced up at his silvery face, noting the mischief glinting in his eyes. "We, *ragazzo mio*, are going to engage in a little matchmaking."

Matchmaking? I flung the word away quicker than I used to spit out pills.

"Sì," Giorgio persisted as we started up the cobbled street. "Hugo needs somebody, and here she is, sent from the heavens. I don't know how it all works, Cicero, but I know magic when I see it."

I wanted to contradict him. Magic? No. It was all me, scheming my way back to him. Sometimes, I tell you, I would give my tail to be able to speak Italian. I'd certainly give my dewclaws. We turned into an alley and Giorgio's old car appeared, and with every step he looked happier. "It's like Sophocles once wrote," he said. "You remember Sophocles, don't you?"

I tilted my head and maintained my stare as Josie picked me up, cradling me in her freckled arms, her dress wafting in the wind.

Giorgio gestured as he climbed into the back of the red convertible, speaking on behalf of Sophocles now, long dead. Like him, I suppose. "One word frees us of all the weight and pain of life," he declared. "And that word is *love*." He grinned, I must say, like a fool.

Madonna mia, I thought as Hugo turned the key.

We were in for a wild ride.

CHAPTER SEVENTEEN

Josie

Sorrento, Italy

Josie climbed into the car beside Hugo, holding her dog close, and frowned slightly at what she discovered there.

The car had a symbol on the steering wheel she recognized. She glanced around the convertible in surprise. Her first impression of it had been simple: that it was quite a cute car, like something from another era, and that it would be delightful to explore the Amalfi Coast with the wind in her hair. But now she took in the yellow stamp on the steering wheel, a tiny rearing horse crowned by the Italian flag, confused. Was this car, of all things, a Ferrari?

Hugo flicked on a pair of sunglasses and turned the key with his one ambulatory hand. The engine rumbled to life.

Josie lowered her own sunglasses from her forehead, feeling the need to talk about this relic of a car, to ask questions, though she was unsure how to do so politely. She had little interest in cars, really, and even less knowledge about them, but she'd lived with Mark and Charlie long enough to know this was no normal vehicle. What was it worth?

If Mark were here, he'd tell her down to the penny. He would also lose his mind at the sight of its tan leather interior, its gleaming wooden dashboard, its rounded hood that shone like a cherry, no evidence of its recent crash remaining.

A larger, and more pressing, question tailed those concerning the Ferrari: Who exactly *was* Hugo Caruso?

He glanced over at her, smiling as he rounded a corner and accelerated up the cobbled street, shifting and steering with his one hand as if it were nothing, passing under a raft of bougainvillea shading a wall. "It's a little noisy," he said over the mounting wind, "but you'll have beautiful views the whole way to San Pietro."

"San Pietro?" Josie felt her frown return—were they not going to Positano?

"Ah," Hugo said, his hair lifting in the wind. "*Scusami.* San Pietro is a quick stop on the way to Positano, where I have an errand. We might make a few stops, if you don't mind—I'd like to buy ingredients for a picnic."

"I don't mind at all," Josie said, taking it in. "That sounds lovely." All the better, she thought, actually. More stops meant she'd get to see more along the way.

And already, there was much to see. The road wound steadily up, framed for a time by either buildings or stone walls, both interrupted, here and there, with churches or cobbled lanes snaking off into neighborhoods. But as they climbed, the buildings thinned, and then the houses grew farther apart, and soon they left Sorrento and its environs behind entirely, weaving into dramatic, sun-strewn hills.

Lemon groves, draped with shade cloth, dotted the landscape, terracing even the steepest inclines and rolling right up to the road. Olive trees, too, silvered the rocky countryside. Josie turned in her seat, holding Cicero tightly in her lap, taking in the view spreading in their wake. The rugged slopes dove all the way back to Sorrento, which decorated the land's edge just before it dropped off into an endless blue. Lazy clouds shaded the hills here and there, casting shapes like little continents, moving slowly.

"It's just beautiful," she called over the wind, pivoting again to see what lay ahead. Hugo nodded, his smile widening, and he shifted gears to snake past a moped.

Good lord, Josie thought, eyeing his one working hand moving between the wheel and the shifter, his knee doing its bit to hold them steady, and she cupped Cicero a little closer. She came from a place with straight roads and flat land and mostly automatic transmissions—she couldn't imagine accelerating up this road, one-armed. This road which, suddenly, dropped off into a veritable cliff on one side. And yet the Mediterranean opened wider beyond the cliff, and she found she couldn't muster too much anxiety. Her customary worry was strangely quiet up here, in these sunbaked hills. Besides, Hugo appeared to be nothing if not capable.

Cicero, for his part, seemed content if unimpressed by the outing. He'd given up growling at Hugo, though he certainly glared and stiffened if any appendage of the man came too close. Now Cicero sniffed at the breeze for a while, and then he closed his eyes and leaned against Josie, his warm little body still upright, napping in the sun.

"Tell me about living in England," she said as the wind shifted, making it easier to chat. "What made you decide to leave home?"

"It began as a study abroad program," Hugo said, downshifting as they made a sharp turn, switchbacking up another incline. "When I was twenty and attending university. I wanted to learn another language—I've always loved language." He smiled and shrugged—a gesture that punctuated many of his thoughts. "So I went to London for what was only meant to be a year. Soon after, I married an English woman, and the rest is history, as they say."

Josie nodded, assembling this new information into what she knew of the man sitting beside her. He'd been married? Her own fractured marriage rose in her mind, and she wanted to ask him about his, to learn what had happened, but she stifled her curiosity. It was too personal.

"I always wished I could have studied abroad," she said instead.

He glanced at her, interest flickering in his brown eyes. "*Sì?* Where would you have gone?"

"Here, of course." She grinned, and he nodded as if in approval.

"You must have missed it," she added, "when you lived away. I can't imagine leaving this place voluntarily, not even for England."

He hesitated, as if trying to select a response from many options. "I did miss it, very much. When I left, I suppose I wanted to experience more of the world. And I did not"—here he downshifted, thinking for a beat—"I did not want to take over my family's business. So that, I suppose, is why it took me so long to return. I wanted to escape that possibility."

"What was your family's business?"

"We grew olives, to make olive oil." He briefly met her gaze. "And lemons for *limoncello*."

"Does that mean you grew up on a farm?" Josie turned more fully toward him, taking in his tousled hair and sunglasses, his hand guiding the wheel, the sleeve of his white shirt rolled up to the elbow, his watch catching the light on his tan forearm. If asked to picture a distinguished Italian man driving a Ferrari along the Amalfi Coast, Josie figured people would imagine this exact human. And yet he'd been raised on a farm, like her?

"Sì," he said. "We had a lot of land, most of it planted with olives and some with lemons—a somewhat unusual childhood, I suppose, though not around here. What about you?"

"I was raised on a ranch," she countered, and he looked fully at her for a second, the same recognition flashing through his brown eyes. "We grew hay and soybeans and raised cattle."

"Davvero?" He slapped the wheel with the heel of his hand. "Usually, people from outside Campania cannot imagine my childhood when I describe it! In London, almost nobody understood, really."

Josie nodded. It didn't matter whether the farm was in Italy or Kansas, or whether it produced olives or soybeans. She knew farms. And knowing farms, she understood something fundamental about Hugo's life, as he likely did about hers. They would both remember how hours evaporated during the growing season, the way growing seasons had organized life, the way calluses formed on hands, the pressure of weather and harvest and pricing and pests. The way a bad year could break you. Josie understood family businesses, too, including the way entire families bled and sweat and cried into them, trying to build something for the future.

And she understood, all too well, not wanting to take one over.

"Your ranch," he added, "was it like a Western ranch? Like we see in movies?"

Josie laughed. "With cowboys and horses, you mean?"

"Sì!" His eyes glittered.

She shook her head. "No, not many of those exist anymore." They turned a corner, and she tried to corral a curl the wind had whipped from her bun. "We had a horse when I was little, but it was mostly for fun. A few people do still use them to manage cattle, but we had machinery to help with the work."

"Tractors, you mean?"

"Yes, we had tractors." *And mud,* she thought. *And old pickup trucks and endless chores.* As a concession, she added, "People do wear cowboy hats. Like in the movies."

He laughed, echoing, "cowboy hats," as if she'd made a joke.

"What was your childhood home like?"

He glanced at her, his dimples deepening. "Heaven," he said simply.

She smiled. "And you said that your father left it to you? Will you return there?"

"Perhaps." Here, his smile faded a bit. "I haven't decided," he confessed, shrugging. "It's a big house, *sì*? Too big for only me. And I have my shop in Sorrento. I've actually been speaking to a real estate agent about it, but . . . I'm not sure."

She thought that over for a second, her first thought one she would not put to words: How could you sell heaven? But then, Hugo leaned forward a bit as if to get a closer look at the road, and they both abandoned talk of his childhood home. "Ah," he murmured, downshifting, *"siamo qui."* "We're just about there."

He slowed precipitously, turning onto a gravel road. The Ferrari wound up someone's driveway, gliding into the shade of overgrown olive and orange trees and coming to a stop before a beautiful, somewhat crumbling house perched against a cliff rising behind it. In its front yard, the land dropped toward the distant sea.

"Who lives here?" she asked, but before Hugo could answer, and before either of them had emerged fully from the car, a tiny, elderly woman appeared in her open door.

"Buongiorno!" she called, gleeful as she tottered down the walk toward them, raising a hand like a woman releasing a handkerchief in the wind. She wore a dark dress and the same heavy shoes Josie had seen on the feet of other older Italian women, and her hair gleamed silver in the sun. She looked like a person who might be interviewed for a documentary about Blue Zones or the secrets to longevity. Even so, she made her way down her uneven steps with little trouble, clasping her hands together with evident joy as she reached Hugo, a swift stream of Italian ricocheting between them.

She was so tiny she had to reach up to him, wrapping his jaw in her hands to draw his face to hers. Once feasible, she kissed both of his cheeks twice. Hugo, in turn, kissed hers, and then she spotted Josie, standing there with Cicero on his leash. The woman released another torrent of language Josie couldn't comprehend, smiling as if her day had been truly made.

"Josie," Hugo said, grinning, "this is Signora Pisano. A good friend of mine." He turned to the older woman, saying, *"Questa donna è mia amica, Josie, Signora Pisano."*

The woman clapped her small, gnarled hands, then took Josie by the shoulders and pulled her in for dual cheek kisses, her lips dry and a bit whiskery. Josie wasn't sure if she should reciprocate—one didn't kiss strangers in Kansas. But before she could worry, the woman was chattering on yet again.

Whatever she said made Hugo laugh heartily, and then he looped his good elbow through the tiny woman's, gestured to Josie to follow, and escorted Signora Pisano back to the house, his leather bag between them.

Inside, Josie took in a simple room with a beamed ceiling, spartan furniture, and a sparkling view of the sea. Cicero sat leaning against her ankle, and Signora Pisano peeled abruptly away from them, shuffling into her kitchen as if something had been agreed upon, humming in a tremulous tone as she went.

"She's lived in this house for eighty years," Hugo said quietly, settling beside Josie and gazing out at the sea. "She moved in just after the war."

Josie glanced at him, charmed but bewildered. What were they doing here? "How do you know her?"

"Oh!" He appeared to realize his omission of pertinent details. "She's a customer. She used to come to my bookshop once a week, but in recent years she's been unable to drive there. She's ninety-eight years old, I believe. She's been a widow for at least twenty."

"So . . ." Josie tried to piece together what he was saying.

"So I bring books to her. Every week, I choose a book I think she'll like, and I drive it here. She usually sends me away with food, because I won't take her money. That's what she's doing in the kitchen. She'll add something for our picnic, I'm sure."

Josie glanced at the tiny woman, busily wrapping a dish at the counter, and her heart prickled with warmth. "She must love you," she said quietly, but Hugo shook his head, his dimples appearing with his smile.

"Other way around. I love her, actually. Though I'm sure she's fond of me as well. We talk about books sometimes, and she tells me about her life—a life we could hardly fathom, Giuseppina."

And then Signora Pisano was back, pressing a full basket into Josie's arms while Hugo fished a book from his bag, stood close to his tiny friend, and read the back cover copy to her. Her eyes sparkled as she clasped the book to her chest, nodding, and then she was patting Josie enthusiastically on the arm, still speaking to Hugo, before they headed for the door.

"What was she saying, back there?" Josie asked a minute later as they retreated down the walk.

He chuckled, reaching the car a step ahead of her, hoisting the basket into the back seat and holding open the door. "I explained that you're helping me with my wayward dog. She thinks you seem like a lovely girl."

Josie smirked. "I'm hardly a girl."

He rounded the car, took his seat, and caught her eye. "To her, we're teenagers."

And then they were off again, snaking down Amalfi Drive, coasting with the wind.

~

They didn't reach Positano until it was nearly lunchtime, because, as promised, Hugo had two more stops planned. First, they pulled into what appeared to be a hobby farm, its terraces and outbuildings tucked into a crevice between two mountains that jutted out to sea. There, Hugo was embraced by an old farmer with a big mustache and a bigger laugh, and they left with fresh figs and cheese. The next stop was a tiny, terraced vineyard, run by another old man who might have been the brother of the first. There, Hugo purchased a bottle of pale wine, fending off the vintner's efforts to slip a second into his satchel. Everyone they met, Josie realized, treated Hugo like a beloved nephew, or even a son, their adoration of him as clear as the southern sky.

"These aren't relatives, right?" Josie asked as they saw the first signs for Positano. "They're just people you've met?"

"Sì." He shrugged, clearly confused by her question. "I stop now and again, purchasing goods. And they stop at my shop, when they're in Sorrento, and I match them with books." He didn't seem to think their effusive warmth was strange at all. Josie tried to imagine people embracing

her as she shopped in Kansas, the butcher or cashier coming around the counter to kiss her cheeks or clap her on the back. She stifled a giggle.

As they neared Positano, the road hugged steep, jagged cliffs, and the sea spread everywhere on the other side, flashing in the strengthening sun. Boats scudded across its surface, drawing white lines across blue water.

"We're nearly there," Hugo called over the wind whipping past the windshield, tossing Josie's hair from its bun, smelling of salt and sea. Birds flickered high overhead, dipping and rising, and Josie's heart, here on this cliff face drenched in sun, felt as if it, too, had wings.

Positano, when they reached it, appeared like something from a postcard. The town draped precipitous hills, its colorful buildings terracing the slopes all the way down to the sea. Hugo slowed as they descended, downshifting on narrow streets lined with shops, restaurants, terraces, and tourists.

"Look for parking," he said as they slowed to a crawl, inching along behind a pair of hatted older folks wearing backpacks.

The sides of the narrow street were lined with mopeds, parked like dominoes, and cars nuzzled so close together Josie couldn't imagine how they'd ever extricate themselves. There wasn't a spot anywhere, and she was about to comment on what appeared to be a futile search when Hugo exclaimed, "Aha!"

He hit the brakes, backed up, and grinned, his dimples deepening. "A *miracolo*. Luck is with us, Josie."

He insisted on hefting the picnic basket despite possessing only one working arm, and so Josie took Cicero's leash, and they were off, winding on foot into Positano's steep streets.

It took only a handful of steps for Josie to fall in love with the town. She and Hugo walked along passages too narrow for cars, scaling steps and gazing into shops, stopping now and again to wander inside. Hugo invariably remained outside, chatting with shopkeepers who sat on stools in their doorways, enjoying the midmorning sun, apparently not overly busy yet on this summer Tuesday. Then she, Hugo, and Cicero carried on, meandering without purpose.

Anywhere a flower could grow, Josie spotted one. Oleander bushes graced terraces and pots, their slender leaves flipping in the breeze, their white and pink flowers bright. Bougainvillea draped walls, petunias hung from window baskets, and, down by the water, palms swayed.

"Why didn't you become a botanist?" Hugo asked as they strolled toward the iconic church in the center of town. Had he noticed her looking at all the plants? Cicero, stern as ever, glanced between them as if trying to follow along.

"Oh," Josie said, "life intervened, I guess. I was in my second year of college when I got pregnant with my son, and then I married his dad."

Hugo studied her for a step. "And could you not finish college, as a mother and wife?"

She hesitated. "It was more complicated than that." A tiny twist formed in her chest, her body itself remembering. "Raising my son was a little more challenging than I'd bargained for."

Hugo chuckled, running a hand through his windswept hair. "That's what I hear from most parents. And your husband?"

She glanced at him, catching his warm, brown gaze for a second. "We're divorcing." She wasn't sure what his question had actually referenced, so she tried to smile, her cheeks heating as if she'd turned a dial. *Divorce.* She hadn't said the word aloud much, since it had become her reality.

Hugo nodded, his own smile fading. "I am sorry. I know how hard it is."

Again, they caught each other's eye, and Hugo shifted the picnic basket.

"I should carry that, really," Josie said in a rush, yet he shook his head, his dimples returning.

"*Assolutamente no.* But you can tell me more about yourself. What do you love about botany, Giuseppina?"

It was a kind question, a way to rescue Josie from her flaming cheeks and shaking voice. Yet she realized, at the same time, it was astute. She did love plants. She loved them in a way most people couldn't comprehend. Yet as Hugo studied her, awaiting her response, she thought he might have an inkling. He seemed like a person who understood deep interests, no matter how unusual.

"Well, there's so much to love, really." She bent, picking up Cicero, worried about the heat on his little toes. "I'm fascinated by the way plants interact with the larger environment, for example, and the way we can influence that environment in gardens. I love to plant certain flowers and watch hummingbirds, bees, and other pollinators come to live among them. I love how it's all a complex system, I guess—how the microbes in the soil affect roots and growth and water uptake, how weather and sunlight and heat impact health, how fungi thread between everything, connecting it all—" She stopped herself, glancing at him, worried she'd taken his slight interest and plunged it right over a cliff. But Hugo appeared wholly invested, watching her as she spoke.

"I also love the names of plants," Josie said, shifting course. "Take these, for example." She gestured toward a pair of pots flanking a storefront, planted with flowers and cypress. "Those little pink ones, draping over? They're called four-o'clocks. Isn't that interesting? There are so many quirky names like that, and they all have a story."

"And the story behind these?"

"They usually don't open until the afternoon, at about four o'clock. See how they're still closed? I don't know why, but I love to think of the first person to notice that, the first person to name the flower."

He smiled. "I understand this. Four-o'clocks. It's quite charming, *sì*?"

She couldn't suppress her grin. And she also couldn't suppress a sense of surprise that Hugo didn't seem bored by this line of conversation, that he wasn't hurrying her to the point. That he seemed, instead, right there with her.

It was very different from what she was used to. The few times she'd beckoned Mark outside over the years, eager to show him the garden, hoping for a bit of appreciation, he'd stuffed his hands in his pockets, raised his brows over the rim of his glasses, and said little. When she'd spoken of her interests with any detail, she'd immediately felt as if she were a child and he the bored parent, barely indulging her. He'd change the subject, and she'd accept it, deflating. Her passions were quirky, she told herself. Not everyone wanted to hear about them.

At that moment, Hugo's phone rang in his pocket. "Apologies," he said to Josie, setting down the picnic basket so he could fish it out and take in the screen, "I need to answer this."

"No worries," she assured him. They stood in the shadow of the Chiesa di Santa Maria Assunta, and Josie pivoted, taking in the church's regal dome overlooking the sea. Hugo spoke into his phone in swift Italian, drifting away a few steps, listening to his caller. And though she wasn't trying to eavesdrop, Josie heard a woman's voice on the other end.

He glanced at her, raising his brows apologetically as the woman prattled on through the phone, and Josie gestured toward the church in explanation. Then she headed inside to take in its ornate, gilded sanctuary, walking around it twice to give him time to finish the call, trying not to wonder who the woman was. It was none of her business, certainly. When she emerged back into the searing sunlight, Hugo was hanging up. Moments later, they carried on down to the beach.

Hugo found them a pair of lounge chairs under an umbrella, and Josie sat, her sundress wafting in the wind, her sandals off, her feet bare in the sand. Cicero spread out under her chair, relishing its shade, too sleepy in the day's growing heat to fuss about Hugo's proximity.

"What do you think," Hugo whispered, glancing at the dog. "Should I try to pet him?"

"Absolutely not." Josie laughed. "We're making progress, but I'm pretty sure he'd still love to remove your remaining arm."

Hugo chuckled, pouring them each of glass of white wine and lifting a pair of plates from his leather bag. Josie helped him lay out the food on the feet of their loungers: lasagna and a hearty loaf of bread from Signora Pisano, with an *aperitivo* of cheese and fresh figs. A feast.

Josie was on her second glass of wine, her inhibitions dulled, when she finally asked a question that had been lurking much of the day.

"What happened to your English wife? Did you get a divorce, too?"

"We did." Hugo squinted out at the sea with its swimmers and bobbing boats, thinking for a moment. "I suppose," he said, hesitating, "more than anything, we never understood each other. She did not know my soul, and even after so long, I don't believe I knew hers. Do you understand what I mean?" He glanced at Josie, uncertainty in his gaze.

She nodded.

"We were married for ten years, but when we spoke to each other it was like a person hitting a ball over a net, again and again, and the other just . . . missing it. She was a mathematics professor, and I worked as a carpenter, so I was often alone in my shop. I became quite lonely." He shrugged. "She was not too sad, or surprised, when I finally wanted to leave."

Again, Josie nodded, considering her own life. She'd thought Mark understood her soul. How could he not, when he had seen it bared so many times? He had watched her give birth to their child. He had witnessed her sitting next to Charlie's bed, night after night, praying to a God she wasn't sure she believed in. Later, he'd seen her get up every day and head off to a job that didn't inspire her, that tired her, yet which she rarely complained about because it allowed her family to thrive. That, too, was her soul, out on her sleeve. She had thought, all along, that he'd been right there with her.

He had not.

"I understand what you mean," she said finally. "I think my marriage might have been similar."

Hugo nodded, studying her. When he spoke, something like sorrow laced his voice. "Perhaps all marriages are this way."

"No." She shook her head, frowning, turning this over in her mind. "No, they can't be."

"Can't they? I often think of all the couples I've known, and how many of them seemed perfectly happy on the surface. And then, later, I'd discover that they weren't at all. Either the marriage would fall abruptly apart, or there would be confessions of hidden secrets over a pint in a pub. I don't know, Giuseppina. At this point, I struggle to believe in the kind of enduring love we were all raised to chase."

"But Hugo, surely some couples remain in love." She sounded, even to her own ears, naive. Yet she thought of her parents, tottering around the farmhouse in matching slippers, drinking Folgers coffee together on cold winter mornings, arguing about current events. Hadn't they truly loved one another?

He shrugged. "Maybe? I'm more inclined to believe that love comes and goes, fading once it has served its function in our individual lives. It's our imagination that turns love into something more than a practical arrangement, *sì*?"

Josie frowned, mulling this over, and Hugo sat up a little. "I think," he mused, "my philosophy has become something like the worldview of Camus—that life is meaningless but worth living, provided you recognize it's meaningless. Perhaps that's true of everything—love included."

Josie looked from Hugo to the glittering sea, considering this, feeling the nudge of familiar terror deep within. When Charlie was small, she'd spent harrowing nights bent over his hospital bed, trying to believe that her world would right itself, that what was happening couldn't be, that there was rhyme or reason to life. That her child *meant* something and would be saved. Yet in her darkest moments, doubts crowded in: Perhaps life was entirely random, entirely incomprehensible. After all, if beautiful children like her own little boy could be snatched away, what meaning could there possibly be? Wasn't that evidence enough for nihilism?

She'd vacillated in her thinking ever since. Because, as a mother with everything to lose, Josie had *needed* her love to mean something. She still did.

"Where does that leave you, then?" she said eventually, catching his gentle brown gaze. "Believing everything's meaningless is a rather hopeless way to live, isn't it?"

"Well"—Hugo paused, thinking—"an existentialist might tell you that there is no meaning in the world apart from the meaning we give it.

There's a difference there." He shrugged. "I used to be different—more of a romantic. And all that left me with was pain, in the end. Now, I suppose I'm something of an existentialist, and it suits me. It's freeing, honestly. After wasting years trying to force a marriage to be more than what it was, it's a relief to imagine that the relationship served a purpose, but that there was no significance in it beyond that. That we are, fundamentally, alone in life, and can thus enjoy and learn from what comes. *Capisci?*"

Josie studied him. "Fundamentally alone," she echoed, and he laughed.

"*Allora*, that does sound bleak. What I mean is, we come into the world alone, and we bounce off each other and interact, but existentially we are responsible for our own journeys. There is no outside force organizing us." Again, he shrugged. "I don't need to attach meaning to much anymore—that's all. I cannot do that again."

Because, Josie thought, *it's too painful. When love means something, its loss does, too.*

He was protecting himself, she supposed, taking a sip of wine. The sun dipped below the umbrella, casting them in light, and an idea started to kindle within Josie. Perhaps she could try living like Hugo, though, just for a bit. She couldn't adopt his larger philosophy—for her, that was a dark path, one she'd already flirted with. But what if, for just a summer, she tried living in the moment? What if she overthought nothing and simply, as Hugo said, bounced along?

"Fair enough," she said eventually, offering her glass for a refill. Hugo obliged, and she held the glass aloft, watching the petal of liquid catch the sun. "To enjoying what comes."

He reciprocated, clinking his glass against hers. *"Cin, cin,"* he said, his grin finally stripping the sorrow from his eyes.

They finished the bottle of wine and most of the food, laughing and talking as the sun arced across the sky. They avoided serious conversations for the rest of the afternoon, instead discussing food, books, dogs, the countries he'd visited, and those Josie would like to see. She kept thinking of the summer ahead, solidifying her new mission to live in the moment. For so many years, her life had required planning and seriousness. Everything, it had seemed, meant something. She thought of Charlie.

Sometimes everything had meant everything.

She squinted at the sea, its waves gaining momentum as they splashed onto the beach, sending sparkles into the sky.

Now, for a few weeks at least, Josie would allow herself to be free.

CHAPTER EIGHTEEN

Josie

Sorrento, Italy

The next morning, Josie woke from a dream in which she sat on the beach, next to Hugo Caruso, drinking wine and laughing as the sun sank from the sky. The dream was, she realized as she sat up in bed, a mirror of the day before, her subconscious repeating the sequence as if longing to relive it.

She blinked, befuddled, comprehending what had woken her. On the nightstand beside her bed, her phone began to ring for a second time. Someone was trying to reach her, repeatedly.

She picked up the phone, rubbing at her eyes, and saw the name on its screen.

Charlie.

Something dipped in Josie, hard and fast. *Live in the moment,* she told herself even as she knew that her life at home was about to claw her backward. Because she intuited, even before Charlie spoke, that this would be about her and Mark. That he was on to them.

"Mom?" He didn't wait for her to say hello.

"Charlie?" She swung her legs from the bed, her feet hitting the cool floor, worry rising in her chest like a flock of resident birds. "What's wrong? Are you okay?"

Outside her window, the sea was just beginning to silver. It must be very early, though the day was over in Charlie's world.

"I'm fine—it's okay, Mom, don't worry. I'm just fucking confused."

She stared at the sea, still shaking off sleep, focusing first on what mattered most: He was safe. He knew reassuring her was of foremost importance—Charlie understood that his mother's worry was like a reflex, automatic and always there.

But *fucking confused*? Indeed, the shoe Josie and Mark had been holding aloft must have finally dropped.

"I went home today," Charlie continued, his voice both puzzled and slightly accusatory. "I was going to check on the house for you guys—you know, water the garden, bring in the mail, maybe spend a night there to escape my roommates." Charlie had many roommates. Josie pictured them, peppering the old house he lived in near his university, as noisy and messy as mastiff pups. "Anyway, *Dad* was there. He was in the kitchen when I showed up, making himself a peanut butter and jelly sandwich. I walked in, wondering why the front door was unlocked, feeling like something was off, you know? And he was standing there in his boxer shorts like he'd just woken up, making a goddamn sandwich, and it was noon. And he's supposed to be in a different country, with you."

Oh God. Had Jen been there? Had Charlie walked right into the shame of it all?

"So I asked him what was going on, and he wouldn't tell me anything. He wouldn't tell me why he came home from the trip early, why you didn't—not anything."

"What?" Josie had been pacing the tiny apartment, gazing out at the sea while Charlie spoke, but here she stopped dead. "What do you mean, he wouldn't tell you anything?"

"He just said to call you. That he needed to get to work—at *noon*, Mom—and that I could hang around the house if I wanted to, but he had a shit ton of work to do, so he was going to leave. Those were the words he used—*a shit ton of work*, like he's a fifteen-year-old kid. I've never seen him act so weird. I asked where you were, and he said Italy, and then he went to the bedroom, pulled on a pair of pants and a shirt, and left. With his sandwich."

Josie clenched her jaw. The *coward*. Mark, who'd started this whole mess, was leaving it to her to break Charlie's heart.

"Are you really in Italy all by yourself?"

Josie hesitated. "Yes, I am, kiddo." She never called him that anymore. A lump rose in her throat.

"Why did Dad come home without you?"

Again, she struggled. "Well, to be honest, he never came here in the first place."

Charlie was quiet for a long moment. "So," he said finally, "you've been lying."

She nodded, trying to conjure the word *yes*, but Charlie plowed on.

"Is Dad having a nervous breakdown or something?"

Josie sighed. Her chest was a nest of hornets, buzzing higher and higher. "He might be, Charlie."

"Why didn't he go with you? I don't understand what's going on."

Charlie was twenty years old. He was a biochemistry major and was preparing for medical school in a couple of years. He was smart, and kind, and so funny Josie often cried with laughter in his presence. He'd had a few girlfriends who he treated perfectly, he'd been adored by teachers, he loved his friends, and they loved him. He was, since his birth, Josie's whole heart. And even though he was now grown and flown, as people say, in this moment he sounded like her boy.

She didn't know how to tell him. She didn't want to tarnish what he believed about his father. She didn't want to throw this curveball into his life at all.

Josie thought of Hugo, who could no longer believe in lasting love. Good lord, how she didn't want that for Charlie.

But she couldn't lie anymore.

"Charlie," she said carefully, listening to his faint breath from across the world. "Your father and I are getting a divorce."

For a long moment, there was only breath. And then Charlie—who was an idealist, who'd believed in the strength of their little family as fervently as she had, who, like her, had used that strength to survive—hung up.

~

Josie sat for a long time staring at the silvery sea, feeling Cicero's eyes on her, her heart aching, her worry growing. Would Charlie be all right? She pictured him going to bed, alone in his drafty rented room. He'd have to return to his summer classes when he woke up, to finish his labs and work in the student union to help pay for his tuition and then study amid the clamor of all those roommates—he'd have to do all of this under the weight of his family's sudden disintegration.

She shouldn't be here, gallivanting across the world, should she? When Charlie was most certainly hurting? Surely that's not what a good mother did?

She'd always tried so hard to be a good mother. From the moment Charlie was born, it had become Josie's calling.

And when he was five, it had become her life's mission.

The mission had started the summer before Charlie was supposed to begin kindergarten, and Josie was planning to return to college to finally finish her degree. After her graduation, she'd imagined, they might have another baby, and she would nurture a career, and life would go on as she'd always planned.

But, during a bright week in July, Charlie had come down with a cold, and everything changed.

It was very hot that week, and Josie sat with her boy, sweating on the couch under a whirring fan, reading *Winnie-the-Pooh*. It was their favorite, and usually Charlie would laugh at Eeyore's gloomy disposition and terrible manners and Tigger's boundless energy and Pooh's boundless appetite. But that day, Charlie simply sat snuggled against her, pale and listless, his big eyes glassy as he followed her finger across the page. Worry nudged Josie, deep down. Charlie coughed, and she kissed his nut-brown head, reached for the thermometer she'd used earlier that day, and took his temperature.

It was right at one hundred. Not too bad, she mused, but the worry wouldn't retreat. Perhaps, she thought, he was too hot? Maybe she'd take him outside for a bit, and together they could cool off in the sprinkler, and then she'd put him down for a nap.

Josie asked Charlie what he thought about this idea, and he roused himself from the couch, unfolding his thin, pale limbs, nodding with enthusiasm.

"We'll just take it easy," she said through the bathroom door as she changed into her own suit, as eager for the cool mist as he was.

"But we'll dance," he called from his bedroom across the hall. "Right, Mommy?"

She grinned, they emerged in the hallway at the same time, and she took his little hand.

It wasn't until they were outside in their bare feet, and Charlie was leaning over the to turn on the spigot, that Josie noticed it. Across his lower back, and spreading onto his belly, was a rash. It looked like a swarm of tiny pinpricks, purple and red. Josie knelt as he neared, preparing to take her hand and run through the sprinkler. She studied the rash for a moment, vivid on his ceramic skin.

"Do these spots hurt, kiddo?" she asked, meeting his luminous eyes.

He shook his head, frowning. Again, worry nudged, harder this time.

It can't be anything too serious, she thought as they skipped, together, through the cool water, his slippery grip tight on hers. Kids get rashes. They get colds. Fevers.

Still, when they went back inside, and Charlie disappeared down the hall to strip off his wet suit, Josie called the pediatrician. She listened to Charlie humming a song while she talked to the receptionist, who asked whether she could bring him in the following day.

"Do you have anything today?" Josie interrupted, her heart beating up into her words. She was being a helicopter mom, she thought as she waited. She was being ridiculous. Still, her pulse hammered harder. She walked down the hall, the phone to her ear, while the receptionist looked over the schedule. When she poked her head into Charlie's room, he was already asleep on his little bed.

"We need to come today," she repeated, and the receptionist, perhaps hearing something in her voice, found them a slot.

Two hours later, Charlie was sitting on the paper-covered exam table in the pediatrician's office, his sandaled feet kicking listlessly, his hands knitted into a polite, tight clasp in his lap. *He was going to be a wonderful kindergartener,* Josie thought, her heart swelling as he caught her eye and smiled with pursed lips. He always tried so hard.

An hour after that, she held those little hands tight in her own, kneeling before him while tears rolled down his cheeks and a phlebotomist drew his blood. "Please, Mommy," he choked through his tears, "make them stop."

And several hours later—Josie lost track of how many—Charlie was checked into Children's Mercy Hospital in Kansas City.

~

It was called ALL, Acute Lymphoblastic Leukemia, Josie learned at Children's. Charlie's white blood cells, the oncologist explained patiently that first night, had gone rogue in his bone marrow. Cancerous cells were reproducing swiftly, crowding out his red blood cells and platelets, causing his rash, his persistent cold, his fatigue.

It would be, the doctor admitted, a long road.

Josie sat very still while he spoke with her and Mark. She held Charlie's hand where he lay in his hospital bed, in the oncology unit, as if they hadn't woken up in their own house just that morning, expecting to get groceries and read stories, to do laundry and make ice pops and maybe, if his fever abated, visit a park. Now she wondered how much Charlie understood of what the doctor was saying. She wondered, in fact, how much she herself understood, and whether Mark, sitting beside her, was processing the doctor's steady words.

Josie felt as if someone was pouring freezing cold water over her, continuously. Like she was trying to hear through an actual waterfall, through snowmelt, like she was gasping and choking and struggling to breathe while she gripped her child's tiny hand, attempting to appear as if everything was okay. Charlie's eyes, lidded with fatigue and too many tears, studied her, weighing her expression, looking for clues about how frightened he should be. And so, Josie sat very still, listening and nodding—she would not let him see her fear.

For the next two months, Charlie remained in the hospital, and all through those harrowing days, Josie didn't let him see her constant terror. She waited until Charlie was asleep to cry, or she sequestered herself in the bathroom or hallway. When she was at his bedside, which was his every waking minute, she read him the entire Winnie-the-Pooh series, laughing at the silly parts, twice. When he endured procedures—and there were so many, many procedures for her tiny child to endure—she held his hand tight in hers, or wheeled his chair down the hall toward whichever department had hailed them, ignoring the nurse to make jokes and kiss the top of his downy head and privately fret over how he would tolerate sedation, or a spinal tap, or an MRI, or a blood or platelet transfusion, or chemotherapy. Mark, too, stationed himself at Charlie's bedside, but when it was time to fetch clothes, or get a breath of fresh air, or coffee, Josie sent him. She couldn't leave Charlie, not for a moment.

"What do you want to be when you grow up?" she'd ask him at times over the ensuing three years, when they were in and out of the hospital and clinics. She willed him to think of his future, especially when the day they were in seemed endless. He would blink his eyes, so large in his thin, pale face, and consider the possibilities. Sometimes he wanted to be an astronaut. Other times, a fisherman. But one day, toward the very end of his treatment, Charlie surprised her.

"I want to be a doctor," he said seriously, pursing his little lips.

A doctor? Josie would have thought that, after all the trauma he'd endured, Charlie would want nothing to do with hospitals or clinics ever again.

"I'll cure sick kids," he said in his high, grave voice, and her heart ached. Many of the doctors they saw had become something like friends to Charlie. Now, she understood, they were also his heroes.

And I, Josie thought to herself, *will be your guard. I will shield you from future danger, from future pain.*

Charlie's seriousness had never left him. He grew, entered remission, and though he became quite funny as a teenager, making his parents and friends and teachers laugh until they cried, there was always a gravity to him. An undercurrent, as if he knew what life was about, and which things mattered. As if he had a mission.

Like Josie.

This was why she had gone to work instead of ever considering returning to college. She chose a job with solid medical benefits and set out to do that job well. Health insurance notwithstanding, they had staggering medical debt and many appointments peppering their family's future.

As years progressed and Charlie grew into a golden young man, Josie's fear for him lessened, but it never vanished. No, Josie understood, she would likely always remain more vigilant than was strictly necessary. Because the kind of fear she'd known is one that never goes completely away.

~

Josie's memories were interrupted that morning, as she watched the silvering sea outside her window, by another phone call.

"Mark?" she said, hearing the crack in her voice. She wiped her eyes. She hadn't realized she'd been crying. For a heartbeat, her anger for her wayward husband was gone. His voice felt like a line she could grab on to, one that ran through both of their pasts, one that connected them no matter what.

"Jo," he said from across the world. "Has Charlie called you?"

She wiped the remaining tears from her eyes. "He did. He said you wouldn't talk to him."

Mark sighed heavily. "I didn't know what to say," he confessed finally. "I'm embarrassed, Jo. I didn't want to disappoint him."

"So you wanted me to disappoint him, then?" Her voice sharpened.

"No," he backtracked. "That's not what I meant. I just mean that he's going to see me differently, as a father and a man. I've set a bad example, Jo, and I'm ashamed. Seeing him . . . I don't know."

She held the phone for a long moment, saying nothing, her eyes on the flash of sea. She heard Cicero hop down from the bed, and turned to see him trotting into the living room, his nails faintly clicking.

"Jo," Mark tried again, and his voice was gravelly. "Listen, I made a mistake."

"Lots of mistakes," she countered, thinking of the many times he'd likely taken the other woman to bed. Cicero's nose found her hip, bumping at Josie where she sat, her cheeks still wet, her hand tight on the phone. The dog stood up on his hind legs, nuzzling what he could reach of her, and Josie automatically patted her lap. He leaped up, settled in one turn, and then he stared at her, hard. When Mark's voice resumed, his head cocked.

"Josephine," Mark managed. It was clear now that he'd been crying as well. "Would you consider taking me back? Please, Jo, I love you. I made a terrible mistake."

Josie could not answer him. She felt very still, as if every cell in her body were made of marble. She'd believed her marriage to Mark meant something, and then he'd made her a fool.

Cicero shuffled on her lap, reaching up tentatively to lick her chin. Had their love meant something, despite his betrayal? Could it still?

"I don't know," she said finally. "I'll have to think about it, Mark."

And with that, she bid him goodbye and hung up the phone.

~

Two hours later, Josie was leaving the apartment, Cicero's leash in hand and tote bag on her shoulder, when she spotted something poking through the lid of her mailbox near the front door. She frowned slightly, confused, and glanced around the courtyard where the mailboxes lined one wall. It was silent, aside from a bird chirping somewhere high overhead, welcoming the day. The lemon trees lifted their leaves to the sun, proud in their pots, and all the other apartment doors remained closed. It was too early for the postman, whom she'd seen making afternoon rounds.

Who had put something in her mailbox?

She flipped open its lid and withdrew a book. *Giardini mediterranei* was printed across its top, and the cover showed a beautiful garden overlooking the sea. Josie's heart swelled a bit, warming with the morning sun. She opened the book, finding a note tucked inside.

> *Thought you might enjoy this. It's full of gorgeous pictures, and perhaps the captions can help you learn some Italian. Would you care to come to my place for dinner, tonight at 8:00?*

A laugh rose in Josie—just one. She didn't know why, but suddenly she felt better. She took a deep breath, standing there in the morning light. She didn't know what she would do about her husband. She didn't know what she should do to help her son. She flipped through a few pages of the book, taking in photos of fig trees girded with lavender, delicate rock gardens, stands of cacti overlooking the sea. All she knew was that today she was in Italy, a place she'd longed to see, and there was nothing she could do about her shattered life. And so, like Hugo, she would live in the moment and try to forget the rest.

"Shall we go see Hugo tonight?" she asked, meeting Cicero's perceptive stare. She smiled, and he tilted his head.

"All right," she said as if he'd answered, tucking the book in her tote and heading toward the door. "But first, today we are going to be brave, Cicero. Today, we are going to Napoli."

CHAPTER NINETEEN

Cicero

Napoli, Italy

Matchmaking, I thought darkly as Josie removed the book from her mailbox. *Dio mio.* The book put me in mind of Giorgio's scheming the day prior, which hadn't relented for the entire trip to Positano. No, he'd sat in the back seat of the car for the journey's duration, narrating the sparks he imagined kindling between Josie and Hugo, while I perched on her lap and forced my attention elsewhere.

Neither of us comprehended what they were saying, of course, the words consisting largely of gibberish. So Giorgio smiled along with their smiles, and he leaned between the seats to study facial expressions when their voices fell, commenting like an overzealous sportscaster.

"Ah, Hugo said something she approves of," he'd exclaim. "What a lovely smile she has!" Or: "Cicero, what do you suppose they're discussing now? It's gotten awfully melancholy all of a sudden, don't you think?" And later: "Bravo, Hugo! Taking her to see your elderly friend was a good move. Though perhaps it wasn't calculated? You know, Cicero, he has a much bigger heart than I ever gave him credit for."

Giorgio's face, difficult to see in the morning light, darkened at this, and his voice dropped so low I flicked my gaze to him, concerned. "There was so much I didn't see," he murmured. "Why is death required for such clarity?"

For most of the drive, I listened to Giorgio's commentary half-heartedly, either sniffing at the wind or attempting to sleep in Josie's arms. I was overjoyed to have Giorgio at my side once again, yet I was less than thrilled by his sudden line of interest. Josie was too good for Hugo, I yearned to protest. She was light and kindness and warmth embodied. And Hugo? *Allora*, I saw him as something akin to a snail vandalizing a garden—a veritable pest. Once, Hugo's hand, working the shifter, moved a little closer than I desired it to, and a growl rose in my throat.

"Cicero!" Giorgio exclaimed, snuffing out the growl like a cigar butt. Shock was clear on his translucent face when I glanced at him. "*Ragazzo mio*, what has gotten into you?"

It's true, I was out of sorts. When Giorgio was alive, I neither cursed nor growled nor bit at people, not counting my puppy days. And now I found reason to threaten *bastardi* quite frequently.

"We're *gentlemen*, Cicero," Giorgio admonished. I regarded him for a long moment, piecing him together in the brightening morning; ghosts, you understand, fade in daylight, becoming a bit like dewdrops shimmering in the sun.

Certo, I wanted to protest, I was a gentleman to the core. Yet I had been through a lot, of late, and such hairpin turns would surely make even the most dapper dog a bit prickly. In the end, I decided to endure the trip to Positano by sleeping as much as possible. And, alas, the day had passed.

Now here I was, leaving the apartment with Josie on a brand-new day, imagining that the hours ahead would be unsullied by Hugo's presence. Yet before we'd even left the building, he ambushed us with a gift. The book in Josie's hand smelled distinctly of Hugo's shop: pine, dust, paper, and ink.

No genius was required to deduce who'd left it. And with the book in her hand, Josie appeared, for the first time since waking, utterly happy.

This worried me, my friend. It worried me deeply.

Josie was tucking the book into her tote when Giorgio arrived, gliding through the door before she opened it, the shape of him fragmenting and reassembling like sand through a sieve. Which, I can assure you, is quite disconcerting to witness. Nevertheless, my tail began its wagging at the sight of him, and my heart filled with a heady mixture of joy and relief, and I only remembered to contain outward signs of my delight when he grinned, held up a finger, and commanded me to refrain.

"You must behave normally," he counseled, not for the first time. "Act as if I am not here, *ragazzo*. We don't want her to think you're addled."

He fell into step alongside us as we left the building, emerging in the quiet streets. It was early, still, but something seemed to prod Josie forward that day. Ever since those crack-of-dawn phone calls and her subsequent distress—which was, I confess, distressing to me as well—she'd moved with fresh purpose. We headed down the street, aiming for the center of town, and I trotted along gamely on my pink leash.

"Did she like the book?" Giorgio asked, studying not me, but Josie, walking briskly in her tennis shoes. "Last night, when Hugo passed the *Giardinaggio* bookshelf on his way upstairs, he stopped in his tracks. Then he plucked that book up and wrote a message in it, and I tell you, there was color in his cheeks. A glint in the boy's eye, Cicero! I couldn't imagine what he was up to until I followed him across town and watched him convince a neighbor to put it in Josie's box. He's smitten, *ragazzo*. I'm quite sure."

I glanced at the heavens for help but caught sight of Giorgio's expression in the process. His silvery face, still plain in the morning light, broke my heart a little. He appeared so hopeful and so anxious, all at once. But why? I'm something of a savant when it comes to human beings, *certo*, but at times their interpersonal calisthenics outright stump me.

"She has to be the one for him," Giorgio persisted. "Why else would I be here, stuck haunting everyone, when I should be off flirting with the other angels? I'm here to help him fall in love with this girl, *veramente*. She and Hugo are of a kind."

I met his gaze, forcing my head not to tilt lest I reveal that I was a haunted dog. I considered his words, *of a kind*. Well, Josie was exceedingly kind, but that's as far as I was willing to go with it. Of a kind with Hugo? Bah.

"Do you know that he called Bettina last night?" Giorgio asked, and I wanted to exclaim, *How could I possibly know such a thing?* Sometimes I felt as if Giorgio was speaking to himself rather than to me, which was downright offensive. To make matters worse, my loyalty, for the first time in my life, was split. I had always agreed with Giorgio. Always. But when it came to Josie, I found that I simply couldn't.

It was terribly confusing. And adding to my bewilderment, who on earth was Bettina?

"Hugo told Bettina that he'd made a new friend, an American woman. He said she's the most genuine person he's encountered in years."

My head did tilt at this, and rather hard, but Josie, intent on the cobbles unfurling before us, didn't notice. *Genuine.* The word caught within me like a leaf on a fence. It was a word that fit Josie like a good pair of shoes. How Hugo could have summed her up so well, I did not know.

And I didn't like it. No, I wished more dearly than ever that I could speak actual words. With a rather heroic effort, I withheld a frustrated bark. I had too much conflicting history to agree with Giorgio about this presumed courtship, too many questions to concur that Hugo should know Josie at all.

Furthermore, why was Giorgio suddenly so invested in Hugo's life? This son, who'd made him angry and sad for so long, who had always been a grave disappointment? This son who'd caused Giorgio to sigh at length during his final years, and to scrawl out mysterious pages of writing in his office, and, in his darker moments, to sob on the *terrazza*? Why did he still care about Hugo, whom I'd known only, until recently, as a slammed door?

As the embodiment of regret?

Remember, my friend, I am nothing if not loyal. And for years I'd hated Hugo Caruso out of solidarity with my best friend. Because Hugo had caused Giorgio absolute torment. I bore witness to it, and I'd done my best to fill whatever hole this wayward *cretino* of a son had left in my generous owner's heart.

And now here we were, pretending none of that had occurred.

A brand-new ghost and a bereaved dog. *Matchmaking*.

~

When Josie and I reached the train station, Giorgio slipped away, explaining that he'd see me later. He wanted, he conveyed with excessive delight, to observe Hugo's preparations for the damned dinner date that evening. I bid him *a più tardi* with a tilt of my head, then faced the day with Josie.

The outing that evolved from that moment, thankfully, was so *bellissima* that I was able to abandon my mixed emotions for its entirety, letting them evaporate like mist in the sun. Josie removed her new book and placed me in the tote bag while we boarded the train, intermittently flipping pages and gazing out the windows. I sensed her heartbeat quickening as the city, finally, grew up around the tracks, the view becoming both grittier and busier. Her breaths shallowed, too, as she placed the book back in the tote, lifted me into her other arm, and made her way from the train into the station. We wove through throngs of commuters and tourists, and, finally, emerged in the sunlit streets of Napoli.

Between Josie's rapid pulse, shallow breaths, and the way her palm cupping my torso began to sweat, I realized that she was devolving into panic. Panic, my friend, is something most animals understand well.

We're all born with a healthy instinct for fear, and I've noticed a few humans get a good, life-preserving dose of it as well.

Even so, sometimes such fear is counterproductive. I recalled that Napoli is known to be, as Giorgio used to say, a bit *frenetica*. Was this what unnerved her? No matter, I mused: We could handle it. So I reached up and gave Josie an encouraging lick on the chin. *Go on,* I thought, hard, when she glanced at me. *You can do it.* I held her gaze for a beat, and she nodded.

"Okay, Cicero," she said, the words followed by her usual nonsense. But I got the feeling she was gathering her courage and that we were about to set off.

And set off we did. Carrying me, Josie wound through crowds and into the chaotic streets, looking up and all around as she walked. People were everywhere, moving in currents and eddies, interrupted often by whizzing mopeds cutting through the drifts like speedboats. Josie leaped aside several times, averting disaster, and then carried on. Her pulse steadied. Her breath normalized. I gave her another lick to keep her going.

We walked up and down streets for quite some time, taking in the shops and the general bustle. Eventually, Josie retrieved another item from her tote, one that I knew was there because I'd sat on it on the train: her notebook. Usually it lived on her nightstand, and she often tossed it a rueful glance. Today she flipped it open, read whatever was written inside, and nodded again.

And so we followed the plans Josie had written down. We went to a museum and stood in front of paintings, among them a depiction of four largely naked men. They wore, it seemed to me, bedsheets, for the most part, which failed to cover much of anything. Not that I've ever truly understood the concept of clothing, mind you, but these days you don't see men running around in ropy sheets. The men appeared to be struggling—wrestling, perhaps?—and I stared at them alongside Josie, utterly confounded.

"Caravaggio," she murmured, along with some other unintelligible tidbits. She stood there so long I could only surmise that this painting was her favorite. I adore humans, certainly, but at times they're utterly ridiculous.

After the museums, there was pizza, the highlight of the day. Josie allowed me to sit in my very own chair, pulled right up to the table, and to dine on my very own slice. The mozzarella was *perfetta*, the crust like a dream, and I adored Josie with renewed fervor. Folks in my old village used to scold Giorgio for sharing with me, and—pardon my speech—I always wanted to tell them to fuck off. What if *they* were never allowed pizza on the premise that it was bad for them? Pizza, it's well known, isn't bad for anyone.

Post lunch, there was more walking through what I assume was the *centro storico*, though the modern world with its rampant mopeds and commerce was enthusiastically present. We saw what I imagine was a castle, and a seaside full of boats, and about ten million people going in every direction. I only had to threaten one the entire day. He was a sly man who smelled of cigarettes and, while bumping up behind us on a crowded street, snaked his hand a bit too close to Josie's tote. I snarled and snapped, and his hand pulled back so fast you'd think I was a wolf. Josie pivoted, confused, but the man had already fled. *Il bastardo.*

Allora, all in all, the day was a rousing success. When we finally reboarded the train to head home, we were tired and, I daresay, rather pleased with ourselves.

If only, I thought as the train rocked back toward Sorrento, the day were well and truly over.

But no. We had an unfortunate dinner date to attend.

CHAPTER TWENTY

Josie

Sorrento, Italy

"Ellen?" Josie said into her phone, biting her lip. "Say something, will you?"

They'd been talking for a half hour—that is, Josie had been talking, while Ellen mostly listened. No sooner had Josie and Cicero returned from Napoli, opening the door to the apartment and walking into its relative coolness, than her phone had rung. Josie had stared at Ellen's name on the screen for a second, contemplating whether she was finally ready to answer, to tell her friend all that had transpired, to begin to process it.

Then she'd answered. And it had all come pouring out.

"That asshole," Ellen said in a half whisper, as though in some kind of shock. "I can't believe it, Josie. Good lord. But you know what?"

"What?" Josie bit her lip a little harder, waiting.

"Good for you."

Josie laughed, surprised. "What do you mean?"

Ellen's tone took on a ferocity that was typical when she was angry. She always moved quickly from fury to conviction, and Josie could imagine her expression hardening, the flash in her dark eyes as she spoke. "I'm so glad you went to Italy without him, Jo. I'm proud of you. Now, go have dinner with this man you met and don't give Mark a second thought—he hasn't provided you that courtesy for a long time, from the sound of it. Okay? Now go."

Josie glanced at the clock on the wall and nodded as if Ellen could see her. She'd begun the conversation by saying she didn't have much time to chat, that she had something like a date, before explaining all the rest. And now Ellen was right—she had to jump in the shower if she was going to be on time.

"Okay, I'm going. Thank you, El." Her eyes stung a bit. "I'm sorry I didn't tell you right away—"

"Oh, for God's sake," Ellen snapped. "You told me when you were ready. Off to dinner with you, my love. And be sure to kiss this Italian bookseller, Jo. That's an order."

~

Not an hour later, the sky over Hugo's street glowed pink when Josie walked down it, freshly showered and clad in a pale-blue dress she'd bought the previous winter in Kansas. She'd imagined wearing it while sitting across from Mark at some cliffside restaurant, their feet finding each other under the table, their well-worn romance rekindling.

Despite Ellen's rage at Mark, and her overt affirmation regarding this dinner date, guilt curled within Josie, deep as a sprouting seed. They'd been married such a long time. She thought of Mark as he'd been during their phone conversation that morning, his voice laced with tears and something akin to panic. She pictured him fixing a peanut butter and jelly sandwich in the kitchen, wearing only boxer shorts, at noon. Unravelling, clearly.

Furious as she was with him, her heart ached with the image.

Mark had long been, Josie had to admit, her rock. He was like the shore, always there, never changing, while she and Charlie were out on a boat facing wild seas. But why had it been like that? She frowned a bit, passing under the orange trees, Cicero pacing at her side. Why had it been Josie and Charlie in the boat, and Mark somewhere off in the distance, providing a steady port?

For the first time, she allowed herself to imagine him—*really* imagine him—falling for Jen the Realtor. Little Peter McPherson's mother, for God's sake. The thought had been too painful to look in the face, until now. Yet, with minimal effort, Josie remembered Jen, with her severe bangs and statuesque bearing. He couldn't have chosen someone more unlike Josie.

Was it because he'd been lonely, out there serving as a steady berth?

The notion rocked something within Josie. She tamped the feeling down, spying the blue door and the windows flanking it, gold in the fading light. She would put thoughts of Mark away for now, shelving him like a troubling book.

When Josie stepped inside, inhaling the scent of pages and pine, a noise made her jolt. A deep, sonorous bark ricocheted through the shop, followed by a woman's voice calling, "Michelangelo!" First Josie saw the dog, trundling toward her, as large as some ponies. Drool snaked the floors in his wake, and he lifted a joyous face while Cicero froze on the end of his leash.

"Ah, Michelangelo," the woman exclaimed again, *"stai zitto! Ascoltami!"* She was a step behind the enormous dog, struggling to restrain him via a dragging leash, grinning up at Josie all the while. "Sorry, sorry!" she said in English, and only then, as the woman tugged Michelangelo down and looked fully up, did Josie recognize her.

It was the woman who'd once given her directions, with the Bernese mountain dog.

"No worries," Josie managed, a noodle of drool now gracing the skirt of her dress. The dog half howled, half barked an overzealous welcome, his collar now firmly in the woman's slender clutch, and Josie laughed, drool and all.

"Is his name Michelangelo?" she asked, bending to pet his generous head.

"*Sì, sì,* Michelangelo. He did not get a long-*ah* walk, so he is terrible now," the woman explained, pressing her hand to Michaelangelo's gigantic bum to encourage him to sit. He dropped onto his haunches, good-naturedly panting, and Cicero took a delicate step closer to Josie. The woman mimed fanning her face, adding, "Because it was so *caldo* today. Hot!"

"So hot," Josie said. "Well, he's a beautiful dog." She glanced around, vaguely wondering where Hugo was and why this woman was in his bookshop after hours. She remembered the phone call Hugo had received in Positano, a female voice echoing through the speaker, and then what he'd said on the beach. *We are fundamentally alone in life, and can thus enjoy and learn from what comes.*

Just how many women did Hugo enjoy?

As quickly as it came, Josie batted the question away. It didn't matter what Hugo Caruso did or who he did it with. He was not part of her real life.

"We met once before, *sì*?" the beautiful woman exclaimed, pulling Josie from her thoughts. "With *questo cane carinissimo*, in the street?"

"That's right," Josie managed, laughing as Cicero took yet another step away from the boisterous pair, effectively hiding under the skirt of her dress. "My name is Josie."

"Piacere." The woman flashed a dazzling smile. "I am Bettina."

As on the day they met, Bettina looked like she'd fallen from a fashion magazine. She was dressed in tall boots, a pencil skirt, and a silk blouse, with a scarf draped over her willowy shoulders. "*This* tiny *cucciolo* is Cicero?" she asked, bending to get a better look at him, incredulous. "The scary dog?"

Again, Josie laughed. "This is him. I'm helping Hugo make friends while I'm here."

"*Madonna mia,* Hugo," Bettina muttered, rising and rolling her eyes.

As if he'd heard, Hugo's voice called from upstairs. "Josie? Are you here?"

"She is here!" Bettina called up before Josie could. "*Sbrigati*, Hugo!"

Hugo appeared on the stairs as Bettina finished ordering him about, his reading glasses catching the light, an amused smile spreading all the way up into his eyes. "Apologies," he called in a rush, thumping down. "I have water boiling for *la pasta*."

At the sight of him, something rose in Josie like a gentle tide.

"Cosa stai cucinando?" Bettina asked as he crossed the shop, giving his outfit a once-over as if she yearned to adjust it, and Hugo raised his unslinged hand like a teacher asking a class to simmer down.

"*Cacio e pepe.* Now, English only, please," he commanded, turning to Josie, a bit out of breath. "Welcome! Apologies for making you wait—I didn't know you had arrived." He glanced sidelong at Bettina, adding, "And more apologies still for my nosy friend here."

"Not at all," Josie said as he grinned, and Bettina swatted his good arm.

"Sciocchezze," she muttered. "And what is *nosy*? *Come il naso?*" She shook her head as if to knock implications of the unknown word away. "No, no—Michelangelo and I walk past every night on our *passeggiata*. And now we must go on. Michelangelo needs *esercizio*."

"It was so nice to meet you," Josie said as Bettina tugged on her dog's leash, murmuring, "*Andiamo! Andiamo* Michelangelo!" while prodding the beast up from the floor, where he'd been splayed like a rug.

"So nice!" Bettina echoed. "We must go for a walk-*ah* sometime, *sì*? With our dogs?"

Josie nodded, and then Bettina blew toward the door like a breeze, wandering on, Michelangelo lumbering in her wake.

"Ciao, ciao!" she called, and she was gone.

"I'm so sorry," Hugo repeated as the door closed. "I told her not to come by, but she listens to nobody. Did she overwhelm you?"

"No," Josie laughed. "She's lovely. How do you know her?"

He gestured for her to follow, speaking as they started upstairs. "We're just good friends."

Josie wondered what that meant to Hugo, but then they stepped into his upstairs apartment and the thought left her. He loped off toward the kitchen where steam ballooned from a burbling pot, and Josie turned, taking in her surroundings. The apartment was beautiful. Like the bookshop, it was trimmed and furnished with glossy wood, the walls a fresh white, all of it softened by potted plants. Artwork hung, here and there, framed in the same polished, hand-hewn wood. The space was an open concept, with a kitchen on the far end where Hugo, currently, stood at a center island, dropping a nest of pasta into the steaming pot.

"Did you do all of this woodwork yourself?" Josie asked, running her hands along a bookshelf that matched the windowsill above it, the joinery seamless.

Hugo glanced up, his glasses fogged. "*Sì*, years ago. With my father."

She bent to unclip Cicero from his leash and wandered over to the kitchen. "Was your father a carpenter, too?"

Hugo laughed, putting a lid on a pot and picking up one of two glasses of red wine, offering it to her. "No, no," he said, taking his readers off and setting them on the counter. "He served as, well, a conversationalist while I worked. My father's greatest talent was talking, really. He helped a bit along the way, *certo*, but mostly he drank wine and coffee and steadied the odd board while I sawed. And he told me stories."

Josie took a sip of her wine, savoring its tang. "Stories?"

"From the village, about people I once knew. I had been away a long time, when we renovated this place." Something passed over his brown gaze. It reminded Josie of the clouds crossing the hills they'd driven through together, casting their shadow shapes. For a moment, it seemed as if Hugo wanted to say more but wasn't sure what, exactly.

"Your father must have been happy when you returned to Italy," she ventured, and Hugo shrugged.

"It wasn't a happy time." He hesitated for a moment as if gathering thoughts. "I wanted to come home for a long time, but I finally came when my brother died. He was older than me, and he had an accident on a motorcycle while on vacation in Torino."

"Hugo, that's awful. I'm so sorry."

Josie stepped toward him, but again he shrugged. "It's all right. It was a long time ago, now. Anyway, I came home, opened the shop I'd always wanted, and here I am."

And after his return, Josie recalled him saying the day they'd met, he hadn't seen his father in many years. But why? She couldn't ask, of course; there was more to the story, the pain of whatever had ensued clear in Hugo's face, though he tried to hide it. Another question loomed, as well—why did he never mention his mother?

Just then, a lid on one of the many pots began to sputter. "Ah, the sauce," Hugo exclaimed, the vibrance returning to his eyes. "Josie, would you help me with this?" He turned, pulling a black apron from a hook, and held it out. "I cannot tie it, with only one arm."

Josie pinched back an amused smile, setting her glass down. She stepped close to Hugo and lifted the apron over his head, pausing to straighten the strap. And, as her fingers brushed the nape of his neck, his eyes met hers. This close, she could see darker flecks spreading through the brown of his irises, like sunrays. His gaze was warm, and kind, and heat rose so suddenly within Josie it was as if his stare was indeed the sun, casting its rays on her. This close, she could sense his heart beating, faintly.

Stop it, Josephine, she thought, hard. Inhaling, she pulled her gaze from Hugo's and straightened the apron across his chest and slinged arm. What was wrong with her? Longing tugged in her belly, swift and sharp as a fishhook. Hugo smelled of soap and pine, as though the wood he shaped had also shaped him. He smiled faintly, his eyes still on her, his lips curling at the corners, and she felt her own mirroring smile.

"Turn around," she managed. She placed her hands on his shoulders, encouraging him to pivot. "I'll tie the back." Her cheeks flushed as she tightened the apron strings around his waist, forcing herself not to notice the shape of him. Exactly what, she wondered, did living in the moment mean to her? Did it mean giving in to longing, whenever it struck? Her cheeks flushed deeper, and just as she was pushing the question away, Hugo's phone rang where it lay on the counter.

Paula flashed on the screen before he could silence the call.

And the strange, suspended moment between them was gone. Josie found her wine, taking a hearty sip, and Hugo moved to stir the sauce.

A timer dinged. Hugo lifted the lid on the pasta, frowned, then turned back to Josie, sheepish. "Will you help me drain it?"

She laughed. "How would you get along without me?"

"I wouldn't. There's another apron." He tilted his chin toward the hook while he fetched a colander from the counter. "To protect your pretty dress."

Josie donned the apron, glancing at his medley of pots and some half-chopped vegetables on the counter. "Why don't we finish cooking together?" she said. "I mean, you have a lot going on here, Hugo."

"Grazie a Dio," he chuckled. "I didn't want to admit it, but I really need your fully functioning arms."

And so, they took turns sipping wine and lifting lids, stirring and chopping and chatting.

"Tell me about your life in America," Hugo ventured while she washed a tomato. When she hesitated, he seemed to sense that the question was too broad and rephrased. "This library you work in, what is it like?"

"Well"—she shrugged—"it's in a middle school, so I pair books with newly minted teenagers every day."

Hugo's brows shot toward the ceiling. "Teenagers? *Madonna mia*, Josie, I sensed that you were a brave woman, but I didn't know how brave."

She smiled, looking up from the tomato. "Oh, they're not so terrible, actually. Teenagers get a bad rap, but in reality, they're usually sweet, and always funny. They're just figuring themselves out, a lot of the time. That's where most of the trouble comes from."

He nodded, stirring a buttery sauce. "Isn't that true of all of us?"

It is, Josie thought. Adults and adolescents weren't entirely different in that regard. Everyone, really, was just figuring life out along the way, stumbling and getting back up again and again.

"And you probably understand teenagers," he continued, "after raising a son?" He glanced at her, slowing his stirring. Yet again she had the feeling he was piecing her life together in his mind, a cartographer making a map.

"I'm sure it helped." Josie picked up a bunch of basil and started separating the leaves, layering them with the sliced tomato. "Though Charlie was the easiest of teenagers."

"Tell me about him."

She paused, thinking of what to say. She was usually a bit guarded about Charlie, unwilling to discuss his entire story with anyone who might react the wrong way. And what was the wrong way? Josie wasn't sure; perhaps any way that made her feel unseen, that made her feel as if this core experience of her life, this defining struggle, was misunderstood.

Yet despite all of this, she found herself talking to Hugo about Charlie as she would anything else. "He's funny and lighthearted on the surface, but underneath that he takes life very seriously. He wants to be a doctor."

"Impressive young man."

Josie nodded. "He really is. But you can't understand Charlie, or me, honestly, without knowing about his childhood. When he was five years old, he had cancer. Leukemia."

Hugo set his spoon down, holding her gaze. "Cancer," he echoed, shaking his head.

"It was hard," she said, simply. Words failed her, as they often did when it came to this.

"How long was he sick?"

Josie cleared her throat. "It took three years to get him into remission, and of course there were lots of checks in the years following that. It shaped his childhood, really."

"And your adulthood." Hugo's brows gathered. *"Vero?"*

She nodded.

"You know," he mused, thoughts moving through his eyes. "Earlier, I said I hadn't realized how brave you were, Josie. Maybe I have an idea, now."

And, strangely, she suspected that he did.

"Shall I start bringing food to the table?" she asked after a moment of quiet, shifting the subject, and Hugo shook himself from his thoughts.

"*Prego.* Yes, let's eat."

Together, they carried their meal to his glossy, handmade table. He'd prepared caprese salad, *cacio e pepe* made with fresh pasta, and whitefish in a buttery sauce with sauteed vegetables on the side.

"I did not forget Cicero," Hugo declared after dishing up, turning in his chair to glance at the dog across the room. Cicero was where he'd been since his arrival: curled up on the corner of Hugo's couch, his eyes following Josie around the room. Now Hugo held up a plate with a slab of fish on it, grinning at the suspicious dog. Cicero's nose lifted into the air.

"He can't help himself," Josie giggled, watching Cicero unglue his body from the couch to leap down, his gaze bouncing between Hugo and the fish.

"He may hate me," Hugo said as the dog made a decision, trotted over, and sat, neatly, before him, "But he likes my cooking. Eh, *ragazzo*?"

Cicero's head tilted sharply sideways with the word.

"What do you suppose he's thinking?" Josie whispered.

"He's wondering whether he can push me from this chair and take my place," Hugo whispered back. "Across from you."

They met each other's eyes, and he smiled faintly, setting the plate on the floor.

"When exactly do you go, Josie? Back to America?"

She hesitated. She found she didn't want to say it, as if admitting her time was so short would make it true. Which was ridiculous.

"Six weeks," she said finally. "I leave in mid-August."

He held his fork aloft, digesting this. "Could you stay longer? If you wanted to?"

If you wanted me to, she found herself thinking, and then she bumped that thought away. Despite their earlier conversation, she was not a teenager, for God's sake. This was not a romance novel. It was real life, and she had a cheating husband who wanted her back, and a brokenhearted son, and a lonely father, and a drained bank account. She had serious, real-life problems to tackle.

"No, honestly. My life is . . ."

"The divorce."

She nodded, her cheeks heating. Why did she have to blush whenever that word was spoken?

"May I ask," Hugo said after a long moment, "what happened?"

Josie took a hearty sip of wine. The room seemed warm around her. She reached down to Cicero, who was happily eating now, and gave him a pet. "Three days before we were supposed to board the plane for this trip together, I discovered my husband was having an affair. He said he wanted to leave me for the other woman, and so I came to Italy alone." She smiled, belying the crush of feelings and pain behind those words. Although, here at Hugo's table, sitting across from his tender, thoughtful gaze, the story felt a little less heartrending than usual.

He frowned, taking it in. "The fool."

"But doesn't it fit with your theory about love? That it can never last?"

Hugo's frown deepened, his forkful of pasta suspended in midair. "*Certo.* Indeed, it does. But he's still a fool."

And he asked no more about Mark.

They ate their salad and pasta and fish, laughing and talking like old friends, and when the dinner was gone and Hugo stood to fetch dessert, Josie got up as well. She wandered around the room with her wineglass, stretching her legs, looking at things. As she was liable to do, she found herself in front of the bookcase, bending to read titles. They were all in Italian, of course, so Josie scanned through them, searching for anything familiar. She was straightening when she noticed a pair of small frames leaning on the bookshelf, as beautifully hewn as everything else.

She picked up the first, examining a photograph of a lovely country house perched on a hill, backlit by the sun. "Is this your childhood home?" she called, and he glanced up from the kitchen counter.

"*Sì,*" he said. "*Bellissima*, is it not?"

It really was. She set the frame down, catching Hugo's eye.

"Will you really sell it?"

He shrugged, placing used dishes in the sink, his smile fading. "I truly don't know," he confessed, wiping his hand on a dishtowel. "Our family lived there for generations—if I'm honest, it would feel like selling part of my soul. But I don't know. It's a big house. And, for me, full of ghosts."

Josie caught his glance for a second, then let it go. She sensed his confusion over the villa, his reluctance to say more.

So she moved to the second frame, setting her glass down and picking it up.

This frame displayed an article from a magazine called *Fine Woodworking*, and in the picture above the text there was Hugo, much younger, grinning for the camera beside a gorgeous table. She scanned the paragraphs beneath it, wherein Hugo was featured as not so much the carpenter he'd claimed to be, but an artist.

"Hugo!" she called a second time, pulling his gaze from the counter where he arranged something on a plate. "Don't tell me you're famous?"

He laughed, his dimples deepening as he picked up the plate and headed for the table. "Not at all. That's just an interview from a long time ago, when I lived in London."

Josie set the frame down, joining him at the table. "But you're not a simple carpenter." She smiled quizzically. "You were overly modest when you described your career in England, the other day."

Hugo shrugged, and if she was not mistaken, his cheeks reddened. He gestured for her to pick up a pastry. "Try that—it's amazing, though I can't claim to have made it."

"Okay, but you have to tell me more about your career while we eat. Did you always want to become a furniture maker?"

He chuckled. "No."

She took a bite of the pastry while he gathered his thoughts—he was right. Amazing.

"It just happened, more or less. I always wanted to own a bookstore—that was the dream. I wanted to build a beautiful shop and spend my days talking about books and ideas with other people. But I also love making things, and when I was a student abroad, I needed a job. So I began by helping an older man, and eventually I married and grew up and took over his business when he retired. It just evolved, I suppose. And I did enjoy it. I've always been interested in how things go together—not just the materials and geometry of a piece, but shapes and weights, colors and the power of negative space—" He seemed to catch himself, shrugging. "Eventually, the furniture I made developed something of a following."

He was an artist, truly, Josie surmised. He picked up a second pastry, urging her to do the same. "Have two."

"And do you still make furniture?" she asked, selecting a cookie.

"*Sì*, I build things in a friend's garage. I'm lucky, really—I'm able to carry on with both of my lifelong interests."

Though it seemed there was more to his story, Hugo stopped at that. And despite wishing to know more, Josie sensed a reticence whenever his past surfaced, and also the sorrow that seemed to move in him, here and there, like weather. There was something more to all of it, she thought, but if he didn't want to discuss it, she certainly wouldn't ask—even if she longed to know more. Because that was the truth: The more Josie got to know Hugo Caruso, it seemed, the more she wanted to know. He was like a novel she couldn't stop reading.

Somewhere beyond the apartment's windows, cathedral bells chimed, signaling the time, echoing through the dark city streets. It was, to Josie's astonishment, midnight. She dusted the icing sugar from her fingers and met Hugo's gaze.

"I need to go," she said apologetically. For a moment, her words hung in the room, and somehow she knew they were both thinking the same thing: Did she?

The hook in her belly tugged, hard, and for a second, she imagined his broad shoulders under that white collared shirt, his tapered waist. For a half breath, she wondered what his chest looked like, his hips, his biceps. She wanted to give in to the tug, finish the wine, and see his bedroom.

But no. She stood, and he nodded, resigned, ever the gentleman.

Minutes later, Hugo held the blue door open for her downstairs, then followed her out into the cobbled, moonlit street to walk her home. She glanced at him as they started off, his hair tousled from the humidity of steaming pasta and cooking pots and skillets. For several strides they remained quiet, walking side by side, though they kept glancing at each other at the same moment, neither of them looking immediately away. The moon hung low over the tiled rooftops, frosting everything it touched.

"*Bellissima*, isn't it?" he said quietly, and without thinking about it, Josie reached over and took his hand. He squeezed, and she squeezed back, and she couldn't explain, even to herself, what had compelled her. She thought of the moon pulling waves up on the sea, far below, and felt that same pull in her own chest.

Josie was walking a dangerous cliff edge, she knew. Tottering. She wanted to let go of her delicate balance, forgetting all that held her. She wanted to fall into Hugo Caruso's arms.

When they reached the door to her building, Josie turned toward him, hesitating. Words formed in her mind. *Would you like to come up?*

No. No, no, she admonished herself. She could not ask that question, not to this generous, interesting man. If he were someone less wonderful, someone she was not in danger of falling for, perhaps. Because if she fell for him, there were only unhappy outcomes ahead for Josie: She had a life to tend to at home, and a faraway man only cluttered that up. And, of course, Hugo didn't believe in love the way she knew she still did, deep down.

Fool that she was.

Hugo took a step toward her, and despite her internal tottering she did not move away. No, as if driven by gravity, Josie took a matching step. She landed right next to him, her chest brushing his, so close she had to look up into his eyes, dark in the night.

"Can I kiss you?" he whispered.

No, she thought, but what she said was, "Yes."

Her cautious heart leaped in her chest, and he leaned down as she stretched up to meet him. He smelled of pine and soap and a hint of red wine and icing sugar. His lips found hers, warm and soft, the curl of his smile still there as they joined, melding together, as seamless as two lovers who'd known each other for a long, long time. Josie's heart pounded, her breasts pressed against him, and his hand found the small of her back. It was warm and strong, and he pulled her inward until their bodies blended, knitting together, and they kissed in a way that made the world disappear.

Nothing existed but Hugo, with his warm mouth and bounding pulse and firm, strong grip. Nothing existed but his good heart, finding hers.

When they parted, it was only slightly.

His eyes met hers again, inches away. Neither of them said anything. There was nothing to be said. They simply held on, for one breath, two, and then Josie took a small, tentative step back. Their hands, as if moving instinctively, found one another, fingers lacing.

I could fall for this man, Josie thought, the words desperate within her. She felt the truth in them. What was she doing?

"Thank you," she whispered, mustering her voice. "For the lovely dinner and company."

"The privilege was all mine." Hugo smiled, hesitating, seemingly unable to let her go.

Beneath them, Cicero lost his patience. He growled, long and low, and then he barked.

And the spell was broken.

They both glanced down at the dog, who stared up from the end of his pink leash, his disapproving stare catching the moonlight.

"I think he's furious," Hugo whispered, and she laughed.

"Mortally offended, I'm sure." She inhaled, trying to slow her pounding heart. "I guess I'd better get him inside. Clearly, it's past his bedtime."

Hugo nodded, still holding on to her hand. Josie squeezed; she, too, didn't want to let go.

Yet she did.

She was just about to turn away from him, finally heading to the door, when he reached for her once more, catching her fingers.

"Can I see you again?"

Her answer came on its own. "I'm counting on it."

"Next week?" He thought for a second, as if calculating. "I wish it could be earlier, but I have some pieces to finish and deliver, and a doctor's appointment. Tuesday's the soonest I'm free."

"Tuesday it is, then." She smiled. *"A più tardi."*

Hugo chuckled, his eyes dancing in the darkness. "You're learning."

Without thinking, Josie reached up and lightly kissed his rough cheek, and then she turned to vanish through her door, Cicero in tow.

When she stepped into the darkened courtyard, the lock clicking softly behind her, she wanted to both laugh and cry, and if anyone had asked, she wouldn't have been able to explain why.

PART THREE

CHAPTER TWENTY-ONE

Cicero

Sorrento, Italy

The night after Hugo cooked dinner for me and Josie, I could not sleep.

I lay awake on the pillow next to Josie's, eyes open, stewing. Self-doubt was nothing I welcomed, yet here it was, lumbering around in my brain with all the insistent menace of a delivery truck. Some dogs invite such doubt—you know the type. They go around with their tails between their legs, flipping over to show their bellies at the slightest whiff of adversity, sometimes even *peeing* in fear—such indignity!—always ready to bend themselves to the will of others.

I am no such dog.

My doubts all concerned my old enemy, Hugo Caruso. Loath as I was to admit it, I lay awake that night considering the possibility that I'd been a poor judge of character regarding the man, that I'd been, not to put too fine a point on it, wrong. Now, my opinion wasn't shifting due only to the slab of buttery fish he'd given me, though that certainly didn't hurt his case. No, there was more to it. I'd watched Hugo carefully all evening as he interacted with Josie, and I saw signs I couldn't reconcile with the villain I thought I knew. There was warmth in his eyes, for one, every time he looked at her. And he moved with a gentleness of spirit, an air of consideration all animals recognize. Usually, people with this grace, this thoughtful way of existing in the world, win over those of us with four legs and intuitive hearts instantly. So why hadn't Hugo won me?

Giorgio.

I sighed on my pillow, audibly. All my life, I had taken as fact anything Giorgio told me. He was a genius, after all, my leader, and my soulmate. He was, as all dogs know their people to be, perfect.

Yet now that our lives were utterly transformed, I was grappling with new, fleeting moments of irritation with my sainted friend, and also with a quite unwelcome question: Was Giorgio sometimes wrong?

It was Giorgio himself who interrupted my stewing in those wee hours, calling from the next room.

"Psst! Ragazzo!" he whispered, forgetting that his voice couldn't wake Josie. "Cicero!"

I lifted my head and blinked toward the open door, thinking, and then I shifted up onto my paws and leaped to the floor. I had questions for Giorgio, *sì,* questions I couldn't volley. Yet if he was here, seeking me out, perhaps he had something to say.

I padded out into the living room, where I found Giorgio sitting, cross-legged, in a shaft of moonlight. He shone like snow at midnight, his smile glistening.

"Cicero," he whispered, "come and sit, boy. *Dio mio*, it's good to be seen, my friend. You're the only living creature who ever looks at me anymore. The only one I can speak to and be heard."

I settled beside him, just beyond the shaft of light, and watched sorrow darken his face, as though it moved through him, rising and falling, trapped within. I tilted my head. He'd been at Hugo's dinner as well, of course, sitting on the couch beside me, uncharacteristically silent all evening. He'd fallen back when Hugo walked Josie home, and was all but invisible, far down the street, when they kissed. Propriety, I knew, weighed heavily on his shimmery shoulders.

"I will remain out here," he whispered now, still observant of propriety at this late hour. "To give the lady privacy. I know she cannot see me, but still, it seems ungentlemanly to be present while she sleeps. I wouldn't be here at all if I weren't so lonely, Cicero, my boy."

I settled further, placing my head on my paws, watching him. He seemed, like me, to be rather more unsettled than usual. Anxious.

"I'm happy about these two kids," he said quietly, his eyes casting to the moon beyond the window. "Hugo and Giuseppina seem like a good match, *sì*? Our matchmaking is working, my friend. Although—" He hesitated, appearing even more mournful than he had a moment before, and he sighed, heavily. "Although, Cicero, I cannot claim to have done anything, really. I'm not matchmaking. I'm not helping my son find his way. I'm not doing *anything*." He scowled, still staring at the moon, his voice dropping to a whisper. He was again speaking to himself and not to me, I realized with no small amount of bemusement. What was I? The furniture?

"Ragazzo," he whispered, "what does it all mean? Why am I here at all? What is my purpose?"

These were questions I'd heard from humans all my life. My irritation grew. The poets love to ask what it all means, all the fucking time. Philosophers adore pondering why they're alive at all, and what they're meant to do. I knew this, because Giorgio used to read written accounts of their never-ending angst, eventually lowering the book in question to blink out at the sunset, struck.

I was never struck, mind you. I know what the purpose of life is.

"If I wasn't meant to do something," Giorgio persisted, louder now, "I would have gone where all the other dead people go. *Capisci?* Surely I was marooned here to *do* something, not to just watch it all unfold around me. I still think Josie is the answer, Cicero. She's the answer to Hugo's broken heart, the brace he needs. But what if Hugo requires my help in winning her? What if she goes back to wherever she came from, and I can do nothing to stop it?"

Here I lifted my head, blinking, alarmed. Go back to wherever she came from? What on earth did Giorgio mean? I glanced around the dark apartment, then swiveled my ears to check on her, breathing in the next room. She came from *here*, this set of rooms, did she not? A blinding panic rose in me, like a geyser. As it dropped, it left dread in its wake.

What did I not understand about my new companion, my new circumstances?

Instead of explaining them, Giorgio rose to stand, walked over to the kitchen table, and crouched before it, leveling his eyes with its surface. I stood, too, tilting my head, wavering again between irritation and this new, seeping dread. What was he doing, anyway? Had my brilliant friend lost the sauce?

He squinted his translucent eyes, staring at a pencil on the table as if he could catch it on fire, and then he raised a finger to touch it. He moved the finger forward, a clear effort to influence the pencil, but his appendage went right through the object of its desire. Giorgio's scowl deepened. He remained crouched, furiously focused, and tried again. And again. And again.

He was still trying to move the pencil when I finally fell asleep, deeply unmoored, my fur gilded by the moonbeam as it slid across the floor.

I woke, hours later, to a dim room, a vanished moon, and a triumphant shout from the table. I jolted at the noise, my head shooting up in time to catch the second of Giorgio's declarations of victory.

"Aha! I've done it, Cicero!"

I cocked my head.

"It was a matter of focus, of calm—a bit like trying to balance on one foot. Watch."

I did watch, my gaze moving from his bushy brows, dropped low over his eyes, to his pointer finger touching down on the pencil yet again. Only this time, the pencil moved, skittering all the way across the table right before my stunned stare.

I sprang up, wagging my tail, delighted for him. I had no idea what he might do with his new, pencil-moving skills, but he was happy, so I was happy.

"Cicero, my boy," Giorgio declared, rising to stand, "I am no longer an ineffectual ghost. No, *ragazzo*, from now on I will touch the living world once again. I will tip the balance, so to speak, if the balance must be tipped."

I had no idea what he was prattling on about. But if tipping the balance had anything to do with making sure Josie never left me, I was all in.

At the very moment I thought this, a new sound pricked at my ears. I turned my head to the front door, cocking it a bit more to the right with every soft beep emanating from the outer hallway. Giorgio watched me for a second, then he, too, turned to the door, listening.

"Someone's here," he whispered, and my heart galloped forth. I stood my ground, growling long and low, the hair on my back lifting like a porcupine's spines as the final beep sounded.

Indeed, someone was out there. Someone who knew the door code.

Before I could bark, the door swung wide.

CHAPTER TWENTY-TWO

Josie

Sorrento, Italy

Josie woke to Cicero's frantic, furious barking.

For half a breath, she lay still, staring around the quiet, darkened bedroom, bewildered. What time was it? Out the window, the sky was no longer black, but the cobalt of dawn. In the living room, Cicero's barking reached such a crescendo Josie didn't hear the front door open.

But she heard it close.

Her heart lunged into a sprint. *Someone was in the apartment.* She clutched the sheet to her chest while swinging her legs to the floor, her instincts dueling: Part of her wanted to hide in bed, and part of her wanted to find a rolling pin with which to hit the intruder.

Before she could do either, a shriek tore through the morning quiet.

"Motherfucker!" a man shouted, and everything within Josie sank like a battleship.

Mark.

"Jo? Are you here? Christ, get him off me!"

She sprang from bed, and a moment later she was pulling a rageful Cicero from Mark's pant leg, which, as he scrambled backward, hung like a windless flag from his knee.

"Good lord," she sputtered, heaving the dog up and away despite his struggling. He resumed barking, so ardently Josie couldn't say much to her surprise guest who now hid behind his roller suitcase, gaping at her and the dog.

"Cicero!" Josie commanded, gathering her senses. *"Stai zitto!"* She borrowed the phrase she'd heard several locals, including Bettina, utter, guessing Cicero might understand the Italian command to quiet down. He did. Stunned, he snapped his jaw closed and tilted his head, his bright eyes studying her in the darkness, his hackles still high on his little white back.

"Mark?" she managed, shaking her head as she took him in. His glasses were askew, his silver-streaked hair a mess, and his mouth hung slightly open. "What in God's name are you doing here?"

"I told you I was coming," he stammered, glancing at his mangled pant leg. "What is this *dog* doing here? He's horrid, Jo. Christ."

"You did *not* tell me you were coming." She cupped Cicero closer, feeling his heart throttling under her palm, her own pulse slowing. She frowned, hard. "You said you wanted to, and I told you not to. Many times."

"Well." He ran a hand through his ruffled hair, glancing around the dark apartment. "I rented this place, too. I have a right to be here."

"No." She shook her head. "We rented it with my mom's money. And then you went off and slept with someone else, so I'm quite sure if my mother is watching you from the great beyond, she's in no mood." She spun around, heading toward the bedroom, obeying a rising desire to put space between them. She needed to gather herself, to *think*. Behind her, the suitcase's wheels began to roll.

"Change your pants," she called over her shoulder. "Those are ruined. And don't follow me."

"Ow!" he exclaimed, and she pivoted again, anger and bewilderment roaring through her, expanding with every second. She couldn't *believe* he was here.

"What now?"

He was glancing around as if trying to get his bearings. "Did you just throw a pencil at me? I looked away and—"

"Oh, for heaven's sake, Mark—"

"No—I'm serious, Jo. This pencil just came winging out of nowhere and hit me on the cheek. You didn't throw it?"

She studied his lanky figure as he pivoted, searching the emptiness behind him. When he glanced at her, his eyes were both startled and defensive, not unlike those of middle schoolers when reprimanded. She couldn't believe he'd boarded a plane without so much as texting her. That he'd barreled his way back into her life, even though she wasn't at all ready to face him. That his admission of error on the phone the other day, his plaintive confession that he'd made a mistake and set a bad example to their son, was enough for him to believe he'd been forgiven.

He never stopped to consider what she hadn't said.

"Of course I didn't throw a pencil at you." She met his gaze and held it firm. "Maybe it was my mother's ghost, Mark. Haunting you."

And with that, she turned on her heel, went to the bedroom, and slammed the door.

~

A half hour later, she emerged, clad in a sundress, Cicero in one arm and her tote in the other. She couldn't stay in the apartment, not for another second. She needed space to think.

Mark was splayed across the couch, his suitcase parked nearby, fast asleep. Cicero took one look at him and resumed growling, an engine without a muffler rumbling angrily in Josie's arms. Still, she paused, staring at her husband. After their call yesterday morning, he must have caught the first plane here, traveling through the night. Again, she pulled up the words he'd said on the phone, holding them in her mind as if to examine them.

Would you consider taking me back? Please, Jo, I love you. I made a terrible mistake.

Despite her fury, she softened, fractionally. She'd told him she wasn't sure, yet he'd apparently gone straight to the airport. Was this a grand gesture to win her back, or to absolve himself from his transgressions? And good lord—how much had that last-minute plane ticket cost? She stared at his familiar body, draped across the too-short sofa, his glasses on the coffee table, until Cicero paused his growling and gave her a questioning lick on the chin.

Right, she thought. He needed to visit the shrubbery.

Once outside, Josie gave in to the urge to walk. The sun was up, and birds flitted through the palms and bougainvillea softening the street as she forged down it, putting distance between herself and her apartment.

What was she going to do now? She thought of Hugo, last night. She thought of the way his brown eyes, so warm and tender, caught hers. The way he looked at her when she spoke, as if really digesting her words, really seeing her. The way her world full of problems had melted, like frost in the sun, when he kissed her. Would he want to see her again if he knew Mark was in Sorrento, sleeping on her couch?

Should she want to see him?

She sighed, winding down the narrow, cobbled roads until she spilled out onto Corso Italia. As her fury settled a bit, like sand on the ocean floor, her emotions moved in new waves. She paused in the middle of the street, still quiet around her, and closed her eyes. Mark had been her husband for *twenty* years—seeing him had infuriated her, certainly, but that wasn't all. There were other feelings, too.

How many times had they eaten toast together at dawn, chatting and passing a saltshaker filled with their mutual favorite—cinnamon and sugar—back and forth across the table as butter melted into their bread? How many times had they tiptoed past Charlie's bedroom door, hoping not to wake him, giggling on their way to bed? She knew his laugh, bright and abrupt. The way he quieted at dinner parties, suddenly shy. She thought of how he'd taught Charlie to tie his shoes, and to ride a bicycle, years later than most children, once he was in remission. The way he'd taught Charlie to drive, carefully and patiently, the summer he'd turned sixteen.

They'd had a whole life together.

Josie opened her eyes and stepped back, leaning against the wall of a building, bewildered. It had been easy to ignore that life when Mark was across the globe, actively betraying her. But now that he was here? Now that he wanted her back? Josie had no idea what she should do.

Here and there, shops opened around Josie as she stood against the wall, trapped in thought, watching the day begin. Cicero settled next to her ankle, leaning his weight against her, patiently waiting for her to resume their walk. But Josie felt immobilized, unsure of what she was meant to do next, both figuratively and literally. What should she do with her life? And, more immediately, what should she do right this moment? Where was she going?

"Josie?"

A high voice rang out down the street, pulling her from her darting thoughts. She turned, realizing she was close to tears, and blinked them swiftly away. Bettina, walking Michelangelo, was coming down the street.

"Josie!" she called again, brightening. "*Buongiorno!* How *fantastico* to see you! Do you walk here in the morning? We come every day to the *pasticceria* down this way—"

Bettina neared and then stopped abruptly, shading her eyes as if to see Josie better, and Michelangelo walked the final steps to sniff at poor Cicero's bristling backside.

"Josie?" she asked. *"Tutto bene?"*

Bettina must have sensed the tears threatening to spill from Josie's eyes. She swiped at them, sniffing, and tried to smile. *"Tutto bene,"* she echoed. "I'm all right."

"Was it not . . . good last night? With Hugo?"

Josie managed a laugh. "No. I mean, yes. It was wonderful. He was . . . wonderful." She was adrift, speaking without thinking, and she could feel Bettina's dark, perceptive eyes taking her in, trying to understand.

"Allora," Bettina said after a moment, speaking briskly and offering an elbow for Josie to link arms. "Come. *Sì?* We will get a *caffè* together. We will talk."

Moments later, they sat at a bistro table in a small piazza. Pink bougainvillea draped an overhead wall and birds hopped through it, tipping their little heads this way and that. Michelangelo watched them, half interested yet utterly unmotivated, drool dripping from both sides of his mouth while Cicero sat primly in Josie's lap.

"Tell me everything," Bettina commanded, tucking her glossy hair behind both ears. She leaned forward a bit, her espresso pinched delicately between her fingers, slim legs crossed. And, surprising herself, Josie did.

She told Bettina about her husband's infidelity, about her solo trip and how daunting it had seemed, and about meeting Hugo. Here, Bettina nodded, as if she'd heard a version of those events.

"And now he is here? Marco?" Bettina asked when Josie finished, her dark eyes sparkling, enthusiastically aghast. *"Madonna. Che bastardo!"*

Josie giggled through a swallow of cappuccino. "*Che bastardo* indeed." She looked down at Cicero, giving his caramel-patched back a pet. "I don't know what to do."

"Well, you must still see Hugo." Bettina spoke with surprising authority, and when Josie looked up, Bettina caught her eye and held it. "Hugo is a good man, *capsici*? And your Marco threw you away."

Again, Josie giggled. "Not to mince words."

"*Cosa significa*, mince words?" Bettina's brows crimped, but she batted a hand before Josie could answer, her curiosity fleeting. "Even if you accept your *traditore* of a husband back, you must take the chance to fall in love. *Sì?* How can you be sure if you do not try another man?"

Josie pursed her lips, stifling her amusement. *Try another man.* She knew what Bettina was attempting to say. Mark couldn't expect her loyalty, certainly, after he'd betrayed her so grievously. And how, indeed, could she go back to him when she wasn't sure at all whether it was the correct choice?

Perhaps spending time with Hugo would provide clarity. Besides all of that, she wanted to. If she was honest with herself, she wanted to see him again, very much.

"So," she ventured, "I should carry on with what I was doing before Mark arrived—"

"*Brava.* Pretend he is not here." Bettina flapped a hand as if swatting flies. "See Hugo. Tell him nothing about Marco being in Sorrento."

Josie bit her lip, meeting Bettina's sharp stare. "I feel like I should tell him. Won't he find out?"

Bettina shrugged. "Maybe. Who cares?" She smirked. "Josie. You should do whatever you want. *Sì?* You owe nobody *niente*."

Josie frowned, thinking, trying to decide if Bettina was right. If she told Hugo that her husband was staying in her apartment, would he shy away? Bettina must think so. Yet wasn't it immoral to keep this development from Hugo?

But then Josie thought of his phone, ringing so frequently with female callers. She thought of his declaration that one must live in the moment, enjoy what comes, and take nothing too seriously. He, himself, would likely tell her not to worry about Mark, to do as Bettina instructed and pretend her husband was not here, if that's what she wanted.

To take life less seriously.

Josie emptied her cappuccino and set the ceramic cup down, decision made, matching Bettina's smile across the table. She would do it.

Josie would carry on trying out another man.

CHAPTER TWENTY-THREE

Josie

Sorrento, Italy

"Jo! You're back," Mark exclaimed as Josie came through the door, later that morning, her dog in one arm and her tote in the other. Arching out of the tote, graceful as a swan, was a white orchid in a ceramic pot. Josie brushed past Mark, setting the orchid carefully on the windowsill where its petals could turn to the light, sensing all his questions mounting across the room. Slowly, bracing herself, she turned to face her husband.

He stood before the kitchen table, his arms crossed over his chest, one leg jiggling slightly under his shorts, his eyes bright with hope. "Josie, listen," he said. "My arrival wasn't what I'd envisioned—I'm so sorry. I was planning to surprise you, to wake you gently, and perhaps we'd go out to get a bite and talk, but I guess that dog of yours had other plans."

He tried to chuckle, yet it came out forced. Still, his familiar half smile lit up his face, the expression that told her he was unsure of himself, not certain which direction to go, but trying. It was when, usually, she would fill in the gaps for Mark, wrap her arms around him and reassure him, soften the moment until they had a laugh. He didn't always get it right—they both knew this. But with her help, he got there eventually.

Except, she thought as she stood in the living room, unsure of how to respond, for the time he'd gone to another woman. Had Jen, also, filled in the gaps for Mark, fitting into him like the puzzle piece he needed?

"I don't know how to feel," she said honestly, pushing a chunk of hair behind her ear and sighing. Cicero was, yet again, bristling in her arms, his stare trained on Mark like a sniper's scope. "I don't think you should have tried to surprise me, Mark. You've given me enough surprises lately."

"I know, I know, and I'm sorry. I really am, Jo."

Josie sighed again, and her gaze fell from him to the table behind him, which he'd set with two wineglasses, a bottle of white, and an assortment of meats, cheeses, olives, and crackers he must have ventured out to procure. Her heart softened, just a sliver.

"Can we just sit and talk?" he persisted, his half smile trying again. His eyes, behind the flash of his glasses, reflected the blue sea beyond the kitchen window. "Please?"

Josie set Cicero on the couch and held a hand up in front of his fierce little face like a stop sign. "Stay, Cicero," she said in her most commanding tone, and, surprisingly, he settled into a reluctant curl.

"You think he'll come after me again?"

Josie stifled the urge to laugh. Her husband gazed at the little dog as if he were venturing too close to the rim of a volcano that just might erupt.

She shrugged. "Maybe. But I think he'll listen for now."

"Where did he come from?" Mark asked, still with an air of wonder, as if Josie were harboring a tiger.

"Pompeii," she said simply. "There are lots of stray dogs there, and we both needed a friend. Anyway." She glanced over the table, eager to change the subject lest it wander to Hugo. "I see you went shopping."

"I did." He brightened, tipping the wine to pour her a glass. "Proud of me? I found a little grocery store while you were gone. Where did you go, anyway?"

"I had coffee with a friend—"

"A friend?" Mark's smile weakened, and his pupils seemed to dart back and forth the tiniest bit, as if he was reading her. "Was it the man you mentioned?"

Josie took a long sip. Did he have the right to ask such a question? After he'd concealed months of secret trysts with the mother of their son's childhood friend?

"That's none of your business," she found herself saying, surprising herself. Uncharacteristically, she didn't give in to the urge to backtrack, to tell him it was only a female friend, to start building a bridge across the gap between them. "Anyway, after coffee I wandered around for a while, and I found the cutest flower shop tucked into a corner of town I hadn't seen before."

Mark, she could tell, was trying to look interested, though his mind was not on the flower shop, but the coffee date.

"The shop was owned by an elderly woman," Josie persisted, forcing the details upon him, knowing he wouldn't really take them in. "She was darling, but didn't speak much English, so we sort of mimed things and played charades and laughed. I stayed a while. It was the loveliest shop. She had garden plants on racks outside—way more than I would expect from such a little store. It was interesting to see what people might grow here, ornamentally. And inside, the shop was full of cut flowers and orchids."

She smiled, picturing the alcove of the shop she'd stumbled upon. Its interior was decorated with a chartreuse and purple color scheme, filled to the brim with healthy, splashy flowers and a scent so divine she could have stayed forever. She and the woman perused the orchids together, speaking words neither could comprehend, and yet fundamentally understanding one another. They were plant people, people who shared a passion, something Josie recognized in the dark glitter of the old woman's eyes. The shop,

Josie thought as she finally selected her orchid and carried it to the counter to pay, was exactly the sort of place she'd once dreamed of opening.

"Sounds nice." Mark nodded, then turned to the cheese.

Something tiny, like a little balloon, deflated in Josie's chest. She watched her husband as he cut a piece of hard cheese for a cracker, his brows furrowing with the effort. And, despite herself, she couldn't help but wonder how Hugo, if he were sitting opposite her now, would react to her mention of the flower shop. Would he ask questions? Would he see, in her story of that shop, the bit of Josie that had always dreamed?

Inadvertently, she glanced at her phone where she'd set it alongside the orchid. There was a text on it she had yet to reply to, a text that burned in her mind.

Giuseppina, it read, Are we still on for Tuesday? I thought we might visit the island of Capri. We'd be gone all day, so you'd need to pack a bag with swimming things and, perhaps, something to wear to dinner. Sì, o no?

She hadn't yet responded. When it had flashed onto her screen as she was walking home, the orchid bobbing in her tote, a knot of feelings rose in her, tugging tighter with each step. *Capri,* one of the ropes whispered, tightening. *Go.* And the other rope, quite a bit longer, pulled harder. *No,* it hissed. *Not with Mark here. Figure your life out, Josephine.*

She'd told Bettina, and herself, that she would try out another man, and she'd meant it. So why did it feel so difficult to answer the text, to let herself go a bit, to fall toward Hugo and let whatever may happen, happen? To live in the moment?

Why, when Mark had already severed their vows, did it feel so much like cheating?

"I'm glad you've been having a good time here," Mark said from across the table, pulling Josie from her thoughts. "And I'm sorry my surprise came off badly this morning. I flew over because, like I said the other day, I'm sorry. So sorry. I hope we can repair it, Jo. We owe it to Charlie. And we have too much history to just give up on such a good thing."

"But you already gave up on us." The words emerged without thought.

Mark's eyes swung up to hitch on hers, a startled blue. She studied his face, a face so familiar it was a bit like seeing herself. She knew what he'd looked like at twenty-two, and on the day he'd graduated from college, and on the day he'd landed his first real job, and then when he'd become a father, and when he'd lost his own parents, one by one. She'd walked beside him, every step, for so long. Something wrenched within her, like a crowbar digging into her chest, pulling on her heart.

"Mark," Josie managed, feeling like she might cry but stifling it. "What happened to Jen? I thought you had a whole future planned together. And now, suddenly, you're here?"

"I cut it off." He spoke swiftly, like they were words he couldn't wait to say. "I came to my senses, Jo, and ended it."

She blinked at him, digesting this. Another question, even more crucial, whispered within her. It was one she'd needed to ask since the moment she found the roses.

"Mark, how could you have done that to me?"

He shook his head, his eyes filling. "I don't know."

And, she suspected, this was the truest thing he could say to her.

"It's just that, after Charlie left," he said, "I felt like I was staring down the barrel of a gun or something. That I was standing on tracks, waiting for the train to come. Maybe in decades, maybe sooner—I don't know. I felt like my life had become one long slide toward death, that there were no new adventures left—"

"But we had *this* adventure, this one right here—"

"I know, but that was for you." He blinked at her, and she had the impression he was, strangely, naked before her. His veneer had fallen abruptly away. "It was for you, Jo. Italy. And after all those years of working in that damn, stark office, doing something I hate every day, paying the bills and shoveling snow and raising the kid—I don't know. I didn't know who I was anymore. I didn't know what I wanted."

Josie stared at him for a long, long time. She, too, had shoveled snow. And all the rest.

"Didn't you think of me?" she said finally, her voice a cracked whisper. "When you went to her?"

He lifted his gaze, and his eyes were so mournful, so lost, that for a second, she couldn't feel anger anymore. All Josie could feel, in the weight of his gaze, was grief.

He reached a shaky hand toward his wineglass, but before it fully connected, the glass tipped, oddly, all the way over. It hit the table, sending a splash of wine across Mark's torso and puddling, inauspiciously, in the groin of his shorts.

"What the—" he sputtered, and Josie sprang up, as she always did when there was a spill, to fetch a dishcloth. She knelt, on reflex, to mop up the wine, and then, one knee on the marble floor, stopped herself. She glanced up, meeting Mark's bewildered eyes, and handed him the cloth. He nodded, started dabbing at the wine, and Josie retook her seat.

"I'm gonna need to change," he muttered, swiping at his shorts, scowling. "I don't know how that happened—I don't even think I touched that glass."

Josie frowned with him, equally confused. She must have seen it wrong. He must have bumped it over. She glanced toward the couch, finding Cicero's sharp stare nailed to her, his dark, perceptive eyes following her every move. She had the strange sensation that he had questions for her. What, she thought, would Cicero say if he could somehow understand who Mark was, who he'd been in her life, and what he'd done?

"Mark," she found herself saying, turning back as he dabbed up the last of the wine. "I'm not sure what your plans are here, but I have my own agenda."

He looked up sharply. "Agenda?"

"Just," she managed, forcing the words out, "I made plans before you came. Like you, I'm figuring out who I am, now."

He blinked at her, stunned.

"For the next few days, I'm going to visit some local towns on the Amalfi Coast I've been meaning to see. Alone. And next Tuesday, I won't be here, either," she said. "I'm not sure I want to spend much time with you, anyway. I'm not over it, Mark. You should find things to do, places to go, and figure yourself out. Just like I am."

His mouth opened and closed once as he took this in.

"I need time," she added. "And space."

Mark began to speak, but whatever he meant to say emerged as nothing but a sputter. He shook his head, as if rousing himself from a stupor. "What do you mean?" he finally managed. "What am I supposed to do while you're out doing who-knows-what?"

She sighed, rising from her chair, everything within her incongruous. She felt like her entire interior was a shattered mirror, the angles and reflections conflicting. "I don't know, Mark. You're the one who wanted a divorce."

She felt him watching as she crossed the room, his gaze heavy upon her back. Still, she went into the bedroom, paused in the doorway, and motioned for Cicero to come. He leaped from the couch in one fluid movement and was beside her in a blink. Then Josie closed the door.

She went to the bed, lay down, and cried.

~

"Dad?" she said into the phone, a half hour later, when she heard Mark clomp across the apartment and bang out the front door. "Are you there, Dad?"

He'd answered on her second attempt to call; after the call had gone to voicemail she'd simply dialed again, hoping he'd pick up, desperately needing to hear her father's familiar, gravelly voice.

"Jojo?" He fairly shouted into the receiver, as though the distance between them might necessitate more volume. "You there, Josephine?"

"I'm here."

He chuckled. "Sorry I didn't pick up right away—couldn't find the damn phone, but it was right there on my nightstand. If it was a snake, it woulda bit me."

Josie wiped a tear from her cheek. It was so, so good to hear her dad's voice, though it occurred to her he sounded a bit beleaguered by sleep. "I'm sorry—I didn't think about how early it is there," she confessed, but he cut her off.

"No worries, you know I rise with the sun, Josie girl. Though not sure how much I'll get done today—from the sound of it, it's rainin' out there like a cow pissin' on a flat rock, and on a day we were planning to cut hay, of all things."

Josie giggled. She'd heard this saying, and so many more, since early childhood. Her mother used to chide her father, hissing, *Little pitchers!* but it never curbed his love of a colorful idiom.

"The weatherman isn't worth his salt, I swear," he continued. "Can't recall a summer so wet."

"Sounds awful," she commiserated, feeling as though she could sense his nodding through the phone, his enthusiasm. The weather was among his favorite topics.

"The sky's been ugly enough to make a freight train take a dirt road, Josephine. Now, how you gettin' along? Been to Rome, yet?"

"Not yet." She sniffed. "But I'm just fine, Dad."

"It sounds like you've been crying, kid. Tell me why you called at the ass-crack of dawn."

She giggled again through the tears she was trying so hard to withhold. "Well," she began, "Mark arrived this morning. He caught a plane without telling me and walked into the apartment, at dawn, as a surprise."

Her dad was silent for a moment. "A surprise?" he asked finally, his tone gruff. "Hell's bells, Jojo. What kind of surprise is that?"

He understood, as she knew he would. A bad surprise, that's what it was.

"I don't know what to do, Dad," she confessed.

"I'd kick him out," he said without needing to ponder it. "The man betrayed you, Jojo. He doesn't deserve the ground you walk on. Send him packing, that's what I say."

She nodded, eyeing Cicero beside her on the bed. She had the odd feeling that, if the dog could speak, he would convey something similar. But she couldn't send Mark packing, not really. She needed to give it a chance, no matter how mad she was. Didn't she?

"I don't know," she said after a moment, the weight of it all heavy upon her. "What will I do without him? Work at the library forever and live in an apartment somewhere? Struggle to make ends meet for the rest of my life?" She could sense her dad preparing to interject, so she spoke faster. "Also, there's something else. I'm not sure if I should tell you this, but Mom isn't here anymore, and I guess I need someone to tell."

"And I'm the next best thing. Shoot."

Josie hesitated. "Are you sure you're ready for it? It's girl talk, Dad."

"Ready."

She inhaled, feeling Cicero's stare still pinned upon her. "I met a man here, Dad. It's obviously nothing serious—we've just spent a couple of days together, but—"

"Is he nice?"

Again, Josie hesitated. "The nicest," she said finally. "I think he's a good man, Dad."

"Then go out with him," he barked. Josie held the phone out briefly, looking at it as if it might be possessed, and then, frowning, requested clarification.

"Dad? How can you be so sure I should do that?"

She could feel something through the phone, something like impatience and urgency.

"Because I want you to be happy. And listen, Jojo—I'm not saying this man is the one, or even that you need a man in your life, kid. I'm not saying anything like that. All I know now is that Mark *isn't* the one for you. I swear to God, I won't let him darken my door again, and I hate that he's darkening yours. So you should play the field. If the man's nice, you should go have some fun."

Josie thought of Hugo, with his kind eyes.

"But if he doesn't treat you well, move on," her father added. "Listen: You think you're old, but you're so very young, kiddo. Take it from a truly old man—you have a lot of life left to live. And I don't want you living it with someone who doesn't value you like he should."

Here, her dad paused to cough, the sound low and wet, before carrying on. "I mean it, Josephine. I've done nothing but think about that husband of yours, and how in the devil he could have hurt you so terribly. And I've decided I hate him. You need him like a submarine needs a screen door, regardless of what job you'll have or house you'll live in." Again, he paused, coughing, and a bit of worry niggled up into Josie's consciousness.

"Are you okay, Dad?"

He chuckled at the question, but she felt the levity, this time, was forced.

"Why are you asking me that? I'm fit as a fiddle."

"Well, you're coughing—"

"Just a cold. Been a little tired, Josie girl, but it's nothing. Don't you worry. I want you to go out with this nice man and give it a chance. All right? It's what your mother would say, if she were here."

A bubble of sorrow rose in Josie, popping as she tried to speak, and the word came out as a sob. "Okay."

"Okay," he repeated.

She lay back on the bed to stare at the ceiling, and Cicero shifted to nestle against her. "Okay," she said again. "I will."

"All right, then." The emotion dropped from her father's voice. "Guess I'd better be off then, Jojo. Day's waitin', weather be damned."

She smiled at the ceiling, imagining him anticipating his Folgers, waiting in the kitchen, and the paper he would fetch from the gas station and then read, over coffee, while rain pounded the old farmhouse roof.

"Sounds good, Dad. Off you go to get things done."

"Off like a herd of turtles." He chuckled. "Get out there and live, kid. And Josephine?"

"Yes?"

"I love you. Don't you forget it, now."

Josie watched the call blink off, her heart full, and then, before she could change her mind, she swiped to her text messages. The most recent had come from Ellen, sometime in the last hour. Did you kiss the bookseller?

Josie laughed, typed only yes, aware that this would spur a torrent of follow-up questions. A tiny flame burst to life in her chest as she stared at that yes, remembering the kiss.

Then, she swiped back to her texts, finding Hugo's question, still unanswered.

Sì, she typed. I would love to go to Capri with you.

CHAPTER TWENTY-FOUR

Cicero

Sorrento, Italy

"Go," Giorgio whispered, again forgetting that nobody aside from me could hear his voice. "Go while nobody's looking, Cicero, and piss in his suitcase."

I blanched, frankly shocked. I hated this new American in our presence, it was true, but to relieve myself indoors? Had Giorgio lost his mind?

"He'll stink if you do it," Giorgio whispered enticingly, going so far as to drift over to the suitcase, its lid open against the couch where the American had been sleeping for several nights. Josie and I had left him to sightsee during the day, boarding buses and visiting the places they took us, mostly villages and churches and new beaches, but at night the man was still always here. Sometimes he and Josie talked, but their voices sounded tight. Once, he'd prepared a vat of pasta when we got home, but unlike Hugo he'd set none of it aside for me, the ingrate. Twice, when we arrived, tired and footsore, he was still on the couch in his underwear, as if he hadn't left it all day despite the heat of the sun and the glorious, beckoning blue sky.

The hatred between us seemed to be mutual, which made me distinctly uncomfortable in my own home. Whenever Josie wasn't looking, the American *bastardo* threw dirty looks in my direction with eyes, I noted, that were increasingly red and puffy. Josie, saint that she is, visited a *farmacia* after one of our outings, bringing the *bastardo* something for his inflamed eyes. I'd heard her say *allergie* to the pharmacist, so I put the pieces together fairly quickly. The American was allergic to me? *Likewise*, I wanted to declare. Every day that he inhabited the couch, claiming my corner as if he had a right to it, I became a bit more allergic to him.

Now Giorgio gestured, grinning, his expression like a mischievous child's. "I would do it myself if I still could, my boy. Take the only opportunity you'll ever have to perform such an act with my blessing."

So, my friend, I did. I'm ashamed to admit that I trotted right over to the suitcase, first glancing toward the closed bedroom door, where Josie was still dressing for the day, and then toward the closed bathroom door, where this new *bastardo* was taking a shit. And then I lifted my leg on his open suitcase. It was early, and Josie had yet to whisk me out to the shrubbery, so I had an entire night's worth saved up.

"Bravo!" Giorgio exclaimed, obviously delighted. "Now, go and wait by the door so you can get out fast when she's ready. *Sì?* You need to escape the premises before he notices."

Now, this made me worry. What would the man with the blue eyes do if he caught a sniff of my indiscretion? I shivered a bit, there on the marble floor. He deserved whatever came to him, certainly. I couldn't understand a word he said, of course, but there was more to my disdain than how he looked at me. I saw something I didn't like in the way he looked at Josie, too. I also didn't appreciate his frustrated movements, and the snap of energy between them, like static unable to reach ground. And, superseding all his other trespasses, I recalled the way he'd left Josie crying on her bed the afternoon he'd appeared in our home. Did he comfort her? No. He'd simply stalked out the door.

Veramente, I loathed the man.

Even so, I was instantly ashamed of my actions involving my full bladder and his suitcase. I'm a gentleman, as you're well aware by now, trained to live a proper, dignified life. Never once had I committed such an act, and I could say with confidence that I did not like the resulting shame growing in my fearful, pulsing heart. So I sat by the door, tail tucked, shivering more and more, awaiting my pink leash as though it was an absolution.

Biting those that deserve it is one thing, my friend. But as I learned that day, indecency is something else entirely. Never again would I lower myself to it.

The bathroom door opened in synchronicity with the bedroom door, and the man came out with a towel wrapped around his waist, the gray wool of his chest silvering in a stripe of sunlight. He placed a hand on each hip, speaking again to Josie, and I could tell he wasn't pleased. My nerves skittered. I glanced between him and the suitcase. Josie said little, yet I was delighted to hear a hint of stridence in her tone. When the *bastardo* turned toward his couch, aiming for the suitcase beside it, Giorgio sprang into action.

"Dio mio," he murmured, and then he concentrated hard, reaching a hand toward the towel. In one graceful swoop, Giorgio released the tucked corner of the makeshift garment, and it didn't just drop to the floor, but flew several feet across the apartment.

The American sputtered something, bewilderment clear on his face as he moved to retrieve his wayward towel, his pale bottom white as a snake's belly. My tail began to thump as Josie bent, heedless of this new drama, and clipped the leash to my collar. She rolled her eyes as the man said more, as if to convey that she was tired of his claims of torment, that he was, clearly, full of shit.

He wasn't of course, having just taken care of that.

My tail wagged harder as we left the apartment, though from relief or misgiving, I cannot say.

~

Later that morning, I perched in Josie's arms, Giorgio glimmering beside me, on a small ferry sputtering across the water between Sorrento and the Isle of Capri. The sun was on my face, and salt air met my nose, and two of my favorite people were by my side. I was, for the moment, entirely happy.

Then Giorgio spoke.

"She has been here for what, four weeks now?"

He gazed out, taking in the waves scudding across the blue sea, and the boats glinting in the sun, and the gulls wheeling overhead like dandelion seeds on the wind. Despite the beauty engulfing us, I could see that he was brooding.

Four weeks? I tilted my head. I'm not one for keeping time, you see. It all blends together for me, like one continuous river upon which we float. How long was four weeks?

"If it has indeed been nearly four weeks," Giorgio continued, "she only has four left. And then, *ragazzo mio*, she will return to America."

My head tilted so hard the world turned sideways. What? What on God's green earth was he talking about?

"With the American *bastardo*," Giorgio added, looking at me pointedly. "This is not what we desire, *capisci*?"

I wanted to bark, many times, but I held it in. I glanced between Giorgio, silver as a teardrop, and Josie and Hugo, chatting obliviously in the wind. Hugo was different today; his blue arm garment was gone. Josie had exclaimed over it, as if shocked, though I didn't know why—people inexplicably change their clothes all the time, don't they? I studied her now. Josie was planning to go to America, wherever that was, with our awful visitor? Instead of with me?

This was, in a word, devastating.

"He's her husband," Giorgio explained, as though sensing my need for clarification. At this, I was doubly shocked. How could such a thing be true?

"Cicero," Giorgio said, turning fully to me on the ferry deck. "I've always spoken to you not as a mere dog, but as a friend and colleague, *sì*? When I was alive, I did so because I was lonely. Still, I've always known you were listening to some degree. It wasn't until recently, when I came back from the dead—or whatever this situation is, really—that I understood how much you comprehend. I've come to believe, in this new state of mine, that you, and perhaps all animals, understand more than any human realizes."

I wanted to roll my eyes. Really, he was just learning this now?

"And because my confidence in you has grown so, I'm telling you that we must act in whatever way we can. *Capisci*, Cicero? If there's an opportunity to help Josie fall in love with Hugo—to truly fall in love with him—we must take it. Because, my friend, love is the only force that might keep her here. We shall tip the balance, as I've said before."

I considered this. Was this why he was teasing the American? Not out of spite, but to knock him off-balance? And what else, I wanted to implore dear Giorgio, could we do?

"First, you must show Josie that you approve of Hugo finally. You must learn to like him, Cicero. I was—" Here his face darkened, sorrow floating through it yet again. "I was wrong, when I was living, to talk the way I did. I will explain this to you when we have more time, and tell you everything that happened, *ragazzo*, unvarnished. But now the boat must dock."

I looked from him to the sea, narrowing before us as a rocky bluff of an island rose abruptly into the sky, its shore embroidered with jaunty buildings.

I would do it, I promised the wind and sea. I would do whatever I could.

I understood, now that I'd seen a glimpse of the grief and frustration that awaited Josie wherever she and her ridiculous husband came from, that she must stay not just for me, and not just for Hugo.

She must remain in Sorrento for herself.

CHAPTER TWENTY-FIVE

Josie

Capri, Italy

From the moment they stepped onto the island of Capri, Josie felt like she'd stumbled upon magic.

She followed Hugo from the ferry dock onto the port-side street, turning several times to take in her surroundings, joy bubbling up in her chest like a singing kettle. Across the water, she could just make out the mainland, still shrouded in morning mist, and distant Mount Vesuvius reaching for a scrap of summer clouds. Turning again, Capri rose before Josie, all pale limestone bluffs laced with greenery, and white seaport buildings with signs like *Farmacia*, and *Gelateria*, and *Noleggio motorini*.

She and Hugo stepped back as a pair of fishermen hoisted a rowboat from a line of them, propped along the quay, and walked it toward the harbor. *"Buongiorno!"* one called under a mustache like a broom, catching Josie's eye.

"Buongiorno!" she echoed him, grinning.

"Now," Hugo murmured, speaking half to himself. "To find the spot Francesco parked the mopeds . . ."

"Mopeds?" Josie asked, setting Cicero down to stretch his legs and falling into step alongside Hugo, still so entranced by this first glimpse of Capri she wasn't fully listening.

"Sì." Hugo caught her eye. "Two Vespas." He tried to subdue a grin, which only made his dimples dive deeper; he was clearly excited. "My friend Francesco, who lives on the other side of the island, said we could borrow them. He gave me the keys yesterday in Sorrento—he's off to Rome for a bit and will not need them."

"Vespas?" Josie repeated, now paying attention. "I've never ridden one. Are you sure it'll be okay for your arm?" Her gaze dropped to his freshly liberated limb, dubious. It was so strange to see him with two working arms and nothing draped across his broad shoulders.

"Sì, sì," Hugo said, waving off any worry, his hair catching the wind. "The doctor said it's good as new, and riding a Vespa is very easy. I'll show you. Ah—there they are, just up the road, tucked between the boats."

Indeed, a half dozen multicolored mopeds were parked along the marina, their side mirrors glinting in the sun. Before Josie could ask how she would manage it with Cicero, Hugo turned, his brown eyes dancing, and pulled something from his bag.

Josie widened her eyes in delighted disbelief. "Is that an Ergo?"

He flipped it around as if unsure, shrugging. "For babies, I guess? Bettina borrowed it from her sister, who thought a small dog could be carried in it—what do you think?"

"I think he'll love it." Josie giggled. "I used to carry Charlie around in one of these."

"*Grazie a Dio*, because I have no idea how to put it on you."

Within minutes, Josie had Cicero strapped to her back, with his little perky head poking over her shoulder, and the kind of laughter that's contagious bubbled up in Hugo, doubling him over.

"It's ridiculous," he managed through tears, and Josie, too, found herself giggling and then laughing so hard she couldn't breathe. She swiped at tears leaking from her eyes, and Hugo, nearly recovered, patted the encased lump that was Cicero's little body, then doubled over again. *They were like children,* Josie thought, leaning into him and trying to contain her eruptive giggles. Tourists strolled by, glancing at the hubbub, several of them chuckling as well.

"This is absurd," Josie finally gasped, turning to catch the dog's keen eye over her shoulder. "But I love it. Cicero's going to have so much fun."

This set Hugo off yet again, and when he finally reined it in, gasping, his eyes locked on Josie's. For a long moment, they stared at each other, grinning like kids, and then he reached out to thumb an errant tear from her temple. And then he was leaning in, and she was tipping up, and he was kissing her, warm and gentle, and to Josie the whole world felt like laughter and longing, bright as the sea.

"Va bene," he said minutes later as she straddled her Vespa, lemon yellow with a matching helmet. She studied its dashboard as he explained. "It's very easy, *sì*? You just turn the key, and then this hand works the throttle—" Hugo's large hand closed over hers on the handle, his fingers pressing hers down as he turned the throttle in demonstration, and with it, the rope caught within Josie and tugged, hard. She wanted to kiss him again. She wanted to melt into his arms. His eyes flashed to hers, a lively brown. "And these are handbrakes, yes? Like a bicycle. You will balance a moment, also like a bicycle, and when it's moving, your feet settle here. Ready to try? I'll wait here while you go up and down the marina to make sure you've got it."

And so, Josie gave it a go with the engine on, turning the throttle as he'd shown her, and she was off, flying down the quay, the wind and sun on her face, and again she laughed out loud. It was easy, as Hugo had said. Cicero, his head near her ear, opened his mouth enough for his tongue to loll out in pure joy. At the end of the road she turned, carefully, and throttled back to Hugo, the sea blinking beyond her, the boats bobbing and gulls calling overhead. When she neared Hugo, he was on his blue Vespa, and his helmeted head turned to her as he raised a questioning thumbs-up. She flashed a thumbs-up in response, slowing just enough to let him pull out ahead of her.

And they were off.

~

The same word came to Josie, again and again, as she and Hugo sailed the winding, sun-washed island roads: magic. Early in their tour, they slowed to skirt the village of Capri itself, taking in its white-painted shops—some glamorous, others boasting more of a homey charm—yet they didn't stop. Hugo grinned under his helmet when they came to an idle at an intersection, calling over the hum of his Vespa, "Want to walk around, or ride more?" and Josie called back while Cicero laid his head on her shoulder, "Ride more!"

In tandem, they leaned gently to the right, gliding around a corner and gathering speed to fly out of town, motors buzzing. Josie took in the island as it slipped by: the terraced gardens and vineyards, the mountains jutting toward the distant sun, the way leaves hung from grapevines in petticoats, gilded in light. Soon, they began to climb, and all at once the world fell away from one side as the road hugged a rocky cliff face. Below, spreading in every direction, was the wide, sunlit sea.

A bus appeared in the curve ahead, seeming to totter a bit as it downshifted, taking up more than its share of the narrow, winding lane. Yet Josie merely drifted closer to the cliff, following in Hugo's wake, and as the bus passed a thought blew through Josie's mind like a windswept petal. *I am not afraid.*

A month ago, she would not have done this. Her hands would have shaken on the throttle. She would have had to pull over, unmoored by her proximity to death in every direction. Or, if she had managed to drive the Vespa, she wouldn't have even noticed how sunlight danced over the island, or the endless blue sea, or the way her little dog sniffed the wind, or the way her heart sailed in time with the motor humming beneath her. She would have been too afraid.

Much had changed, she realized as Hugo raised an arm to signal a turn, gesturing toward a viewpoint ahead. Josie glided into the tiny parking area perched on the side of the cliff, mimicking Hugo as he killed the engine and rocked his Vespa back onto its stand beneath a stunted palm. Josie was scarcely the same person who'd boarded a plane, terrified and mourning her broken life, not even a month ago.

"What do you think?" Hugo asked, his expression jubilant as he pulled off his blue helmet, his hair standing on end, eyes joyful as they met hers.

Josie's answer came on impulse. She simply went to him, putting a hand on both of his rough, sun-browned cheeks, and pulled him to her, and they kissed in the sun, high over a sparkling sea.

"He's not growling anymore," Hugo whispered as they separated, an air of wonder in his voice, his gaze flicking toward Cicero. "Do you think he's starting to like me?"

It was true, Josie realized with a jolt of surprise. Cicero had been nothing but lovely all day. "Hugo Caruso, I think you've won him over," she declared, and he raised a tentative hand toward the dog's little head.

And Cicero, ears perked, sniffed Hugo's fingers, then gave him a lick.

"Ha ha!" Hugo exclaimed, and then he reached that same hand toward Josie's, threading his fingers with hers. They knit together tightly. "Here is my plan," he said, pulling her close. "We'll drive around the island a while more, so you can see all the sights. And then, we'll go to a little beach I love, take a swim, and then have a late lunch. *Bene?*"

Josie looked up, matching his dimpled smile with a grin. *"Benissimo,"* she said.

CHAPTER TWENTY-SIX

CICERO

Capri, Italy

It was late afternoon when I sat at a circular table across from Josie and Hugo, in my very own chair, with my very own plate before me. Hugo had insisted upon it, causing the waiter to chuckle and shrug, which led me to marvel at the error of my recent ways. How could I have ever disliked this man? This man who bestowed upon me fish and Vespa rides and now lunch? This man who gazed at Josie with such delight?

I tell you, as a rather introverted soul, who'd spent most of a lifetime devoted to one man, it was nothing short of revelatory to observe my inner circle widening. Though, I mused, glancing at Hugo and Josie across the bistro table, these two would be quite enough for my circle, moving forward. Any more would become a crowd.

They both smelled of the sea, a mixture of salt and fish and the tang of pebbles drying in the sun. We'd been swimming, you understand, at a beach the size of a pocket, and now we overlooked it from our bistro table in what seemed to be a very fine restaurant. They had pizza, after all—I'd seen it floating about on waiters' trays heading to other tables. I hoped Josie knew enough to order me a slice.

For now, she and Hugo ate salads, of all things, and chatted in the lively manner of children. They had red cheeks, and salt still glistened on their skin, giving Josie, in particular, a slightly sparkly impression in the blue sundress she'd donned after parking the Vespas.

The Vespas. I tell you, I was in love with those things. Riding high on Josie's back, snugged up tight with my jowls to the wind, had been nothing short of thrilling. I glanced in the direction we'd left them, out the restaurant door, down a few steps, and across the street. We'd parked those lovely contraptions beneath a wall of flowers, and I hoped with everything in my fierce little heart that we'd take them for another spin after lunch.

As I looked toward the restaurant door, Giorgio came ambling in. He'd not been with us on the Vespa ride, of course. It would have been awkward, I suppose, to perch on the scrap of seat left behind Hugo, even for a person who seemed to be made of nothing but light. Giorgio arrived at the table and plopped down beside my chair, sitting with his legs crisscrossed, which made me grateful nobody could see him. It was rather indecent to sit on a restaurant floor, was it not?

"Ah, Cicero, I am sorry," he said, his eyes shining as they met mine. His wrinkled face didn't look sorry, however. He pursed back a smile that caused wrinkles to spray across his temples, like spiderwebs in the sun. What was he apologizing for?

He didn't answer my question right away. Instead, he glanced around, and his expression fell a bit toward sorrow. "Do you know how I found you here?"

I tilted my head. I did not: We'd left him at the marina hours ago.

He smiled, sadly. "I used to take Hugo here, when he was little. With his brother, after their mother left."

His voice was quiet when he said this, and there was something so tender in his words, so careful, a fissure cracked my own happiness like a leak. After their mother left? It occurred to me, then, that I'd never so much as considered the fact that Hugo had once had a mother, or a brother, or any family at all beyond Giorgio. Of course, as a domesticated canine, such family ties are rather flexible. We're born into families, *certo*, but invariably those original mothers and siblings go by the by as we're shuttled into new homes, becoming distant memories.

Was that strange? I pondered it while awaiting my pizza. It had never occurred to me to be sad about losing my own mother, because Giorgio had stepped right into her place. Was it not the same with humans?

Perhaps, I mused, the difference for dogs is that we devote ourselves to those who *need* our love. And those with such needs, such holes in their souls, are most commonly human.

Giorgio looked about, his eyes shining as if with unreleased tears, which, of course, would be the case forevermore. Giorgio could no longer cry.

"Ah, Cicero, life seems so long when you're in it. And then you die, and you see that it was all but a heartbeat. One powerful, wonderful heartbeat."

I stared at him, thinking of this pulse of life I was still in, and all that was contained within it. And I understood what he meant, I think. I could see everything that mattered in one resounding heartbeat: Giorgio. Josie. And now Hugo.

A waiter came, speaking brightly and, to my horror, stepping right through Giorgio's seated figure. A growl erupted in my throat at this stranger violating the ghost of my dear friend in such a manner, whether or not he might deliver pizza to my plate, but Josie reached over to smooth my hackles down, and Giorgio caught my eye and laughed.

"It's all right, *ragazzo mio*. I can't feel a thing anymore. You needn't guard me any longer."

The waiter stepped around the table, moving through Giorgio as easily as walking through a shadow.

I felt a lot of things, my friend. And in that moment, I could not have named them.

"Allora," Giorgio continued as the waiter departed, still failing to leave pizza in his wake. Instead, there was a bottle of wine on the tablecloth, its glass catching the arc of sunlight and the dazzling sea.

"Now, Cicero, I must tell you why I've apologized. It's the Vespas."

I perked up, listening well.

"I've sabotaged them," he confessed, and my head tilted as if he'd jerked it with a leash. Sabotaged?

"It was necessary, my boy—you must forgive me. I found a shard of rock, right there on the road beside them, and with all the meager forces I still possess bunched within my soul, I slashed the tires."

If I could have protested, I would have. This was a rather poetic way to obscure the facts, I wanted to howl. He'd damaged those gorgeous *motorini*? Why ever would he do such a thing?

"I did it," he said, guessing my question, "so Hugo and Josie will remain on Capri overnight. Cicero, they must stay overnight if the future is going to change. Look at them—anyone can see they're falling in love, right before us. There's a glow to their faces, no? And the way they're talking, my boy. I've no idea what they're talking about, of course, but from the look of it, soon they'll be finishing one another's sentences. They need a night. You may not understand, and I have no wish to explain it. You will just have to trust me."

My fury abated slightly. It would be no calamity to stay on Capri for a night, certainly. But to think of those beautiful Vespas, no longer capable of rolling, hurt like he'd taken a nail clipper to my heart.

"He'll go to Hotel Nautilus, I'm sure of it," Giorgio added, again with an air of nostalgia I could not understand. "It's just up the lane. It will be *perfetto*. But for that, Cicero, I will make myself scarce—it would be improper for me to remain in attendance. So, you, *ragazzo*, must carry on with the matchmaking while I wander the island, seeing it now from this side of the veil. I wonder if it will look different?"

He glanced toward the flashing water, shrugging. "Before I leave, Cicero, a tip for you: If they end up in a bedroom together, do yourself a favor and sleep on the *terrazza*."

He stood, glancing again toward the sea, thoughtful, and then gave me a nod before he turned on his heel, shimmering right out of the restaurant and vanishing through the door and down the steps, his duty done.

CHAPTER TWENTY-SEVEN

Josie

Capri, Italy

"I can't imagine who would slash those tires," Hugo said for the third time, shaking his head as they trekked uphill, sweat beading on his brow in the heat of the late afternoon. Cicero trotted along on his leash, jaunty despite the heat, and Josie, feeling surprisingly unfazed about the tires, took in the scenery as they walked. The road spooling ahead of them was narrow and winding, and if they followed it for a half hour it would lead to the village of Capri, perched on the crown of the island. They were not, however, planning to walk that far.

"There it is." Hugo reached for Josie's hand, giving it a squeeze, and she spotted the hotel's sign perched in an oleander bush bordering a wrought iron gate. It squeaked under Hugo's pull, and then, beyond the bushes, the hotel materialized, a small, homegrown sort of establishment, the building island-white and lined with verandas, patios, and gardens, all with a view of Spiaggia di Marina Piccola where they'd gone for a prelunch swim.

"You're sure you don't mind spending the night?" Hugo asked, pivoting away from the hotel, worry flashing in his brown eyes. "I'm not presuming anything, Josie, I promise—we can get separate rooms, if they have space. Or I can sleep on the terrace. I just want to call a mechanic to fix those Vespas, so we can drive them back to the spot Francesco left them tomorrow—"

"I'm delighted, actually," Josie interrupted, reaching up to place a hand on the back of Hugo's neck. It was warm from the sun, dusted in salt from the sea. He tipped his head down to look at her, his brown eyes searching hers, and she smiled. She liked that he didn't assume they'd share a room, much less a bed, but the thought made her want to laugh. All afternoon, she'd known. She wanted Hugo Caruso in every way. And she wouldn't let herself think about how temporary their connection would be, how it could only ever be a summer fling before she returned to her real life. No, she would live in the moment, and in this moment, she was sure.

"Hugo," she whispered, pulling him closer. When she spoke next, her lips brushed his. "There's no need for separate rooms."

Her words struck like a match. The question fell away from Hugo's gaze, and all that was left in its wake was longing, hot and growing. He kissed her, then whispered in her ear, "Well then, let's hope they have an open room."

They did, and when Josie and Hugo walked through the door, Cicero took one look at them and ran to the sunlit balcony, vanishing onto the patio furniture. The door clicked in their wake, and Hugo turned to face Josie, his body close to hers. She felt him against her, the warmth of his chest, his arms coming around to circle her waist, one hand wandering down the small of her back. She pressed into him, pulled him down to her, felt his rough jaw brushing hers and then his lips, warm and soft. They stumbled backward, still kissing, their bodies melding like they'd melted together in the sun. Josie's heart fluttered in her chest, and she felt Hugo's heart pounding against hers, and then his large hands were on her shoulders, pushing the straps of her sundress away, and her hands were on the firm, muscled skin of his waist, sliding down.

The world vanished as they kissed and undressed one another. All that existed was the room, full of golden light, and the blue sea beckoning out the window, and Hugo's lips and eyes and heartbeat and soul. All that existed was the two of them, alone on this beautiful spinning earth, wanting only each other.

~

Later, Josie lay in Hugo's arms as the sun vanished behind a rocky bluff beyond the window. Swallows appeared in the sky, darting and diving, and he tightened his hold on her as if to ward off the cooling air. They wore only a bedsheet, and they fit together as if made that way, their bodies seamless. Josie reached up to touch Hugo's jaw with one finger, tracing it down his neck to the place where his pulse tapped, faintly, under his sun-brown skin.

"Do you have to leave?" he whispered, kissing the crown of her head, his eyes on the swallows. "Truly?"

Josie tipped back slightly to meet his gaze.

"Not for another month."

"A month isn't enough."

Josie nodded. Dread surfaced, as it always did when she thought of home now and all the dreary inevitability of her life there, all the decisions she had to make. The future ahead of her felt like a sheet of paper, crudely cut, that she had to manipulate into an origami swan, making something of it all. When really, she just wanted to crumple it up and start over.

Her voice caught. "How could I stay?"

Hugo shifted, looking at her more fully. "What if you did? Think about it. Perhaps you could get a job here, Josie. And we could just . . . see."

A quizzical smile tilted her lips. "See what?"

Hugo's answering smile seemed to be as naked as he was, as vulnerable. "See if we can make a go of it."

She blinked. Was Hugo, who didn't believe in lasting love, suggesting they try? But how could they? Hope fluttered up in her at the notion, yet there was also fear, its wings just as strong. Even allowing herself to imagine remaining in Italy, with Hugo, would exact a cost, because there was no way anything could come of such daydreams. If only, Josie thought, they could suspend it all and just stay in this island room together, far from the decisions and pressures and responsibilities of their separate lives. If only the moment wouldn't end.

She spoke gently. "I thought you didn't have faith in such things, Hugo." She didn't say the word she meant, because unclothed as she was against him, the word would lay her even more bare: *love.* She shifted her tone to light teasing. "Anyway, what would you tell all the other women?"

His brows tipped up. "Other women?"

"You know—the ones who call you all the time." Josie shrugged. "Paula. Martina. I haven't been snooping, I promise—I've just seen their names flash on your phone when we're together. And it's okay, obviously—"

At once, Hugo laughed, quieting her. His face transformed from confusion to amusement, and Josie pulled slightly away from him, sitting up. "Hugo," she ventured, "I'm not trying to catch you out or anything—from the start you told me that you live in the moment, and enjoy whatever comes your way—"

"Josie," he interrupted, taking her hands in his, "Those women are clients. Martina ordered a table from me, and she's a busybody who likes to check in. She lives near Rome, and she's seventy-five years old. Paula has a custom hutch about halfway finished in my shop." He chuckled again, his eyes bright in the evening light. "She's married to a businessman in Napoli. There are no other women."

His hands were warm over hers, and he squeezed. She sat there, the sheet pooling at her waist, stunned. *There are no other women*. At once, the world tilted before her, and she saw the two of them anew.

She'd felt it, hadn't she? Her cheeks heated with her own foolishness, her own blind spots. She'd sensed, on some unexamined level, that she was his only interest, but she wouldn't let herself believe it.

"I'm sorry," she sputtered. "I just thought, I don't know. Maybe I assumed that because of what happened with Mark, that I should expect . . . I'm sorry—"

He leaned in to kiss her, long and gentle, his thumb coming up to smooth the worry from her temple. When he pulled away, his voice was as serious as it was kind. "You should expect more, Giuseppina. Mark is a fool," he whispered. "He didn't see what he had. And I know we've only just begun. That this is just the start of something, and I'm so afraid it'll end too soon. That you'll board a plane before we've really had a chance. Because I feel like I *know* you, Josie. From the moment we met, you felt like . . ." His eyes flashed as he sought the right word. "You felt like home to me."

Something beat in Josie's heart then, a pair of wings. It was hope again, rising, and she realized all at once that she understood what Hugo meant. That he, too, felt like home. That she'd sensed it almost from the beginning. She nodded, unable to produce a word.

"And I know what I said on the beach in Positano," he continued, squeezing her hands. "About life, and love, being meaningless. I have a hard time with love, Josie." He paused, and behind him, beyond the open window, a flock of swallows spun like a whirlpool, climbing higher and higher. "The truth," he managed after a long moment, "is that I'm not sure anyone has ever actually loved me."

Josie's mouth fell open a little. "Hugo," she managed, taking in what he'd said. "That can't be true, can it?"

He smiled sadly, nodding. "I'm afraid it is. It's taken me most of my life to realize it, but from this vantage point it's rather clear that everyone who was meant to love me really only cared for themselves.

Even my parents. I think I decided not to believe in love because it was less painful than the truth of my life."

Josie shook her head slightly, as if to say again that this couldn't be. He was entirely lovable. "What happened with your parents?" she asked instead, studying him.

Hugo looked away, pulling her to him so they were again snuggled under the sheet, staring out at the sky rather than at each other. And he talked, his voice low.

"I was raised in a villa overlooking olive orchards, as I've told you. The estate had been in our family for generations, Josie. My grandfather, and grandfather's grandfather—they all made olive oil and, later, *limoncello*. It was a large operation, and successful. My father always believed that my brother and I would take over the estate together someday. He was a charismatic man, my father, but there was only one way to live, in his view."

Hugo paused, and Josie tried to picture him as a boy, running through the silvery leaves of olive trees, chasing an older brother he rarely mentioned.

"When I was three, my mother left us."

Josie frowned. "Left you?" she repeated, not because she didn't understand, but because it was unfathomable to her. How could a mother leave her children? Leave the sweet boy Josie knew he must have once been?

Yet there was little emotion in Hugo's voice as he continued talking about his mother, as if this bit of family lore was well worn, long faded. "It's all right—I barely remember her. She's still out there, somewhere, traversing the world like a teenage backpacker. She calls, sometimes. She was selfish, Josie. That's the only way to understand her. But my childhood was good. We had a beautiful home, and space to run and play, and grandparents, and a village full of people who'd known my family for generations. It wasn't until I was a young man and I wanted to go to college and live abroad and chase a different life, that it fell apart. My father reacted very badly when I told him I was going to London. He demanded that I join my brother running the business, but it wasn't for me. My brother was a bit of a bully—I couldn't work with him. And maybe part of me was curious about my mother, and her wanderlust. Anyway, I wanted to leave."

He tipped his head down, catching Josie's eye. "Was there ever any pressure for you to take over your family's ranch?"

She nodded slowly, thinking about this. "My parents never pressured me, though I know they hoped, for a while, that Mark and I would come home and run it. It felt like a trap, really, though they never meant it to. It's just that I was an only child, so without us the ranch won't stay in the family."

"*Sì*, exactly. And did your parents make peace with it, when you didn't come home?"

"They did." Josie tipped up to look at him. "They wanted me to choose my own life, I guess."

Hugo pinned his lips together for a second, as if digesting that, nodding. "My father," he continued, "did not. When I stayed in London, he didn't speak to me for years. It wasn't until my brother died that we tried to repair things, and I came home."

"You must have been devastated to lose your brother," Josie said.

He hesitated. "*Sì*, and no. When I think of us walking to school together, or playing in the orchards, I do feel his loss. But when he died, we'd been almost as estranged as my father and me. At the time, my marriage was falling apart, and I'd wanted to come home for years. And I saw that, without my brother, the estate would fall to nobody. My brother's girls were grown already, living in Milan, and his wife joined them there. So I told my father I would come home and help him. I'd oversee the estate alongside him, but live in Sorrento and open a bookstore, which I planned to run in the offseason. I just wanted to maintain a bit of my own life, I guess. My own dreams. I'm not sure if that's what pushed my father over the edge, or if we were already hurtling that way."

He paused, and Josie turned to see pain in his face, and the way he was pressing back emotion. She yearned to kiss that pain away.

"My father," he finally managed, "let me divorce my wife, leave my work, move all the way home, and build my bookshop before he decided to tell me that he'd sold the estate. Even though I promised to help him run it, preserving it in case my nieces ever returned, or in case I had a family of my own someday." He shook his head, as though newly baffled. "I'd come home, finally, determined to maintain our legacy, and he sold it all out from under me. He kept only the villa and one surrounding acre. One afternoon, he drove to the bookshop to finally tell me this, in his ridiculous Ferrari, bought with some of the proceeds, I'm sure."

Josie stared at Hugo, trying to grasp this. What had his father been thinking? Had it been a way to punish his prodigal son, at long last?

Hugo swallowed. Clearly, that's how it had felt. "The loss of our family's land hit me harder than I ever imagined it would. It was my whole childhood, my roots. When I told him that, he shouted that I'd never wanted it anyway. So I slammed the door on my father." He sighed heavily. "Literally and figuratively. We never spoke again. I thought he'd apologize eventually, that he'd tell me he loved me despite everything. But I'm not sure he did, Josie. So, that's everyone—my parents, my brother, my wife."

I could love you, Josie thought. But she couldn't voice such a thing, so she cupped his jaw in her hand, saying instead, "I'm so sorry, Hugo. You deserved more."

He stared at her, blinking the pain from his eyes, and then she kissed him, long and slow, running her fingers through his hair. He was such a good man, a man who wore his soul on his sleeve, a man who deserved to be adored.

Without saying more, their kiss grew and evolved, and soon they were sliding back onto the pillows together, finding one another again, and Josie tried to show Hugo what she couldn't put to words.

~

An hour later, stars sprinkled the darkness outside, and Hugo turned to Josie, his eyes glittering like the sky. He grinned.

"Want to go for a swim?"

She laughed. "Now?"

"It's only five minutes down to the beach. Why not? Maybe we can get a bottle of wine from the little bar down there and enjoy it with our toes in the sand."

Josie laughed again, and then she swung her legs from the bed, finding she couldn't subdue her smile, and rummaged for her bathing suit and sundress. She felt like a teenager who was sneaking out, dressing beside Hugo in the darkened room. They caught each other's eye and Hugo added, "Maybe the bar can give us a snack, too," and Josie giggled. When had she ever had so much fun?

They peeked at Cicero before they left, deciding to leave him where he was, sprawled across the patio furniture and so tired he opened only one eye to watch them go.

The night air was cool as they started down the road, knitting their hands together, their hips bumping because they were walking so close. Beyond the winding road, the moon hung over the water, spilling its light like a trail scudding across the sea.

Upon reaching the beach, they stripped their outer layers, shivering slightly.

"Pronta?" Hugo asked.

"Pronta."

And, their hands still holding tight, they ran into the sea, laughing as the water splashed up around them, droplets falling like stars. They swam out into deeper water, passing a dark jetty of rock, and emerging, arms encircling one another, in the open sea, laughing and then kissing, bobbing together along the moon's silver path.

CHAPTER TWENTY-EIGHT

Cicero

Capri, Italy

I'm not sure what got into Josie and Hugo, but well after my bedtime I woke to hear them giggling and moving around in the hotel room. It was not a respectable hour, my friend—stars littered the sky, and somewhere in the distance, an owl raised his questioning song. Were we really going somewhere so late? *Dio mio,* I groaned as I heard the rustle of shorts being pulled on and the snap of Josie's sandals on the floor. But then the two of them poked their heads out on the balcony, whispering like they had a secret, and when I refused to so much as lift my head, they left me in peace.

"Aspetta qui," Hugo whispered with a wave, letting me know I was safe to wait. They'd be back, and I needn't rouse myself, thank heavens.

"Cicero?" A voice came shortly after their departure, and I looked to those heavens I'd just thanked. What now?

Giorgio materialized, apparently having climbed the lemon tree flanking our balcony. This was a new one to me—did ghosts really have to climb? All my life, I'd imagined them floating when I saw them hanging around, but what did I know? I raised my head to greet him as he dropped silently onto the balcony floor, my tail wagging on the lovely, cushioned patio settee I'd claimed as my own. Exhausted as I was, I was always happy to see Giorgio.

"How's it going?" he asked, glancing from the balcony railing to the road snaking away from the hotel. "I was sitting out in the street, watching the moon, when those crazy kids appeared. They certainly look happy, eh *ragazzo*?"

He was right. Though I'd taken his advice and retired immediately to the patio, falling into dreams full of Vespas and wind, I could sense that Josie and Hugo had grown closer. I was a dog, after all, a pack animal. And my intuition informed me that a bond was building between them, the kind of bond that transforms solitary souls into family. I wondered if they knew it yet.

Giorgio turned from the view, his face alight.

"They're going to take a swim, I suppose. *Bellissima.* I haven't seen Hugo this happy in years." He turned, settling on the chair opposite my settee, and something like puzzlement edged into his delight. "Of course," he said quietly, "I haven't seen much of him at all for years, Cicero. I was going to tell you the story, wasn't I."

I tilted my head, because indeed, I wanted to hear the story, whether we were ensconced in the wee hours or not. All my life, I'd heard Giorgio grumbling about Hugo, who lived so close yet never called, who never traveled home to see us in the villa. He'd scrawled long letters to his boy—that's what Giorgio always called Hugo, *his boy*—yet the postman brought nary a reply. Giorgio would sit on the *terrazza* those many sunsets with me, and when he wasn't reading, he'd talk, sometimes of his life raising his boys. There had once been, as I've mentioned, two. The stories were as golden as the evening light, and they always ended with a question: What had he done to deserve his remaining son's abandonment?

That question, which I had found utterly unanswerable, is why I'd hated Hugo for so long.

"I'll tell you what I did," Giorgio said now, his fluffy brows dropping low over his eyes. He glowed, that night, like the moon, as though he'd stepped down from that same silver circle to walk among us. "Cicero, when my boys were small, I had to raise them alone, and it was of great consolation to imagine that one day I'd be old and they'd be grown, and we'd all live together. There would be grandchildren flocking about the estate, I imagined, and family dinners out on the *terrazza*, and long days in the orchards with my sons. Then Hugo left, and I was furious."

He blinked, staring at the moon, and revised his sentence.

"No, Cicero, not merely furious. I was hurt. My wife had left, too, you see. Gone abroad, a woman who just wouldn't be pinned down. Now that I'm dead and oddly wiser, I can see that it probably wasn't about me—she always had her own demons, Cicero. That's obvious, now."

He sighed, heavily.

"*Allora*, in light of all that, I was unfair to Hugo. And when he finally moved back, I was newly heartbroken. I had only one boy left, you see, and I could not stop thinking about how it might have been if my younger son had stayed. Perhaps, if Hugo hadn't run off to London, his brother would still have been alive—he wouldn't have felt the need to blow off steam on a death machine up north. Perhaps Hugo would have married a nice local girl, and they would all be on the estate with me, managing it together, like our ancestry demanded of us. It was irrational, Cicero, but my anger didn't abate when he arrived and decided to live in Sorrento part-time."

He rolled his silvery eyes, frustration mounting even now.

"And then he insisted on building that bookshop. I helped him, you know. I held boards and supplied wine and kept him company, but the entire time, my anger grew. The bookshop felt like a second rejection of the life he'd inherited. I thought, yet again, he was turning away from me. From all I had to offer."

I blinked at him, trying to understand what he was talking about. Human affairs, you see, are sometimes lost on those of us who know what is actually important.

"Quindi," Giorgio said, straightening, "I made a decision, without telling Hugo, and I sold the estate. All but the villa, which I couldn't bear to include in the sale. And when I told him, he was furious."

The blue door rose in my mind, slamming.

"He must have felt as if I'd disowned him, a second time. So, twice I felt rejected, and twice he felt disowned. There's a tragic comedy to it, don't you think?"

Tragic, yes, I mused. I raised and cocked my head. But the only comedy I could see here was one I'd observed rather constantly in human company: how often they miss the point.

Giorgio wiped at his wrinkled cheek as if there were tears upon it, but there were none, of course. He glanced again toward the black, glimmering water, perhaps trying to see his boy out there, afloat.

"I always meant to apologize, Cicero," he whispered. "I wrote him many letters to that effect, but I was a coward." He shrugged. "I never mailed them. I stuffed them in an old leather satchel, year after year. I thought I had time to make it right. I thought Hugo had time to find his way. My little friend, I was a fool. All of the things that came between us? The land, the estate, the family legacy? None of it mattered. I should have known that, in the end, I had only one thing left that truly mattered."

He looked at me, long and hard, before he said it.

"Hugo."

I placed my head on my paws, thinking this over. I could have been huffy that he didn't add me to that sentence—that, as his loyal, good boy, I was not included in his appraisal of what mattered. Yet I forgave the omission, because I knew I was his. He was here beside me, after all, death be damned.

And this, my friend, is what humans miss, again and again. They get so lost in all the details of life that they don't see what's right before them, right there every second they breathe air in and out of their lungs.

Somewhere in the distance, an owl called again, his voice full of wonder.

I've told you that I know the meaning of life. All dogs do. Listen: Do you recall how, shortly after Hugo met Josie, Giorgio quoted Sophocles? We were climbing into his shiny little car, and I was growling and bristling and utterly confused, and Giorgio advised me to remember what Sophocles said: *One word frees us of all the weight and pain of life. And that word is love.*

However, this isn't entirely correct. Sophocles was wrong.

Love doesn't free us from the weight and pain of life. Love *is* life.

Capisci? That's it, my friend. Love whoever you were sent to love. That's the meaning of life.

And, when you and I eventually slip into the silvery realm of death, that love is all we shall take to the other side. It was true of Giorgio, was it not? All any of us shall carry with us, when this life finally ends, is the love we had, tucked deep within our traveling souls.

CHAPTER TWENTY-NINE

Josie

Capri, Italy

Josie and Hugo stayed on the island of Capri for three more nights. They were lucky; it was the high summer season, yet someone had canceled a reservation at the last minute on their little, sunlit room. For the rest of the week, time and worry and the outer world ceased to exist. They laughed and swam, ate and made love, walked, and, once they were fixed, rode the Vespas up to the village of Capri. They window-shopped, stopped for coffees and cocktails, and strolled hand in hand through winding alleys, whispering in one another's ears and kissing on street corners.

Josie found herself wishing, again and again, that they could stay on Capri together forever. And then she'd remind herself that, even when they caught the ferry back to the mainland, there was much to look forward to. Over dinner by the sea one evening, they'd made all kinds of plans: For example, the day after returning to Sorrento, they would visit Hugo's childhood home. He had a meeting with a Realtor, and she was going to help him navigate it, help him decide whether to move forward with selling a villa that she could see, every time he discussed it, still held a piece of his heart.

"I'll show you the village," he'd said enthusiastically over dinner, topping off her wine. "It's full of people I've known since I was a boy—I'll introduce you, walk you around to the baker we used to visit, and the butcher, and the bar where my father and Cicero used to while away the mornings. I'll show you my old room."

Josie couldn't wait.

She also couldn't wait to go with Hugo to Rome in August. She'd told him of her itinerary, and he'd leaped upon it.

"I'll drive us," he'd declared, "and then we can see Florence, too, if you like? You'll love Tuscany."

Yes, Josie assured herself over and over, Capri was just the beginning of their adventures.

And still, during their final morning on the island, the world came tumbling back in to snatch at Josie's ankles, pulling hard.

She and Hugo were packing up their room and chatting, yet again, about his new favorite subject.

"What if you really did stay in Italy?" he said, folding his swim trunks. "At least for the fall, and maybe the winter, and then we could figure things out? I was lying awake last night, thinking, and I had an idea for a job in Sorrento, if you want one."

Josie held back an amused smile. Hugo had been brainstorming for three solid days now. He'd imagined her teaching English, though he wasn't sure where this would take place. He'd said she could work in his bookshop, or, if she liked, she could be a professional tourist. "What's a professional tourist?" she'd laughed, and he'd shrugged. It didn't matter what she did, he declared, taking her in his arms and whispering into her ear, his breath hot and convincing.

"Stay."

"Tell me," Josie said now, pulling the blanket up over the bed and smoothing it flat. "What's the new job idea?"

"*Allora*, there's a flower shop tucked off a corner of Via Santa Maria della Pietà, and the woman who runs it is quite elderly. When I last chatted with her, she wished she could find competent help." He caught her eye, his dimples showing. "I don't know why I didn't think of it before."

Josie, straightening the bed, paused. "Wait—I know that shop." Her heart beat a bit faster. "That woman is lovely."

Hugo's brows shot up. *"Vero?"* A smile washed over his face. "Then it's meant to be, Giuseppina."

She laughed, but her heart still beat rather swiftly. "Meant to be? Hugo Caruso, are you telling me you believe in such things?"

"I don't know." He shrugged, hoisting his bag over his shoulder, and came to her, his hands landing on her hips. "But I'm willing to entertain the notion."

Josie was about to say more, was about to request details regarding the woman and her flower shop, when her phone rang. She frowned, taking it from her pocket, and then she stuffed it back in when she saw the name on the screen.

Mark.

He'd called, off and on, nearly the entire time she'd been gone. He'd left voicemails, which were at first merely frustrated, and then, increasingly, angry.

A text immediately buzzed in her pocket, but Josie ignored it as she had all the rest, stretching up to kiss Hugo's cheek despite the concern in his gaze, and then she fetched Cicero's leash. She wanted to ignore Mark, and the tumble of anxiety his calls inspired within her, just a little longer.

It wasn't until she was waiting for the ferry on the dock, and Hugo was off leaving the Vespa keys with a bar owner who would give them to Francesco, that Josie peeked at her text messages.

Several, all from Mark, waited.

I can't believe your audacity, Jo, an early unread message began. I admit I've made mistakes, but I never flaunted them right in front of you like this. After all the years I took care of you, after all the years I paid for every goddamn thing—and don't you tell me you worked, too. Your income was a pittance for an easy job that was barely full time. It was me who allowed you to be out at the goddamn swimming pool with Charlie, or hanging out with other moms over coffee for "playdates" while I was working for a living, and now this is how you repay me? After I apologized and came crawling all the way here to make our marriage right?

Josie scrolled away from that text, feeling sick. The most recent message appeared when her thumb stopped, and her heart dropped at the sight of its opening words. It seemed, that after ranting for quite some time, Mark had moved on to new tactics.

I will ruin you, Jo, the final message read. I'm calling my lawyer. I already have the best, and I will take everything from you if you don't stop what you're doing right now and come back. All the money we have is mine—I earned it. The house, the cars—everything is in my name. You're playing a dangerous game, Jo, running around with your Italian friend . . .

Her hands were shaking by the time Hugo arrived at her side. He studied her for a beat, frowning.

"What happened?"

She shook her head, lost for words. Who, on earth, *was* Mark? How could those hateful texts have been written by the man she'd stayed married to for twenty years?

The ferry's horn sounded, making Josie jolt, and seagulls burst into the air all around. Hugo took Josie's shaking hand, gave it a squeeze, and tipped his head toward the dock.

"Tell me on the boat," he said, seeing that she needed a minute.

They were standing against the ferry's upper railing, watching the sunlit bluffs of Capri recede in its wake, when Josie handed Hugo her phone. "I didn't tell you," she said, miserable, "that Mark arrived in Sorrento last week. He came without asking permission, saying it was a surprise."

Hugo frowned. "What kind of surprise is that?"

"That's exactly what my dad said." Josie smiled despite her anguish. "I didn't want to tell you because I thought it might be weird. He's been sleeping on the couch, and I didn't know what to do, and now . . . well, read the texts."

She buried her face in her hands while Hugo thumbed through the messages, her cheeks hot with shame, her heart pounding out her grief.

She was an absolute fool. Her entire life with Mark had been a lie, a farce—clearly, she'd never really known him.

"I think I understand what you said our first night on Capri," she managed after a long moment, leaning into Hugo's solid, warm body. "About not being truly loved. For all these years, I thought my husband loved me."

Hugo's jaw was sharp as he clenched it, still reading. His brow furrowed tighter with every text.

"He won't do this to you," he said finally. "I won't let him."

Josie smiled, tears stinging the corners of her eyes. It was sweet of him to say so, but how could that be true? She wiped her cheeks dry, watching Capri become smaller and smaller, and when Hugo wrapped his arm around her, she pressed into him. She didn't want to leave him.

Ever.

Maybe, she thought tentatively, she wouldn't. The idea gained momentum in her mind for the first time, lifting like the flock of gulls swooping around the ferry. Maybe she really *would* stay. Could she work in the flower shop until she found her way forward? Could she fight for whatever she deserved from her long marriage from afar? The thought lifted her, buoyed her a bit, and she allowed it to continue. What if she stayed in Italy for a very long time indeed? What if she and Hugo made a life together, for real?

What if it could all be real?

In a flash, a possible future came to Josie: Charlie, flying into Napoli to visit during summers and holidays. Her father visiting, too, perhaps for a month or two at a time, perhaps for entire winters. She could see him tottering around Sorrento's cobbled streets, marveling at all the ways it was different from Kansas, laughing about the strength of the coffee and delighting in the pastries and the wide, blue sea.

Josie imagined Hugo by her side, growing older. The two of them, growing old together.

Her phone rang yet again, fracturing her daydream. Hugo frowned, handing it back to her, and they both saw the name on the screen.

Mark.

"I won't answer it," she said, and Hugo nodded. She could sense protective fury gathering within him. She began to worry, just a bit, about what might happen if the two of them ran into each other.

She put the phone back in her pocket, yet it started to ring anew.

Josie silenced the call. And when she did, it rang again, insistent.

"Oh, for heaven's sake," she sputtered, whisking the phone from her pocket once more. She and Hugo looked at the screen together, and this time Josie's stomach dropped.

Charlie.

Without hesitation, she answered it.

"Mom," Charlie stammered into the phone, his voice raw with panic. Gulls dove overhead, and a wayward breeze buffeted her ear. Josie cupped a hand over the phone to better hear her son.

"Mom, thank God you picked up. I just got Dad a minute ago. Grandpa is in the hospital, Mom." A sob fractured his voice, but he instantly recovered, sounding so grown, so worried, and so far away.

"Listen," he continued before she could speak, "I've been talking to his doctors and the surgeon, and you won't get here before his surgery, but if we hurry, you might arrive before he wakes up. I've also been looking up flights, and I think I found one that could work. Out of Naples, right? If you can get to the airport by two o'clock, I'll book it. Do you think you can do that? Mom?"

Josie found her voice. "Two o'clock—yes. Yes, I can." Her thoughts collided, confused, and she struggled to find words. "But wait—Charlie, what happened?"

She could see her son's serious face in her mind, his blue eyes, often so grave, as he spoke. "He had a stroke, out in the fields, Mom. I need you to hurry."

~

Hugo's foot was heavy on the accelerator as he drove toward Naples International Airport, weaving through midday traffic. In the front seat of the little red Ferrari, Josie sat, stunned cold despite the day's heat, with Cicero perched on her lap. In the back seat, Mark was wedged between their suitcases and carry-on bags, his knees tucked tightly together, his face inscrutable beneath his blowing hair. Once or twice, he laid a hand on Josie's shoulder and she glanced back as if reminded of where she was, taking in her husband's stare behind the flash of his glasses while Cicero, outraged, growled.

"Your dad will be okay," Mark called into the whipping wind of the autostrada, and Josie blinked. Then she turned back around to face forward.

How could he claim to know such a thing?

None of this was about Mark, anyway. Their own little drama had paled since the phone call with Charlie, becoming, rather abruptly, mere background noise. All Josie could think about, sitting next to Hugo as the car threaded through traffic, was her father.

She saw his warm gaze in her mind, and the way his eyes crinkled at the corners when he smiled. She saw his mustache, thick as a push broom, obscuring his upper lip. She imagined his voice, low and gravelly in her ear, reassuring her as if he were in the car beside her.

I'll be all right, Josie girl, he murmured in her imagination, *God willing and the creek don't rise.* Tears stung her eyes, streaming into her hairline.

Hugo moved his hand from the shifter to hers, squeezing. He caught her eye.

"I will get you there in time," he promised yet again, maneuvering the car into a lane of traffic that seemed to be moving a little faster than the rest.

He'd said little else after she gave him the facts of Charlie's phone call; instead of offering platitudes or requesting details she didn't yet possess, Hugo had simply flung himself into action. He'd whisked her back to her apartment, given Mark a cursory nod at the door, and then the two men, unbelievably, had moved in silent synchronicity to help Josie pack. Together, the three of them shoved everything she owned into her suitcase, searched the apartment for anything forgotten, and within twenty minutes they'd traversed Sorrento, bags in tow, and piled into Hugo's red Ferrari. The atmosphere was so heavy in the car, so thick with urgency and fear, nobody commented on the emotional triangle wedged awkwardly between them.

And now, as the road swept toward the airport, Josie cried for her father, and she cried for everything. She kissed Cicero's little head as airplanes appeared in the sky, lifting off, curving into the blue. Cicero turned his nose to her, sniffing her salty cheek, and then he gave her a lick. She saw the question in his bright eyes.

She didn't know how to answer it.

When they pulled into the departure lane at Naples International, it was one forty-five.

"Plenty of time," Hugo said, squeezing her hand and meeting her eye. "Let's get you on a plane." With that, he hurried out to help with the luggage. Mark crouched in the back seat and hoisted the ungainly suitcases to Hugo on the curb before following them out, unfolding his long legs and brushing the wrinkles from his shorts. Both men remained silent as Josie bent over the car, kissing Cicero on his soft head, before joining them. She took a shaky breath, smelling exhaust and hot concrete and sweaty bodies streaming toward the sliding glass doors of the terminal.

Josie glanced at Mark, his eyes wide, but then a lump rose so hard and fast in her throat she turned away from him. She didn't care what he thought, not right now. Her father whispered in her ear. *Get out and live, kid.*

She turned fully and fell into Hugo's arms.

"I will see you soon," he whispered into her ear, and then he kissed the skin beneath her earlobe, and then he kissed the tears from her cheek, and then she kissed his salty lips. "I will," he whispered once more, his brown eyes hitching on hers. "We will be together again."

But there was something so desperate in his stare, and so terribly sad, that Josie couldn't believe his words. She breathed in the hot midday air, holding his gaze, and reached up to wipe a tear from a crease near his eyes. She ran her finger down to touch his lips. She could say nothing.

We will, she wanted to assure him. *We will be together again.* But how could she make such a declaration? More than ever now, she had no idea what her future held. She was sure of nothing. Mark hovered behind them, looking pointedly away, and his threats to ruin her life hung in her mind. Would there be money to travel, to fly back to Italy? No, of course not. Any money Josie might possess in coming months would be spent in court, and if not there, it would vanish as she patched her crumbling life back together.

Aside from all of that, and looming far more heavily, was her father. Her father, who she loved so dearly. Her father, who was fighting for his life at this very moment. She would not leave him. He needed her.

This, she knew, Hugo would understand.

And would he fly across the world, to Kansas, to visit her? Josie ran a hand over Hugo's neck, bringing his forehead down to meet hers, and they stood that way for a breath. No, he wouldn't come to Kansas—his life was here, and they'd met only weeks ago, and it was more than she'd ever expect from him. They were destined to be separated, both by circumstance and distance.

She'd known this from the beginning, hadn't she?

This was, she thought with an ache so fierce she couldn't breathe, goodbye. A sob climbed her throat, and she tried to contain it.

"Josie," Hugo said, smoothing her hair from her face, her tears from her cheeks. "You're going to be all right. Your father is going to be all right. I believe this."

"Maybe," she managed, forcing a smile through her tears. "I hope so." And in her mind, her father's voice whispered again.

God willing and the creek don't rise.

"Take care of Cicero," she said finally, and Hugo's eyes shone with a smile.

"I will."

Able to say nothing more, Josie forced herself to turn, to unlatch her fingers from those of the man who held on to her so tightly, and she followed her husband through the sliding glass doors.

CHAPTER THIRTY

Josie

Kansas City, Missouri

Ischemic stroke.

Josie googled it obsessively while traveling home, sitting silently next to Mark on the plane, her heart in her throat. Google didn't reassure her.

The hospital room, when Josie finally reached it, past midnight, was dark and quiet, and her father lay in the bed hooked up to multiple blinking monitors, asleep.

"He was raking windrows in the hay," Charlie whispered to Josie, dropping to sit beside her on a folding chair, staring at the bed and the screens glowing around it. Mark was somewhere in the hospital, in search of food Josie had sent him to find—she wasn't hungry but didn't want him near. Besides that, upon their arrival moments ago, the nurses gently explained that only one guest, whoever was next of kin, was allowed to remain in the room overnight.

For now, Charlie remained with Josie, ignoring the rule. He reached out for her hand and gave it a squeeze, continuing to tell her, calmly, what had happened. "Grandpa's hired man said they were out working when he started slurring his speech, and then without warning he fell off the tractor. We're lucky he wasn't alone. Paramedics from town were able to get to him fast and administer tPA drugs in the ambulance, which was fortunate. Then, the hired man called me, so I reached the hospital not long after Grandpa did."

"Charlie," Josie managed, her voice cracking, meeting his blue gaze. "I'm so sorry this has all been on your shoulders, that we were so far away—"

"Don't worry, Mom." He squeezed her hand again, his grip strong. "I'm grateful I could help."

Josie blinked at her son, calm and authoritative beside her, speaking in the measured tones of the doctor he'd surely be someday. He already thought like a doctor, too: Emergencies were familiar territory for Charlie, having shaped so much of his life. Bodies were something to fix. She felt his steadying hand on hers, and she gripped it tighter. They'd switched, she realized. Once she'd been the adult, reassuring him as he lay, tiny, in his hospital bed, and terrified. And now here he was, her son, grown and capable, supporting her.

She needed it. Memories crowded in as she sat on her folding chair, struggling to breathe, staring at her father's prone form and seeing her son in her mind, long ago. She carried the trauma of nearly losing him within her, always: His familiar hospital room echoed in Josie's soul like a dim, beeping void.

The past, mixing with the present, made it difficult to think.

"What happens next?" she managed finally, meeting Charlie's serious gaze. "His prognosis, I mean."

"There are a lot of unknowns," he said quietly, ready for the question. "I think we'll know a lot more tomorrow, after some postsurgical imaging is done. When you were en route, he underwent a mechanical thrombectomy to remove the clot from his artery, because his CT scan showed it wasn't fully resolved by the drug treatment."

Josie nodded, stacking this against what she'd learned online. "Will he have brain damage?"

Charlie held her stare a minute. "That's what the follow-up imaging will help determine. Along with how he responds upon waking up."

Despair dropped into Josie like a stone, heavy and cold. She heard, plainly, what Charlie wasn't saying: that his grandpa would be okay. He wouldn't say it if he wasn't sure of it.

"Are you tired, Mom?" he asked after a minute, studying her. "There's a cot in the closet."

She was exhausted but knew she wouldn't sleep. She shook her head. "Are you?"

He shrugged, and she saw that he was. That he likely hadn't paused since he'd answered the call about his grandfather. "Charlie." She recovered her voice and her role as his mother. "Go and take a nap somewhere. Here's a credit card—" She fumbled in her purse, producing one. "If you don't want to drive all the way to the house, just book a hotel room across the street and get some sleep. Take your father with you—"

"No." He held up his hands, refusing to accept the card. "I'm not leaving you alone here—"

"Nonsense." She forced a shaky smile. "I'll be just fine, Charlie, and nothing's going to happen until morning rounds. Right? I slept on the plane, but I can see you haven't slept a wink, and I need you sharp tomorrow. You're going to be my ears—you'll be better at it than either me or Dad. You have a knack, Charlie."

He hesitated, mulling that over, his brown curls falling into his thoughtful eyes. She knew it would appeal to his sense of logic. They would all be better off if Charlie was rested and capable of supporting his parents with his intelligent, cool head. He'd understand that, and she knew he'd do whatever would help her most.

"See you in the morning," he relented a few minutes later, shrugging into his sweatshirt and giving Josie a hug. He was over a foot taller than her, a fact that never ceased to amaze her, and she patted his broad back. He smiled, looking a bit like the funny boy he could still be. "I'll be back first thing."

~

For the rest of the night, Josie sat very still on her folding chair, nodding at nurses as they came and went, her gaze on her father. She'd lied to Charlie, of course: She hadn't slept on the plane, and her eyes felt fuzzy and raw with spent tears. Her thoughts, too, blurred around the edges, as though the darkness outside was creeping into the dim hospital room, enveloping her like fog.

She walked a tightrope, she thought, and all around her was darkness. Somewhere behind her, strung along the rope her feet traversed, was her past. It whispered in her memory, creeping up to snatch at her ankles, threatening to pull her into the yawning abyss, but she kept walking. *Charlie is okay,* she whispered to herself, as she had a thousand times over the years, trying to banish the memories. She closed her eyes and tipped her head back against the wall, unsure which were thoughts now and which were dreams. *He got well.* She knew this was true, but memories of his hospital room beeped within her, and Josie also knew that in all the years since his illness, she'd lived with that beep in her soul, like an alarm going off forever.

She thought of Hugo on the beach, his eyes sparkling and sorrowful as he paraphrased Camus. *Life is meaningless but worth living, provided you recognize it's meaningless.* And she understood what he'd meant. She always had. They were more similar than she'd imagined that day, because like Hugo, some part of Josie was always bracing for catastrophe, some part of her could never believe that things might be okay, that there was meaning holding their spaceship together as they hurtled through an unforgiving universe.

Some part of her, always, had an ear cocked to the distant beeping within.

Hugo. She knew, instinctively, that she'd never see him again. Nor Cicero, her beloved little dog.

She opened her eyes, an ache pounding like a nail into her heart, and stood. She pulled the folding chair over to her father's bed, sitting lightly upon it, and reached for his limp hand.

Tears streamed down her cheeks. She couldn't bear to lose him, too.

She searched his familiar face. Even in sleep, his expression seemed to be smiling, wrinkles created by years of laughter spreading across each temple. When Charlie was sick, her father used to bring food to the hospital—always things that would cause nurses to look askance, should they notice: doughnuts, french fries, potato salad, and ice cream sandwiches. All her favorites from childhood. When Charlie was well enough to eat and stable enough for visitors, his eyes would light up at the sight of his grandparents, his grandpa laden with gifts and his grandma tut-tutting in her husband's wake. And when Charlie couldn't receive outside guests due to his flagging immune system or recovery from a procedure, her dad would leave candy or LEGO sets down at the front desk with a note taped to them.

Love, Me.

Josie choked up, laying her head on her father's limp hand.

"Dad," she whispered, quiet enough not to rouse him, "I can't see my future at all."

She thought of the tightrope in her imagination, the long walk across a thin line. The rope vanished before her into a swirling fog.

No, she couldn't see where she was headed, only that it was dark.

CHAPTER THIRTY-ONE

CICERO

Napoli to Sant'Agata de' Goti, Italy

When Josie vanished behind the glass doors of the bustling Naples airport, I experienced the kind of fear that begins as anger.

I barked, frantic, as her shape disintegrated beyond the reflective glass, my gaze darting between Hugo and the direction she'd gone. "Josie? What the fuck!" I howled, leaping against the windshield in protest, and I would've jumped right out the car door if Hugo's hand hadn't closed over my collar.

What the actual fuck, Hugo? I willed him to understand me. *Go after her!*

I was no fool—I knew what airports were for. They were for people to fly far, far away. I was about to nip Hugo, forcing him to release me, when I caught sight of his eyes.

Davvero, the man looked so sad, so dreadfully heartsick, my fury dropped like a ball, rolling around my innards, spinning a path of confusion.

What had happened between Capri and here? What had I not understood?

"Ragazzo mio," Hugo murmured, speaking for once in a language I comprehended. "Let's go home."

I didn't know what he meant by *home* until we were nearly there. I curled up on the seat of the car Josie had so recently inhabited, smelling what was left of her on the leather. For much of the drive, I imagined I would never leave this seat again. I felt as if I'd lost my heart a second time, when once was entirely too much.

But then, as we drove, my senses whispered. Familiar odors found me on the wind: soil, sunbaked and mineral rich, heavy with centuries of fertilizer. And trees, too, pricked at my nose. Not all trees smell the same—how can I explain it? Various groves of trees, rooted to one place for many lifetimes, forge something like a culture. Their leaves rustle in winds carrying particular particles of dust or sea salt or rock. Their roots grow in those particles, stretching into limestone or loam or leaf mold rich with fungi. They murmur to one another, through their roots and the air and the reach of their branches. Do you believe me? All animals understand the nuance of nature; only humans tend to be skeptics of such ordinary magic.

What roused me that heartbreaking day as we drove was the smell of *our* trees. Trees that had been in our family for centuries, whose trunks Giorgio and I used to walk among daily on our way down to the village.

The weight of despair shifted as I stood, sniffing the wind, and then there it was: my beloved home—the villa.

~

"The Realtor is coming tomorrow," Hugo said as we walked inside, glancing around cautiously, behaving as if ghosts wandered the quiet, echoing halls.

They did, of course. Or, rather, one ghost was in residence. At the creak of the heavy front door, Giorgio ambled out to greet us as though he'd been waiting.

"A day early!" he exclaimed, glancing between me and Hugo, and I saw his misperception. He'd left Capri well before us, again referencing propriety. I had a vague sense of what made him shy away, but it concerned me little. The facts of life provoke no blushes in the canine world, particularly for those of us who've made an unfortunate trip to the veterinarian at a young age. While I failed to understand the need for delicacy regarding the subject, I'd still retired to the hotel balcony nonetheless, exhausted, paying my humans little attention.

Now, in the villa, Giorgio glanced between me and Hugo, his brows raised high in anticipation.

"Where is Josie?"

He looked from me to Hugo, who trudged to the sofa and slumped heavily down. Giorgio's brows dropped fractionally as the catastrophe of her departure fell upon him.

"Cicero—where is she, boy? What happened?"

I hung my head, wondering why he'd ask such a question of a creature who can merely bark, and padded past Giorgio to the living room. I leaped up onto the sofa, curling into a tight ball beside Hugo, turning away from Giorgio's stunned expression.

Hugo tipped his head back. Pinching the bridge of his nose, he remained quiet for a long, long time. Outside, through the doors that led to the *terrazza*, the sun began its dip toward the horizon, gilding the grapevines on the old arbor.

"We should have known," Hugo said eventually, failing to lift his head, failing to open his eyes. "Love cannot last, Cicero. Not for me. I was a fool to imagine it might."

My eyes, too, were closed, so I felt Giorgio, rather than saw him. He crouched before us, very close, his soul so full of urgency it was like sitting next to a lightning rod being struck.

"Did she leave?" he demanded, and I opened one eye. "With that dickhead?"

I couldn't explain, obviously, so I simply sighed. Heavily.

"Gesù Cristo!" Giorgio exploded, leaping up from his silent crouch, spinning in agitation, then pacing the floor. "Why did he not go after her? Why is he sitting here, defeated?"

Hugo, still pinching the bridge of his nose, laughed in a soft, mirthless way, shaking his head against the cushion. "For a minute, Cicero, I did believe it might work. She was so lovely, so genuine—I wanted to believe we were meant for one another. *Madonna*, I hope her father will be all right." He opened his eyes, tipping his head to me, and I met his gaze. "I hope *she* will be all right."

"Dio mio," Giorgio wailed across the room, pressing a hand to his fluffy brows. He shook his head and stared out at the sinking sun, falling quiet. "Her father's sick," he said after a moment, piecing it together, illuminating what had occurred for me as well. "And so she went home, and Hugo has given up entirely on the glimmer of happiness he saw in a future with her."

I cocked my head, and Giorgio sank into a chair. "I failed him," he whispered at long last, lost in thought. "I ruined my boy's ability to believe in love, did I not? First, when I let his mother go. Then when I disowned him. Ours was the final relationship to fail in his life, after so many other failures." He pivoted from the *terrazza* door, bright with golden light, to Hugo on the sofa. "I plundered whatever remained of his optimism."

I tilted my head, turning that over.

"Cicero," Giorgio exclaimed abruptly, gliding over to crouch before me. "We can fix this."

I blinked, doubtful.

"We need to show him that he's wrong, *ragazzo mio*. That love, complicated as it may be, can be enduring." He stood, glimmering in the slanting sunlight. "You can help me. Come. *Andiamo.*"

Despite my throbbing heart, I stood. Hugo glanced down at me as I leaped from the couch, but then he simply shrugged and tipped his head back again. I trotted across the room, my nails clicking on the tile floor, following Giorgio.

He stopped at the front door, turning to glance at his son. "Scratch at the door," he commanded, watching Hugo. "Whine. Act as if you're in danger of taking a shit right here in the house if he doesn't spring up to let you out."

The indecency of such a suggestion! Yet, even while indignation rose within me, I recalled the liberties I'd taken with the American's luggage, and relented. I scratched and whined with gusto.

Hugo lifted his head from the couch, sighed, and roused himself as though he were ancient. He trudged across the villa to open the door, and Giorgio whispered, "Now, run. I want you to take him on our usual *passeggiata*."

I cocked my head as the door creaked wide, and Giorgio clarified. "Go to each of our stops, *ragazzo*. Our morning *giro*. Quick, before the shops close, and you'll see what I'm up to."

I would have shrugged if I could, but instead I turned and took off down the driveway, pausing before a curve to gaze back at Hugo, marooned in the still-open door.

Follow me, I thought, focusing hard, and as if he'd heard, Hugo departed the doorway, appearing a bit lost, and closed it in his wake.

And that's how it went, all the way down to the village. I ran the winding roads, joy rising within me like the dust under my paws despite my bereft heart. I couldn't ignore where I was—*home*! I was home, running down a road I had once traveled every day, breathing in the scent of the whispering olive leaves, wheeling around a corner and seeing the village strung along a hill that dropped, right from the ancient buildings' foundations, into a cliff. It was a beautiful village, and it was mine.

Hugo ran behind me, rousing himself from a lethargic walk into a jog and, finally, the sprint I forced upon him. He must be worried, I imagined, that he'd lose me again. He called, from time to time, over his ragged breath. "Cicero! Wait!"

I did not wait. I didn't slow, fully, until I was well within the village, my paws padding the cobbled road. Our first stop appeared before me.

The village bar.

My heart lurched at the sight of it. The bar was small, a place locals drank coffee in the morning and sipped wine or cocktails at night. There were four or five wooden tables inside and three iron ones on the street. I slowed as I reached it, passing the tables, nostalgia hitting me.

Giorgio had not come with us on this *giro*. He was back at the villa, I presumed, waiting.

Hugo fell into an exhausted walk behind me, panting and wiping sweat from his brow, shaking his head and trying to reach for my collar. I ducked, deftly, darting through the open door.

Hugo followed me into the bar, rather empty at this in-between hour. Berto, the bar owner, turned from where he was drying a glass behind the counter. He was a heavyset man, and I knew him well. He was the one, after all, who'd finally come to find Giorgio on the *terrazza*, stiff with death, and me still on his lap. Before that fateful day, we'd visited Berto nearly every morning of my life, appearing at his bar with the rising sun and sitting at the middle table outside, Giorgio with his cappuccino, me with my *latte*.

Berto blinked his glassy eyes now, turning his rotund belly to the front, and then his face dissolved with unexpected joy.

"Hugo Caruso! Is that really you?" he called, raising a hand to the panting newcomer, and then he was forging his way around the counter like a cargo ship, drying his hands on his apron, laughing out loud with his arms wide.

He embraced Hugo, who seemed a little stunned, and then patted his back with something like fatherly warmth. "Hugo!" he exclaimed again, "I wondered when we might see you next. Have you moved back into the house? I heard rumors of a Realtor snooping around, but I thought no—that couldn't be true. You wouldn't sell your villa!"

Hugo nodded vaguely, glancing around. I followed his gaze, wondering what he saw.

And then I understood.

All the furniture within the shop—the tables and chairs—were his. He'd made them. I knew this, but apparently, he didn't. He shook his head, confused.

"Ah," Berto said, as if he understood the bewilderment befalling this prodigal village boy. "Your father ordered them years ago. Do you not recall shipping them here?"

Hugo frowned. "I do remember these tables, but they didn't come here. Years ago, when I lived in England, a proprietor of a hotel in Napoli ordered chairs and tables—"

Berto laughed, oblivious to any nuance in the situation. "That was your father. I don't know why Giorgio didn't tell you, son, but he ordered things for all of us over the years. Always obscuring the details for you."

"All of you?" Hugo blinked.

"Oh, I have these, and Giuseppe the butcher has some cutting boards—he's hung them up as decorations, claiming they're too fancy to cut anything on—and the bakery has a shelf you made, and the grocer has wine racks. Didn't you ever wonder about all the orders shipping to Napoli?"

Hugo shook his head, puzzlement clear and growing on his face. "I shipped things all over Europe," he said, shaking his head. "But why would my father have gone to all the trouble, ordering so much expensive wood furniture? I don't understand."

"Is it not obvious?" Berto laughed, booming like a tenor. "He was proud of you." He pivoted, lumbering back behind the counter and plucking something off the wall. He handed a small frame to Hugo, adding, "So very proud."

Hugo took the frame, cradling it in both hands. And then he set it on the table, sat down on shaky legs, and after a strange, stunned moment, he wept.

I went to him, leaping silently onto his lap, and his arms encircled me. Every bit of him trembled. I licked tears off his scratchy chin, then glanced at what was displayed in the frame: a newspaper article, carefully clipped and matted, featuring Hugo and a table.

Giorgio had given them to everyone we visited daily, sometime before my birth. I knew this because I'd seen such frames, for years, in the shops we visited. They hung on walls featuring village news, or behind cash registers, a celebration of a local boy who'd made it.

I'd thought nothing of the frames.

Until now. Now, with one of them before Hugo's weeping eyes, I realized for the first time that the little displays *meant* something. Listen: I've mentioned that, as a dog, human relationships often befuddle me—they're overly complicated, ridiculously intricate. Consider dogs, for example. Consider, if you will, me: I either love someone, or hate them, or am indifferent altogether. That's it. When I've decided which category a person falls into, they generally remain there. Only Hugo had switched camps, as far as I recalled. And *certo*, I have my little frustrations, snippets of irritation, even with those in the love camp. But when you get right down to it, when I love someone, I love them without ambiguity. That's how it is with dogs.

But human relationships? *Dio mio.* What I saw in Berto's shop, and all the other shops I trotted Hugo to that evening, was that love between humans can be as clear as a muddy pond. It can be downright murky, full of floating debris and amoebas and sediment, in dreadful need of a filter.

The framed newspaper articles, and ubiquitous furniture made for village establishments by Hugo's oblivious hands, were the filter he needed.

He saw it, that evening. His father, imperfect as he was, had loved him.

~

When we returned to the villa, the sun was fully gone, though the sky was still light enough for birds to show off their final acrobatics of the day.

We clattered inside, me panting, Hugo silent and ruddy cheeked, unable to produce a word. I sensed his thoughts, racing within him, unsure of where to go.

Giorgio seemed unsurprised by his son's shell-shocked appearance. "*Andiamo*, Cicero," he called to me, patting his thigh to emphasize the command. "You have one more job to do. Let's go."

Despite my utter exhaustion and careworn heart, I followed Giorgio across the living room and into his office while, behind me, Hugo slumped onto the couch. As before, he tipped his head back, staring at the ceiling.

The office was where Giorgio had spent most of his afternoons, "working," he claimed, though I never understood what that work entailed. The estate was sold, I well knew because he'd grumbled for years about Hugo's dastardly lack of interest that had led to this sale. Still, he sat at his desk every day, sometimes thinking, sometimes sorting drawers. Sometimes writing letters to his son.

Now he walked right past his desk to a coatrack standing in the corner. Every day of our lives together, Giorgio had hung whatever garments he wore in various seasons on that rack—hats, coats, and scarves were draped over it. There was, also, a leather satchel slung over one of the hooks, though this never came down.

"I need your help," he said now, his silvery eyes catching mine. "Touching the living world wears me out, Cicero. It requires tremendous concentration, and I can only do it once or twice a day. I think I may need to save my energy, so I need you to be my hands. *Capisci?* Jump up for that satchel, my boy, and tug it over. Be careful, now—when you pull it, the entire coatrack is going to tumble after it, so you need to dart out of the way."

I glanced at the coatrack—a tall, wooden affair—dubiously.

"I know you, my boy. You can do this," Giorgio urged, seeing my hesitation. "Also, it'll be worth it. We're convincing him to go after Josie."

That was all it took.

I leaped up like a veritable gymnast, latching my sharp little teeth on to the hanging satchel. The weight of my body brought it down, as Giorgio had suggested, and with it came the entire coatrack, falling toward me like a tree on a lumberjack. I darted left, escaping just before the whole mess crashed to the floor.

"What in God's name?" Hugo called from the next room, and I heard him scramble to his feet.

"Quickly, Cicero," Giorgio urged from his crouch by the satchel. "Come here and open the leather flap. I need you to nose the letters out."

The letters?

I padded over to him, hearing Hugo's approach over the tile floors, and used my teeth to pull back the satchel's leather flap. Then, as Hugo's shadow fell over me, I nosed into the satchel, breathing in its earthy smell, and found paper. I bit, tugging out a loose bundle in my jaws, and dropped it on the tile floor.

Envelopes splayed out before us like a deck of cards.

Hugo's brows fell over his eyes, just like Giorgio's. The two of them, one a silvery apparition, one breathing yet, stared at the pile littering the floor. Without a word, Hugo dropped to sit, his legs crisscrossed, and opened an envelope. Then, minutes later, another. And another.

He read for a long, long time.

Eventually, I settled on the cool floor beside him, my head in my paws, watching as he read the letters, his frown deep, dimples gone.

"They're my apologies," Giorgio whispered finally, his words fracturing the silence that had fallen upon us like the twilight slanting now, blue and lit with dust motes, through the windows. "I wrote to him, all the years he was in Sorrento, as if he were still far away," Giorgio continued, his voice a whisper, his sad, silver eyes on his son. "I told him about the village, and the people he knew there, and our days walking around the orchards and the shops and the hills. I told him about how lonely I was, and all the things I regretted in my life. Chief among my regrets was how I'd treated him."

He sighed, the sound like soft waves climbing a beach, rolling the pebbles around.

"I didn't know how to say I was sorry, so I wrote it down. I never had the courage to mail them."

When Hugo finally lowered the last letter, Giorgio wiped his tearless cheek, whispering the refrain of his strange purgatory.

"I thought there would be time."

Stars winked beyond the window before Hugo finally spoke. He sounded like a man who was coming back from somewhere far, far away.

"He loved me."

His gaze fell upon me, bewildered. "My father," he said again, "loved me, all along. He just didn't know how to say it."

I lifted my head from my paws, staring at him hard. *And now you,* I thought with everything in my little soul, *now you need to say it. Go and say it to the person who matters, the person who should be yours, before it's too late.*

He shook his head over the letter in his lap, and I had the sense that he was going to stand, that he was going to right the coatrack and find something to eat and retire for a fitful sleep, just as he would have before this little escapade, if something didn't happen fast. If something more didn't happen, he would meet with the Realtor tomorrow. He would sell the villa, carry on with his routine, mulling this new information over yet never understanding how it could change his own life. How it could change the way he saw the world.

Something had to happen, damn it.

It was as if Giorgio read my thoughts. Because in a flash he stood, strode to the desk, and scowled in concentration. He pinned his eyes shut for one furious second, and the next a pen was in his translucent hand, floating triumphantly across the room.

When Hugo saw it, his mouth dropped open. He sat utterly still in the twilit room, his stare fixed on the pen coming toward him, his lungs failing to open with fresh breath.

"What the fuck?" he whispered, echoing sentiments I'd had many times that day. I watched calmly, trying to impart my serenity to him so he could think, could follow along, could accept whatever was going to happen next.

All of Giorgio's attention funneled into that pen, which lowered now toward one of the envelopes on the floor. Everything in him propelled the nub onto the paper, and it wavered there once, twice, and he bit his lip. I could see him, focusing like a man struggling to maintain his balance on a cliff edge. The pen began to move. Frowning furiously, his hand as tight on his implement as a preschooler with their first crayon, Giorgio created letters, one by one. He connected them across the paper, like jewels on a string, the lines looping behind the pen's wobbly and inconsistent track.

Oh, I tell you, how I wished I could read in that moment.

Hugo sat stone still. The entire time the pen moved across the envelope, he remained frozen. His face was white in the fading light, drained of color, his brown eyes startled wide. He stared as the pen looped and curved, shaking here and there, and finally clattered to the floor.

Giorgio fell at the same time, collapsing backward, his powers of concentration spent. He lay on the floor like a shiny puddle, staring at the ceiling as if he'd run a marathon, his hands on his forehead, his eyes closed.

"Cicero," he managed, unmoving. "Can he read it?"

Next to the coatrack, Hugo finally moved. Carefully, as though picking up a lit firecracker, he reached for the envelope. He brought it close to his face, squinting, his reading glasses nowhere in evidence. Though even I could see that the letters were large and legible. Perhaps it wasn't glasses he needed to interpret them, but faith.

He cleared his throat, his breath shallowing. He seemed to read the message again and again.

Finally, his brown eyes flicked up, meeting mine. As if he'd finally recalled I was here, waiting on bated breath to learn whatever it was Giorgio had written.

Hugo read the words out loud. "Go to her."

His stare held mine, and, desperate to nudge him along, to push him like a bobsled heading out on its course, I did something very undoglike, indeed.

Clearly and deliberately, I nodded.

PART FOUR

CHAPTER THIRTY-TWO

Josie

Kansas City, Missouri

"Josephine."

Her father's voice woke her. She sat up, confused, from where she'd fallen asleep on her folding chair, her cheek on the edge of her father's mattress. She rubbed at her face, feeling the creases left by his blankets, blinking.

"Dad?" she managed after a second, the world assembling itself before her. "How are you feeling?"

"Oh, just dandy," he said, but his words lilted a bit. He glanced around as if he, too, was confused. "I'm surprised to see you here," he added, and it sounded as if he was speaking around a gumball in his mouth.

A nurse came in, bright as the morning, before Josie could respond.

"Mr. Thompson," she cooed, "how nice to see you up so early."

"Up?" he echoed, glancing at his legs under the covers, and the IV in his hand, freshly baffled. "I'm about as 'up' as a groundhog on grass cutting day, ma'am."

She pursed her lips as if subduing a laugh and bustled about to take his vitals. "Now, the doctor will be by in about a half hour on morning rounds, you two, so you can ask any questions you might have soon." She paused, glancing at the numbers on a thermometer, and added, "Anything I can get for you in the meantime?"

"Don't suppose you have any bacon floating around back there?" he asked, and now both Josie and the nurse stifled amusement. Bacon, he would be aggrieved to learn, was no longer on the menu.

Because Josie, of course, would be fixing his menu from now on. She'd have to move in with him during his recovery, obviously. She stood, frowning a bit as she walked around the bed to straighten the blanket over her father's legs, thinking about Mark with expanding dread. What would she do, now? If her dad was to recover in his own home, he'd need the support of a caregiver. He would need someone to drive him to whatever appointments would be necessary, to make sure he had food in the fridge and clean sheets and the proper medicine with his breakfast plate. She wouldn't be able to return to the school library in a month, that was for sure. No, she would take care of her father, and that meant she'd need support financially. Which meant . . . She sighed, allowing herself to think the question: Was there any way to manage this without Mark's help? Was there an arrangement he might agree to, a way to coexist, a way forward?

"Josie girl," her father drawled, interrupting her thoughts. She glanced up, her hands dropping back to her sides. "Kid, what are you thinking? You look as worried as a cat with a long tail in a room full of rocking chairs."

She huffed out a laugh. His speech was slurry, yet he was not only determined to produce it, but he seemed to be completely himself behind the marbles in his mouth. She returned to her folding chair and gripped his cool hand in her hot one, shrugging.

"Just thinking. We'll see what the doctor says in a bit, but you seem pretty good, Dad."

"Fit as a fiddle." He struggled a bit with the word *fiddle*.

She nodded. "Well, we'll get you home soon, and whatever help you need to get better, we'll sort it out, Dad."

His brows dropped low, and his mustache tilted with a frown. "What are you talking about?"

Josie shrugged again. "I just don't want you to worry. Everything is going to be okay, Dad. I'll come and live with you for a while. Ellen's already setting up a meal train, so we won't have to cook for a bit. And Mark and I will sort out a plan—"

"What in the hell are you talking about?" he interrupted, his eyes going a bit wild under his brows. "You're going back to Italy just as soon as I break outta this place."

Josie cocked her head, much like Cicero did when he was trying to understand. "No, Dad, that's impossible—"

"What's impossible is you talking like you're going to drop everything to take care of me. And you and Mark? What did I miss, Jojo?"

"Nothing," she sputtered, taken aback. "But Dad, you've had a *stroke*. That changes things—"

"I know damn well and good what I had," he interrupted again, half bellowing this time. "Son of a gun, Jojo—I have ears. I've heard everything the doctor's said. Now, I know I sound like a radio with a broke dial, but I'm thinking just fine, and I'm telling you this: You will not be taking care of me."

He blinked, his stare fixed to hers, and a sheen of improbable tears brightened his eyes.

She shook her head, unsure of what to say.

"You've been taking care of everyone else your whole life, Josie girl," he pressed on. "I saw you, kid. I saw your sleepless nights, and the constant driving around to clinics and hospitals, and all those ziplock baggie lunches and Sunday breakfasts and the goddamn laundry that always got folded, no matter how sad you were, and no matter how busy you were. Not to mention the job you held down, helping other people's kids read."

He blinked again, and two tears rolled down his cheeks. He seemed to deflate rather suddenly, his tone softening. "Your mom and I worried. Your mom lay awake nights after she'd come stay to help out. She'd say you had nothing for yourself. Everything you did was for everyone else."

Josie opened her mouth to respond, but her voice caught. She stared at her father, and two tears, matching his, rolled down her own cheeks. She swiped them away and reached to take his hand, which fumbled for hers and then gripped hard, his fingers dry as paper.

"I've seen you, Josephine," he slurred. "And goddamn if it isn't your turn finally. I won't take that from you."

She shook her head, still unable to speak, her thoughts a jumble and her heart aching. But it didn't matter what he was saying, or how true it was. No—she wouldn't abandon him, not when he needed her, regardless of whose turn it was.

The door to the hospital room opened and Josie turned, still gripping her father's hand, to see Mark coming in.

"Where's Charlie?" she asked, her voice hitching.

"He's coming. He insisted on grabbing some coffee for everyone downstairs." Mark glanced between Josie and his father-in-law, taking a few steps into the room and leaning against a wall, his hands slung in his pockets. His eyes were puffy behind his glasses, still tired from the trip. "How are you feeling, Howard?" he ventured, tentative.

Her father seemed to roll something around in his mouth before he spoke, as if preparing. His eyes took on a steely glint as he stared at Mark, marshaling his tongue, selecting his words. "I'm feeling," he finally boomed, speaking far too loud, "like if you don't hightail it out of this room, I'm going to have another goddamn stroke."

Mark took a step backward, blanching. "Howard, I'm—"

"Get out, you son of a bitch," Josie's father bellowed, his command so loud the door creaked open again, and a startled nurse poked her head in.

"Is everything okay, Mr. Thompson?"

"Just swell," he said fiercely, his eyes fixed on his son-in-law.

Mark glanced between the nurse and the hospital bed, shaking his head, his eyes wide. "We're all fine," he assured the nurse, and then he retreated, following her brisk departure from the room. He left as fast, Josie thought with unbidden amusement, as a cat in a room full of rocking chairs.

She turned to her father, giving his hand another squeeze.

"I'll be right back," she said, and he held on to her for a moment.

"Don't you go back to that man."

His body might have been in a hospital bed, but Josie's father still had iron in his backbone.

His frown deepened. "Don't you dare."

Josie managed a smile. "I won't," she said. And, just like that, she knew it was true.

~

"Mark," Josie said a moment later, finding him sitting on one of two chairs down a turn in the hall. "I think you'd better go. You're not helping, being here."

He gazed at her for a long moment, blinking his blue eyes, a blue that had once sent her heart pounding.

"What are we going to do, Jo?" he asked after a long moment, and she heard everything he meant in those words. Were they going to forgive each other? Were they going to try to find a way forward?

She sighed, then turned and took a seat beside him, thinking.

"Mark," she said finally, "it's nobody's fault that our life together became a battle, early on. We had to fight to save our son, to help him thrive, and it was so, so hard."

He reached for her hand, enclosing her fingers in his, and she let him.

"But here's the thing," she said, staring at his hand over hers, searching her thoughts. "When soldiers go off to battle, when they dive into the foxhole together and fight off their enemy, it's awful. Right? Facing the possibility of losing everything, of death, is life changing. It's something that nobody outside the foxhole could possibly understand." She glanced over to find him nodding. "But then, when we'd finally gotten out alive, together, and we had a future sprawling out ahead of us, you betrayed me. You pushed me right back into the damn foxhole."

He shook his head. "I was lost, Jo."

Josie shook her head, too, pulling her hand, gently, from beneath his. "I know. But even if you're lost, you don't hurt the person you fought the battle with."

He held her stare, unmoving, for a long time.

"I can't forgive you, Mark," she said finally. And at last, tears broke loose, chasing themselves down her cheeks.

Mark, too, began to cry. "You could," he sniffed, wiping at his nose, "if you wanted to. We could go to therapy, and work it all out—"

"No." Josie smiled through her tears. "There are some things that can't be undone. Go back to Jen, Mark." She stood, stepping back. "Try again. And let me go."

"No, Josie—" he protested, but she cut him off.

"Let me go," she repeated, and he stared at her for a very long time, stunned, as if he couldn't sever the connection with her. Finally, Josie turned away. She walked back to her father and son, leaving her husband marooned on one of two folding chairs at the end of the hall, alone.

CHAPTER THIRTY-THREE

Josie

Kansas City, Missouri

For the next four days, Josie and Charlie stayed in the little hospital room around the clock, only taking turns a couple of times to travel across the street and sleep in the hotel they'd booked until discharge. And for those four days, Josie could feel her son's questions about what had happened between his parents, yet he asked little. Josie, for her part, only offered the information requested, feeling certain that, in time, he would require more.

"So, Dad cheated on you," Charlie whispered out of the blue on the second day, as they sat near the bed while her father slept.

Josie stifled a gasp. "Who told you that?" she demanded, her pulse leaping. What was the protocol for handling such a delicate situation with an adult child? If there was a manual out there somewhere, what would it advise her to do?

"Grandpa told me," Charlie whispered back, and as if on cue, Howard's eyes opened.

"Damn right I did," he slurred, his mustache moving with each word. "Kid should know the truth."

Josie pursed her lips, unsure whether her father was right. Was it better to lie?

Charlie didn't pursue it. He simply nodded, as if confirming a private thought, and stood up to greet an incoming nurse.

There would be time to talk it out, Josie thought, a bit desperately. There would be time to do it right, to follow whatever guidelines there were for such things, to find a way to preserve her son's belief in his father. He deserved that.

On her fourth day in the hospital, something happened Josie did not see coming, something that upturned her already topsy-turvy world entirely.

They were getting her father ready to leave that morning. Howard was going to be discharged before lunch, and despite his grumbling, Josie and Charlie would head home with him, at least to begin with, so they could manage his medications and therapy.

"He may only need a few weeks of live-in support before shifting to daily checks," the doctor had said brightly that morning, smiling as he addressed the three of them. "I'd like someone to be available for round-the-clock assistance to begin with, Mr. Thompson, and to drive you to therapy for those first visits. But really, you should be able to return to normal activities fairly quickly."

Howard had been lucky, they'd learned over recent days. Exceptionally lucky. His speech was a bit fuzzy, but mentally he was sharp. Physically, he was somewhere in between: He could maneuver quite well up and down the hospital halls, provided he had a sturdy cane.

"Do not, under any circumstance, venture out without your cane," the doctor commanded more than once, and Josie and Charlie had traded amused glances. The doctor seemed to know who he was dealing with.

"I'll use the damn cane," Howard finally grumbled. "And I don't need anyone to drive me to therapy, for God's sake."

Josie and Charlie exchanged an aggrieved look. The ensuing weeks, they both knew, would be challenging in more ways than one.

But, Josie vowed, she'd find a way to manage.

Like she always did.

~

What changed that afternoon as Josie was finally preparing for discharge, was, quite simply, everything.

Charlie was downstairs, collecting lunch while they waited for the doctor's final visit before heading home, and Josie was milling around the room, picking up a bit, when the door opened.

She glanced over her shoulder, seeing Charlie, but before she could greet him, she nearly dropped the empty breakfast tray she'd been about to put by the door.

Because behind Charlie, Hugo appeared.

Josie's mouth dropped open, and her eyes were so wide the air stung them. Was she seeing things? She stood, unmoving, stunned.

"Giuseppina," he stammered, following Charlie all the way into the room and then stopping in front of her, glancing around, his cheeks flushed with uncertainty. He was unshaven, his jaw dark and his eyes tired from travel. "I—" He swallowed, reaching for her hands, and she felt that his were shaky. He squeezed her fingers, searching for words. "I was at the front desk, asking which room your father was in, when your son, here, found me. You'd mentioned which hospital it was, you see, back in Sorrento, and so I came. I wanted to make sure you were okay."

Josie glanced between Hugo and Charlie, wholly shocked.

"I'm sorry," Hugo said in a rush, clearly floundering. "I should have called, or texted you, before coming. I see it now—I shouldn't have come all this way and surprised you at a time like this—" His gaze traveled to the bed, landing on the bewildered eyes of the elderly man still in it. Hugo lowered his voice, looking back to Josie. "I was afraid that if I reached out, you'd tell me not to come, and that would be the end. The end of us. And I could not stand it, *capisci*? But now I see: What kind of surprise is this?"

"A damn good one," her father barked from the bed, making both Josie and Hugo jolt. Charlie hung back by the door, and Josie sensed his watchful eyes moving between her and Hugo. But then, her father was shifting his weight on the mattress, swinging his legs to the floor, and Charlie detached from the door and hurried to him. Howard was fully dressed, in anticipation of leaving, right down to his laced boots.

"Here, Grandpa," Charlie said, holding out a palm to help his grandpa to his feet. Once Howard was upright, Charlie offered him his cane and walked a step behind him as he made slow progress across the room. The cane squeaked on the linoleum with each step.

"Howard Thompson," her father announced as he came to a shaky stop before Hugo, holding out his free hand.

Without hesitation, Hugo responded in kind with a firm handshake. "Hugo Caruso. *Piacere.*"

"Pia-what?"

Hugo grinned, his dimples showing. "It's how we say 'a pleasure' in Italy. It is a true pleasure to meet you, sir. I am a friend of your daughter's."

"I know." Josie's father grinned, his eyes twinkling. "I know who you are, kid."

For a strange second, Hugo and Howard held each other's gaze, and Josie had the sense that they approved of one another, somehow, on sight. The nerves that snapped like static within her relaxed a little, allowing a whisper of joy to creep in. Yet she glanced anxiously at Charlie as he, too, stepped forward, ever polite. He slung his hands in his pockets and stood close to his grandfather, measuring Hugo with his gaze.

"So, what," Charlie said, his brows gathering skeptically. "You came all the way from Italy just to check in? That's a little weird, isn't it?"

Hugo nodded slightly. "It is. Indeed."

Charlie shook his head and turned away, looking out at the parking lot. Josie's father chuckled lightly to himself, pivoting on his cane, and clapped her on the shoulder before moving to stand alongside his grandson.

And Hugo's gaze, awkward and hopeful, found Josie. As she looked up into his brown eyes, something thawed within her. It was all a mess, she thought—everything was happening at once: joy and worry, clarity and confusion, shock and gratitude.

It was a moment, she mused, that was like all of life, really. A bewildering blur.

She gave Hugo a tentative smile, and he lifted her hand to his lips, kissing it silently.

~

"I can't believe you came all the way here," she whispered two hours later, after they'd driven to her familiar childhood home out on the sprawling plains, and finally had a chance to talk in private. She and Hugo were in the kitchen, preparing a plate of snacks, while Charlie and her father chatted in the living room.

"I know," Hugo said quietly, arranging some crackers on a plate and then turning to her, anxiety clear on his face. "It was a crazy thing to do—I know it was. But there was another, even crazier thing that happened back home, something—*allora*, I don't know how to say it. Someday, Josie, I will explain why I got on that plane."

She turned to him, frowning. She didn't know what he was talking about, but when she peered into his face, she spoke without thought.

"I'm glad you came."

He smiled, and she stepped a little closer, mindful of the voices in the other room. "It's so good to see you." Tears stung her eyes, surprising her.

He wiped her cheeks with his thumb, gently. "It's good to see you, too."

"What was the crazy thing?" she whispered, tilting her head. "What happened?"

Hugo hesitated. He placed his hands on her shoulders, and then let them fall down her back, bringing her in closer yet. "I realized," he whispered, ducking so his lips brushed against her ear, "that I am falling in love with you. And I could not let you go."

Like a warm summer wind, it hit Josie: She could not let him go, either. The world around her faded, growing distant. The dim kitchen, the hot day, the hospital and Mark and the bumpy road ahead—all of it quieted as she reached up, silently, to kiss the good man standing before her.

"Do you think we can work it out?" she whispered, laying her head on his chest, tucked up against his chin. He wrapped her up tight in his arms.

"I do."

"But I have to stay, for a while at least—"

"That's fine. If you like, I can stay with you."

She pulled back a little, studying him. "How can you? With your shop, and your business? Can you afford not to work for a while?"

His lips quirked into a half smile, more sheepish than amused. "Giuseppina," he said quietly, "worrying about money is not something I need to do."

She cocked her head, bemused. She thought of the villa he'd described. His family's estate. The Ferrari. Why hadn't she pondered these things before? She guessed, piecing it together now, that it just hadn't mattered much to her.

"Are you telling me that you're wealthy, Hugo Caruso?"

He shrugged, still holding her tight. "You could say that. My father left a generous trust fund for his two granddaughters, and he bequeathed everything else to me. I'll tell you all about it sometime. But now I will be here with you."

She took that in, nodding, and then another question found her, this one urgent. "Wait—where is Cicero? Is he okay?"

Hugo grinned. "He's with Bettina, bossing Michelangelo around. He'll be just fine."

Josie exhaled, relieved. And with that, they gathered up the snacks and walked, bumping elbows, to the living room.

CHAPTER THIRTY-FOUR

Cicero

Sorrento, Italy

My friend, I'm aggrieved to report something I learned the month Josie and Hugo disappeared, leaving me in the care of Bettina.

Not all dogs are thinkers.

All my life up until that point, I'd clung to Plato's opinion of canine intellect, taking it as a point of fact that dogs, as he claimed, possessed the souls of philosophers. That we were a sophisticated bunch, the sort of creature who sees beneath the surface of things. Of course, I'd witnessed some rather unphilosophic behavior from my brethren in the past, but I imagined those were simply uneducated dogs, and that, underneath the rude, and sometimes, frankly, lewd behavior, there were thinkers just waiting for a chance to surface.

Michelangelo disabused me of this notion almost immediately.

There were two terrible things about the month I languished in his company. The worst aspect of that interminable period was that I spent it constantly pining for Josie and Hugo. Most of my daylight hours were devoted to sitting by Bettina's window, staring down from her third-floor apartment into the street, studying passersby. I sniffed the air, despite my status behind glass, hoping for a whiff of Josie coming down the lane. She smelled of lemons and lavender and, oddly enough, laughter. In a pinch, I'd look for Hugo, too, who smelled a bit like Giorgio once did, minus the halitosis, and if he'd rolled in freshly milled pine. The thought of my gentleman friend rolling, like the most basic of dogs, amused me despite my anguish.

It wasn't only scent I sought at the window. I studied the gaits of people walking by, and their shapes, and I began to believe that if I hoped hard enough, if I stared intensely enough, those pedestrians below would transform into the humans I longed to see.

I was, my friend, searching for my family.

"They will return, *ragazzo mio*," Giorgio would coo in my worst moments, perched on the couch beside me, his watery shape failing to make a dent in the cushion. Are you surprised to learn that, even with Giorgio by my side, I was so bereft? This is how it is with dogs, you understand. All of us—*this* I can confidently claim—are the same in this way. We are experts at love. If you've known a dog, you've likely gathered this already.

When we love somebody, it's forever.

"You could go and play with Michelangelo, eh?" Giorgio suggested, more than once, which prompted me to turn more fully away from him, tuck my head between my paws, and huff. Play with Michelangelo? What did he take me for?

Because, of course, Michelangelo was the second most terrible thing about that month. *Madonna mia*, what a roommate! Have you ever had a truly terrible roommate? One who eats your leftovers from the fridge, and sits around in his underwear, and swears when your mother comes by to visit? Well, let me tell you: The worst roommate you've ever had would pale in comparison to Michelangelo.

Every day Bettina would take us for a morning walk, during which Michelangelo would pee on everything stationary and, sometimes, things that were not so stationary. Once, he lifted his hairy leg and pissed all over Bettina's ankle when she was looking away, at which point she screeched, cursed, and hustled us back home as if she were on fire. Never, I tell you, have I been more humiliated in public.

After breakfast, which involved Michelangelo first staring mournfully at whatever Bettina was eating and then trying to steal the kibble from my bowl, we'd be left on our own.

"Have fun, *ragazzi*! See you after work!" Bettina would chirrup from the front door like a deluded kindergarten teacher, and then she'd whisk off to work, abandoning me with her horrendous pet.

Michelangelo never failed to howl upon her departure for at least fifteen ear-splitting minutes. How, I wondered day after day, had he not learned the routine by now? Sometimes I would join in, just to drown out the noise of his bewildered sorrow, awaiting the inevitable thump from the apartment above us and the muffled *"Michelangelo! Stai zitto!"* from its elderly inhabitant.

When he tired of howling, the giant oaf would throw himself upon the living room rug, splayed out like a drunk bear, and I would inhabit my post by the window. My afternoon would be spent soaking in the fumes of the hairy *cretino's* flatulence like Nordic folks steep in a sauna. At dinner, he would try again to steal my food, and when I growled with all the menace I could muster, he'd simply *lick* me, wherever was most convenient for him, gracing my white coat with a ribbon of drool.

Thus, I pined and sighed and whined at the window, desperate for my internment to end.

"They will come back," Giorgio reassured me, over and over again.

Yet as the days turned into weeks, he, too, began to look out the window.

And anyone, thinker or not, would have been able to see the worry growing on Giorgio's translucent face.

CHAPTER THIRTY-FIVE

Josie

Howard's ranch, Kansas

A month passed like a minute.

In late August, summer shifted from sweltering to pleasant, the nights cooling here and there. The light, in early evening, slanted over the mown hayfields, gilding the odd grassy seedhead. And, like the changing season, Josie's father gradually transformed as well.

His words became clearer, though she wondered if he might always have a slight slur to his speech. He was surprisingly dedicated to his physical therapy sessions, practicing his exercises in the living room without fail, and his gait improved. Josie still admonished him to use a cane, just in case, but really, she saw, soon he might not need it.

Another stunning development occurred in the kitchen: He showed interest in healthy meals, going so far as to peer at labels on his favorite snacks, scowling and grumbling in consternation at whatever unwelcome facts he discovered.

Soon, Josie realized, her father might not need her at all.

She suspected, one afternoon, that this was on his mind as well when he called her into the living room, asking her to sit down. Charlie was also there, his elbows on his knees where he perched on a faded love seat, his face brown from the summer sun and dusted here and there with freckles. Like hers. Hugo was not present because he was out fetching groceries. This had become typical—Hugo loved going to the grocery store, always coming home with variations of strange foods he couldn't find in Italy.

"We don't really eat this here, either," Josie would laugh, holding up a box of stuffing or an unusual flavor of chips. "I mean, not typically. Maybe on Thanksgiving?" They'd had some inarguably disgusting meals since Hugo had been visiting, yet his enthusiasm for novelty made her choke down trays of corn dogs, or a Jell-O salad he once found at the deli counter. He'd eaten it with surprising gusto, his dimples showing as he grinned, shaking his head at the notion of marshmallows in a salad.

"Ambrosia," her father had chimed in, equally enamored. "That's what we call it."

Now Josie settled in the living room, glancing between Charlie and her father, and nerves roiled within her gut. It seemed, suddenly, like a premeditated chat. What was going on?

"Time for a board meeting," her father said, which was a term he hadn't used since Josie was in high school. She frowned, taking a seat in the rocking chair.

"Josephine," Howard said, leaning forward with the demeanor of a lawyer about to make his case, "it's time for you to return to Italy."

Josie stared at him, then flicked her gaze to her son. "What are you talking about?"

"I've been discussing it with Charlie," her father said, speaking a bit louder than necessary. "And you never even got to see Rome, did you?"

Josie opened her mouth to respond, but she ended up just shaking her head. No, she hadn't. She hadn't seen half the places on her itinerary, a fact that had stung like a pin in her heart when she left the country so abruptly. But, in the greater scope of things, it hadn't mattered.

"These are the facts," her father continued, adjusting himself to sit up even straighter, leaning forward over his knees to look her in the eye. "You're in love with a fine man, and he lives *there*. And you love it there—anyone can see that when you talk about the place. You were really living in Italy, kid, after decades spent supporting the lives of everyone around you."

Josie looked at Charlie where he sat quietly on the love seat, his gaze on the carpet. She'd worried, obsessively, about how he felt regarding Hugo. With Hugo in the house, she'd sent Charlie back to his rental near the university, releasing him to just be a college student, rather than a caretaker all summer. Nonetheless, he'd come to the ranch plenty of times to see his grandfather. And he'd sat across from Hugo at supper, saying little, and then left abruptly after eating. It had made Josie feel, in a word, awful.

But she also realized something crucial: She would feel awful whether Hugo was by her side or not. Because what was really troubling her son was already happening—she and Mark were getting a divorce. Paperwork had been filed, and a mediator had been hired. It was going forward amicably, so far—Mark had walked back the threats he'd slung in those early texts he sent her in Italy. He'd seen reason. He didn't want to hurt Charlie, and perhaps he realized he'd hurt Josie enough already. And now Josie felt sure of her decisions regarding her marriage, except where they concerned Charlie.

For Charlie, her heart broke.

"I can't go back to Italy," she protested, smiling gently, looking to her son. "Not long term, anyhow, with you two here—"

"Mom," Charlie interrupted, finally swinging his eyes up to meet hers, flicking his overlong hair from his gaze. He cleared his throat. "You should go. You should go and make a life with Hugo."

She shook her head, studying her son's beautiful face. "But you're here, Charlie."

He forced a laugh. "There are planes, Mom." His smile fell as swiftly as it had come, leaving his customary gravity in its place. When he spoke again, it was in a low, measured tone.

"Here's the thing. I'm not happy about you and Dad. Obviously. I think any kid, no matter how grown up they are, is going to be upset about their parents splitting up. It kind of shatters what you knew about your childhood, right?"

Josie felt tears threatening. She nodded, stifling the urge to cross the room and give him a hug. He had more to say.

"And I can't *like* Hugo, not really, because how I feel about him is all mixed up with how I feel about Dad. It's going to take me some time to sort it out. That said, anyone can see that he's a nice guy. And anyone can see that he loves you." He held her stare, his expression fervent. "And I love you, Mom. You never left my side, not for a minute, and I see that. I know what you've been for me."

Josie swallowed a sob. It was difficult to speak. "It was an honor—"

"I know," Charlie said. "I know you loved being my mom and that you sacrificed willingly. But I also know that you chose to put me first. And you put Dad first. And if we let you, you'll put Grandpa and me first even now, but we don't need you to. I'm grown, Mom. You did your job." He swiped a tear from his cheek. "And you did a good job."

Josie struggled to speak around the lump in her throat. "But, Charlie," she managed, "what if you need me and I'm so far away? I don't want you to feel like I left you."

He chuckled through his tears. "Again, planes, Mom. There are planes. But also, I'm an adult. I have years of school ahead of me, and then, someday, a career—I'm going to live my own life now."

"And, Josie girl," Howard chimed in, "it's time for you to live yours."

She turned from her son to regard her father, her vision blurred. "But what about you, Dad? You'll be so lonely—"

"Bah!" he all but shouted, grinning. "That's just what you think. I'm selling the ranch, kid." He gestured around the worn, cozy living room they sat in, then glanced wistfully out the window at his fields. "I should've done it years ago. And then I'm taking myself on a cruise or two. Who knows? Maybe I'll meet a lady who likes to hear an old man talk too much. Maybe when I come to see you in your new life, there'll be two of us." He shrugged, still grinning under his mustache.

Josie shook her head, lost for words, everything within her colliding. Outside, her car appeared down the long gravel driveway, churning up a cloud of dust, glinting in the late-afternoon sun. Hugo was back from the store.

"You've taken care of everyone all your life," her father said, lowering his voice for once and glancing meaningfully toward the driveway. Then he caught her eye, his brushy brows lifting. "Josephine, go on and let someone take care of you for a change."

Josie nodded, wiped the tears from her face, and stood. Charlie managed a smile, then unfolded himself from the love seat, went to Josie, and wrapped her in a hug, so tall now he was able to plant a kiss on the top of her head. Saying nothing else, he loped off toward the kitchen, and she heard the door to the covered back porch open and close.

"Go help Hugo carry in the groceries," her father said, tipping his chin in the direction of the driveway. Josie smiled, a single laugh chasing the last of her tears, and obeyed.

Outside, the light was golden, and a pair of dragonflies traced treble clefs over the tangled garden Josie's mother had once planted along the front walk. Their wings, as silver as dewdrops, winked in the sun.

"Giuseppina," Hugo called from the trunk of her car, hoisting a pair of grocery bags. She came around and caught sight of his face, brown from the Midwestern sun, his eyes dark and lively in the fading light. "Close your eyes," he commanded, setting the bags back in the trunk.

She did. A moment later she sensed him before her, standing close, the warmth of him like an aura that drew her in, again and again.

"Open," he whispered.

When she did, he stood before her with an orchid, snow white, in his hands. Its stem rose in a graceful arch, and its petals, as delicate as the dragonflies' wings, fluttered in the light breeze. "For the kitchen." His dimples deepened with a smile.

And she stepped closer yet, setting the orchid carefully on the ground, and he folded her up in his arms. She breathed Hugo in: pine and soap and salt. Joy.

"Do you think they allow orchids on airplanes?" she whispered.

He peered at her, cocking his head questioningly like Cicero.

Josie grinned. "Hugo," she said, tipping his head close to hers so their foreheads met as they often did just before a kiss. "Let's go home."

EPILOGUE

Cicero

One year later

Hugo and I sat on the *terrazza*, watching the sun sink toward the hills, painting its watercolor canvas across the sky. Overhead, pink and orange slashed through the reliable blue of day, fading, behind us, to black.

It all changed, my friend, while we were watching. So swiftly did the world revolve, always the same, and yet also, somehow leaving something entirely different in its wake every single day.

"*Bellissimo*, is it not, Cicero?"

Hugo glanced at me, a glass of red wine cupped in his hand. He was sitting in his father's chair, gazing out over land that had until recently been in his family for generations, bidding goodbye to another revolution of the planet. Like Giorgio had, always.

Giorgio was with us, too, of course. He sat, cross-legged, on the very edge of the *terrazza*, staring at the traveling sun, his figure backlit by rumpled orchards that swept all the way down to the village that had always been his home, twinkling in the distance.

I glanced from the sunset to Josie, out in the yard, tending her flower garden. She'd moved into the villa, finally, which meant that

I, too, had at long last come home. My heart beat with joy every day, waking up in my very own house with my very own family.

It had taken time, you see.

When Josie first returned to Italy, several seasons before, I'd greeted her with all the excitement of a dog who believed he'd been lost. Wild spins and barks erupted from me without premeditation, like hiccups leaping from my throat. My happiness at seeing Hugo and Josie appear in Bettina's apartment was so vivid I could barely think. Michelangelo barked as well, that oaf. He slathered Josie in kisses and drool, and it was all I could do not to bite him. She was mine, after all.

Yet I needn't have worried, because Josie took me home that very day. Home, for several months afterward, was her Sorrento apartment, which she'd apparently secured for the better part of a year. That was fine by me. We sank into something like our former routine together, though there were several changes. You may recall that I, as a rule, don't welcome change. There were, I must confess, some awkward adjustments.

The first was Hugo's presence, all too frequent, on my pillow on the nights we didn't join him over the bookshop. I was sent to the sofa in the living room far too often, and trust me, I let them know how very unacceptable this was. I'd grumble and, if my mood was particularly sour, nip at Hugo's hand should he try to lift me from the pillow mid-dream. So the task of removing me from the bed usually fell to Josie, who kissed my little head and whispered her nonsense in my ear, shuttling me into the next room.

Eventually, she bought me a sheepskin bed of my very own, which resolved the issue, more or less.

There was also a change in our daily routine, though this I minded not at all. Josie began to work in a flower shop an easy walk away, and I adored the old woman who ran it from our first encounter. She knelt before me, her face as lined as Giorgio's, and she gave me a biscuit.

"Who's a good boy?" she cooed, and I admired her intelligence. Because, of course, it was a rhetorical question. We both knew the answer.

Josie procured a sheepskin bed for the flower shop as well as our apartment, so for the better part of a year, I spent most of my days drowsing on it, lying in a slab of sunlight, monitoring customers who came and went through the jingly door with their flowers and plants. Josie still works there now, half of each week. That, in fact, was why she was out in the garden at twilight during this particular sunset, weeding.

When we moved home to the villa in the spring—another change, if you can believe it—she spent her first week there walking behind a god-awful machine that absolutely destroyed a large patch of grass. The patch in question was my toileting spot, so I was not enthused. Not at all. But then Josie began to plant seeds in the horrific square of dirt she'd created, and lo and behold, those seeds grew. They became plants, and then flowers, and before I knew it, Josie was selling what she grew and I was her unwitting assistant.

We spent a full day every week walking down to the village beyond the orchards, supplying flowers to all the people Giorgio and I once knew. This, I loved. For once again, the butcher would greet me as Josie handed him a vase of flowers for his counter, exclaiming, *"Ciao, bello,"* and giving me a bite of whatever he had on hand. And then we'd stop at the grocery, and the bakery, and finally, the bar, dropping a vase off there as well. The bar was our final destination on the route, so we'd usually pause long enough to enjoy a cappuccino and a *latte*, respectively. It was almost, my friend, like old times.

The second half of each week, we'd return to Sorrento, where Hugo worked in his bookstore over the weekends, and Josie and I would sleep with him upstairs. *Perdonami*—I misspoke. I didn't sleep with Hugo, of course—I had my sheepskin bed there, too. Ours, you see, was not that kind of friendship, though I had become quite fond of that old *bastardo*.

In Sorrento, Josie and I went to the flower shop. Once, I heard her saying to Hugo, in Italian of all things, that perhaps she would buy the shop when Signora decided to retire.

It was her dream, she said, after all.

And so, on the evening Hugo and Giorgio and I sat on the *terrazza* watching the sunset, and Josie weeded her vast garden, all was right in my world.

All was right, until Giorgio rose from his cross-legged seat overlooking the orchards, turning to face me.

"I've had time to think about it, Cicero, my boy. The reason we're all here."

I looked from the sunset to my old friend, something like a premonition gathering in my chest. The sky overhead was awash with color, the sun like a golden thumbprint over the hills.

And I knew. Something was going to happen. Change was coming for me yet again.

Giorgio blinked, his eyes like clear water rushing over river stones. There was movement to him, I realized. Something in him, like the river-water sheen in his gaze, was ready to wander on.

I lifted my head, tilting it sharply, studying his shimmering face.

"I think, *ragazzo mio*, you've known the meaning of life all along," he mused. "Haven't you?" Giorgio gazed at me for a moment, and bats wheeled through the sky beyond him, like bits of night, diving and spinning through the final colors of day. Soon, they would vanish into the coming darkness. "Perhaps that's why humans need dogs, eh, boy? We have it backward. You don't need us as much as we need you, because you show us the way."

He smiled, his fluffy brows, like bits of mist, rising. And he took a step backward. Something was changing in Giorgio right before me. I sprang to my feet, my hackles lifting, a whine rising in my throat.

Hugo shifted in his chair, the wood squeaking, and frowned at me. "What is it, Cicero?"

I glanced between him and his father, my whine escalating. *No,* I wanted to howl. *Don't, Giorgio.*

Yet he took another step backward, wiping his tearless cheek with the knob of his hand, nodding. Smiling.

"It's time," he said, his tone soothing. "It's time, my boy, for me to travel on. I've stayed long enough. Too long, most likely."

I took a step in his direction, barking once.

"Ah," he conceded, "that's true. I needed to stay, didn't I? I had to show my boy that I loved him. That he could be loved. And now I have."

He glanced down the hill, catching sight of Josie's silhouette against the sunset, kneeling among her flowers, weeding the rows. Giorgio's smile grew. "He's going to be just fine. And so are you, *ragazzo*."

Behind him, the sun slid beneath the distant hills, shooting light in every direction in a vivid burst. I heard Hugo inhale behind me, struck with wonder. But my eyes were on Giorgio.

The light called to him. I could see that. One of the dying sunbeams hit his translucent figure like it existed just for him, filling up his form, making him golden. He laughed, standing there, brimming with light.

"Take care of them," he called to me, sounding already as if he was far away. I tilted my head, staring hard. "Show them, Cicero, what life's all about. Remind them when they need it."

He was fading now, his figure traveling with the beam as it weakened, following the sun as our patch of earth spun on. Giorgio was nearly gone. He disintegrated, joining the light, leaving me bit by bit.

"Cicero," he called, one last time, before he vanished. "My boy, I love you."

And then he was truly gone.

I stood unmoving on the *terrazza*, where my beloved friend had died over a year ago, parting from me for the first time. I watched the last shreds of sun fade from the sky, leaving stars glimmering in their wake. Darkness was coming, fast.

And I was okay.

My friend, I knew that, despite the pain beating through my little, loyal heart, I would carry on. Because I had a family to tend to. I had humans to teach, as Giorgio implored me to do.

And I would.

For the rest of my days on this beautiful, tragic, bewildering, swiftly spinning earth, I would show my humans the meaning of life. Remember it, won't you?

Love who you were sent to love.

That's it, my friend.

That, quite simply, is all you need to know.

Acknowledgments

My writing life includes a fleet of wonderful people who offer support, first reads, guidance, and encouragement, and I am forever grateful to every one of them.

Many thanks to my extraordinary agent, Kevan Lyon, for her steadfast advocacy, advice, and friendship. The day I signed with Kevan was my luckiest day as an author. I am also deeply grateful for the insight and enthusiasm of my editors at Little A; thank you to Laura Van der Veer for believing in this book, and to Ali Castleman and Faith Black Ross for their excellent editorial guidance. I am beyond fortunate to work with each of you!

Thank you to the hardworking team at Little A, including Karah Nichols, Jo O'Neill, Rachael Clark, Sarah Engel, Jill Schoenhaut, Jessica Poore, Rachel Norfleet, and Emily Mahon. I am indebted to each of you for your sharp eyes, creativity, guidance, and feedback!

Among my first readers and advisers are my parents, Hugh and Lois Judd. Hugh is an excellent listener and fact-checker, and Lois is always available as a sounding board, quick reader, and bearer of unflinching advice. Thank you for your unflagging support of my career.

I would be lost without Carrie Kwiatkowski, my dear friend and critique partner. For many years now, we have traded stories, critiques, brainstorms, and lots of laughter. I also owe much gratitude to my first readers for this book, including Michelle Campbell, Sasha Smith, and Erin Lietzen.

I am beyond fortunate to be a member of the Lyonesses, a group of brilliant authors and friends. Many thanks for the retreats, laughter, commiseration, and advice shared for this and all books—this gig would not be the same without each of you. I am also deeply grateful for my PNW author friends. Here's to years of lunches, discussions, and writing retreats to come!

For this story, I also owe special thanks to my husband, Jeremey Beck. The idea for the adventures of Josie and Cicero began one evening when we were out to dinner for our anniversary. Over appetizers, I mentioned how I was trying to decide what to write next, and he asked, "Well, what do you feel like reading?" This led to an evening of discussion and laughter and, ultimately, this story. So, thank you, Jeremey, for being an incomparable partner in brainstorming and everything else!

And finally, Finn and Lily, I am forever grateful for you. You bring so much joy, laughter, and heart to both my work and my life. Thank you for being such incredible kids.

About the Author

Photo © 2021 Liza Mahler Photography

Kristin Judd is an acclaimed author of historical and contemporary fiction. A former teacher, she holds a bachelor of arts in English from the University of Washington and a master's in teaching from Western Washington University. When she's not reading and writing, Kristin loves anything that gets her outdoors, whether it be hiking in the mountains, riding horses in the woods, or digging in the garden. Kristin lives in the Pacific Northwest with her husband, children, and many pets, including an opinionated terrier much like Cicero.